My South Seas Sleeping Beauty

MY SOUTH SEAS
SLEEPING
BEAUTY

A Tale of Memory and Longing

ZHANG GUIXING

Translated by Valerie Jaffee

 Columbia University Press   *New York*

Columbia University Press and the translator wish to express their appreciation for assistance given by the Chiang Ching-kuo Foundation for International Scholarly Exchange in the preparation of the translation and in the
publication of this series.

Columbia University Press
Publishers Since 1893
New York   Chichester, West Sussex

Library of Congress Cataloging-in-Publication Data
Zhang, Guixing.
    [Wo si nian de chang mian zhong de nan guo gong zhu. English] My
    South Seas sleeping beauty : a tale of memory and longing / Zhang
    Guixing; translated by Valerie Jaffee.
        p. cm. — (Modern Chinese literature from Taiwan)
ISBN 10: 0-231-14058-4 (cloth : alk. paper)
ISBN 13: 978-0-231-14058-4   e-book: 978-0-231-51182-7
    1. Zhang, Guixing—Translations into English.   I. Jaffee, Valerie.
II. Title. III. Series.

    PL2837.K79W6213 2007
    895.1'352—dc22

                                                    2006030717

Printed in the United States of America
c 10 9 8 7 6 5 4 3 2 1

Contents

Translator's Preface   vii

Part I   1

Part II   83

Part III   153

Translator's Preface

The interaction between fiction and history is never simple. This observation may not be new or uncommon, but it feels particularly urgent when applied to Zhang Guixing's *My South Seas Sleeping Beauty: A Tale of Memory and Longing*. Zhang's novel adopts fantastic storytelling as a theme and emerges from a historical world likely to seem unfamiliar and a bit fantastic to an English-language readership. But readers can take some comfort in the fact that even the author of this remarkable novel is unable or unwilling to dissolve the haze of myth and mystery that renders the world in which he was born so seemingly unfamiliar. Indeed, the exploration of that haze of myth and mystery is one of the signature imperatives driving the contemporary generation of Malaysian Chinese authors, of which Zhang is one of the most prominent representatives.

Zhang Guixing was born in Sarawak, Malaysia, in 1956. At the time of his birth, Sarawak, a region at the northern edge of the island of Borneo, was a British crown colony. In 1957 the British-ruled area at the southern tip of the Indochinese peninsula gained its independence as the nation of Malaya. By 1963 Zhang's home region of Sarawak had, along with the rest of northern Borneo, become part of the rechristened nation of Malaysia. The division between peninsular Malaysia, where the capital city of Kuala Lumpur is located, and northern Borneo, where Zhang grew up, continues to the present day to be more than geographical: peninsular Malaysia is the seat of commerce, industry, and government and the area where the Muslim Malay ethnic majority predominates; Borneo remains less developed economically and is home to a variety of indigenous minority groups.

Malaysia's ethnic Chinese population is divided between the two regions and has borne a historical burden all its own. Chinese emigrants have been settling in the various regions of Southeast Asia for centuries, and in the nineteenth century war and economic disruption in China sent thousands of migrants, mostly from the southern provinces of Guangdong and Fujian, radiating outward to form what is still one of the largest and most influential diasporas in the world. Before the national lines of the twentieth century were drawn, these migrants called all of distant Southeast Asia *nanyang*—"the South Seas." In Malaysia, Chinese immigrants came to control an outsized proportion of trade and financial wealth; as is often the case with wealthy minorities, the Chinese have long been an object of resentment for the Malay majority.

The tensions surrounding the Malaysian Chinese were certainly not ameliorated by the so-called Emergency that lasted from 1948 to 1960. During this period, the Malaysia Communist Party, whose members were overwhelmingly ethnic Chinese, waged a guerilla war against the British and, later, the Malaysian governments. That revolt plays a substantial role in several of Zhang Guixing's novels. In *My South Seas Sleeping Beauty*, however, the Emergency is merely the circumstantial backdrop for a fantastic rendering of the origins of a private resentment within the narrator's family. But to contrast the private resentment that Su Huan, the narrator's father, feels toward his son with the public ethnic hatreds that have helped to shape Malaysia's history is perhaps to trivialize it unfairly. The private hatreds portrayed in the novel are easily as absolute, as violent, and as mysterious in their origins as those that form and dissolve nations.

In 1969, the same year that ethnic riots between Malay and Chinese populations prompted the temporary suspension of constitutional rule, Zhang Guixing graduated from a Chinese-run primary school. In 1976 he graduated from high school and moved to Taiwan, where he would go on to earn a degree in English at Taiwan Normal University. This was a common move for Malaysian Chinese youth of his generation, many of whom were driven both by frustration over the obstacles to their advancement in the Malay-dominated sectors of elite life in Malaysia and by a rather romantic interest in the Chinese motherland and in what it might feel like to live life as a member of the ethnic majority. One might imagine that this interest would tend to lead to disappointment. Taiwan, of course, was not the mainland motherland from which the ancestors of most Malaysian Chinese had departed, and Taiwan itself was a land suffering from the identity crisis that accompanies collective exile. More to the point, searches for motherlands, for homes where history can be clarified and imagined memories can be actualized, rarely have ecstatic endings. In *South Seas Sleeping Beauty*, the move of the narrator, Su Qi, to Taiwan marks a monumental shift in the narrative. At that point, the temporal confusion, proliferation of rumorlike stories, and mythic events of part 1 give way to the more plodding narrative of part 2, in which the pace of time's passage is relatively easy to discern and Su Qi's self-enforced loneliness locks him into an emotional dormancy not so different from the coma that engulfs Chunxi, his childhood love.

Zhang graduated from college in 1980 and remained in Taiwan. In 1983 he renounced his Malaysian citizenship and became a citizen of the Republic of China. That same year, his fiction-writing career, which had begun when he was a high-school student in Malaysia, began to gather steam. Zhang would proceed to devote the virtual entirety of that career to exploring the Malaysia of his memories. His four most prominent novels before *My South Seas Sleeping Beauty*—*Sailian zhi ge* (Siren song, 1992), *Wanpi jiazu* (The clown dynasty, 1996), *Qun xiang* (Herds of elephants, 1998), and *Hou bei* (The primate cup, 2000)—all draw their subject matter from the lives and histories of ethnic Chinese in that country. As David Der-wei Wang has pointed out, Zhang's novels mark a departure from earlier works of Malaysian Chinese literature in several respects: their subjective and imaginative approach to historical experience, their exploration of the concept and process of memory, and their engagement with foreign and distant literary traditions, including the works of William Faulkner, Gabriel Garcia Márquez, and the mainland Chinese writer Mo Yan.[1] *Clown Dynasty* is the

1. See Wang Dewei, "Zai qunxiang yu houdang de jiaxiang: Zhang Guixiang de Mahua gushi," introduction to Zhang Guixing, *Wo sinian de changmian-zhong de nanguo gongzhu* (Taipei: Maitian chuban, 2002), pp. 23–24.

story of the life of an emigrant Chinese family in the Malaysia of the 1930s and 1940s. But the other three novels all, like *My South Seas Sleeping Beauty*, describe the life of a male protagonist in Malaysian Chinese society in the decades in which Zhang himself knew that society. Also like *Sleeping Beauty*, the earlier trilogy addresses the politico-historical turmoil of Malaysia in the fifties and sixties but also shrouds that historical experience in a skeptical fog of cultural imagination and private, uncertain memory.

Zhang is still living in Taipei today. He teaches high-school English and returns to Malaysia only infrequently. It is an open question whether Zhang's relationship with the land of his birth appears more or less ironic in light of the fact that he is only one of a considerable number of Malaysian Chinese of his generation who have chosen a path that mixes permanent exile and continuous homecoming. Writers born in Malaysia who have enjoyed successful careers in Taiwan, and in so doing placed their marginal homeland at the center of the contemporary Chinese-language literary scene, include Li Yongping and Huang Jinshu.

Zhang Guixing is an excellent exemplar of the traits that have drawn readers' attention to this group of authors. His works mobilize the Chinese language in powerful and surprising ways to explore the notion of storytelling even while he engages artfully in the act thereof and to weave stories that walk a dazzling line between sensational artifice and the power of raw sensation. Published in 2001, *My South Seas Sleeping Beauty* is typical of his better-known works in many respects, but Zhang also considers it to be the most accessible novel of his mature period. Given the timing of many of the story's main events, the reader is tempted to discern an autobiographical impulse lurking within the novel. But the work's engagement with and enactment of the sheer magic of storytelling also assures readers that it is as undiluted and consummate a work of fiction as can be found anywhere in the world. This translation seeks to convey to readers some idea of the depth of Zhang's accomplishment.

VALERIE JAFFEE

Part 1

Chapter 1

My little sister's death was the subject of all sorts of stories. People had begun to spread these stories around just when I was getting old enough to understand a little bit about the world.

The first of the stories goes like this: One day, when my sister isn't even a year old, she takes an afternoon nap and then just never wakes up. No one really understands what killed her, but in medicalese they call it Sudden Infant Death Syndrome.

The second story has my mother falling asleep on a swing, holding my little sister, who is just over a year old. My sister slips out of my mother's arms, falls headfirst onto the ground, and breaks her neck with one rapid snap. Until I entered high school, I used to think about that image quite often: of my poor mother on the swing, humming a nursery song. In our garden, a painstakingly arranged labyrinth of vegetation, she is as dignified as the Blessed Virgin, as radiant as a falling star, and I can't bring myself to take my imagining one step further and wonder whether my mother's own mistake might have caused the loss of the little daughter she loved.

The third story goes like this: On a summer afternoon, my mother is pushing my sister's stroller through the garden. She stops beside a pond and falls asleep under a tropical willow. All of a sudden, the stroller slides down toward the pond and plunges into the water, sleeping baby sister and all.

Then there is another, much stranger story. It is a summer evening, and a young Dayak man, who, the story goes, has come to take my father's head, breaks into our house. There, he finds my mother nursing my baby sister and is astounded by her beauty. He seizes her hand and leads her away into the jungle. The young Dayak is handsome and well built, and my mother is no longer quite herself when she is with him. The two of them spend seven days and nights together in a tree house built by hunters at the top of a giant tree. They eat fresh fruit and drink rainwater, and they bare their naked bodies to the sun, the moon, the stars, and the stares of the aboriginal peoples. When my mother comes home again, seven days later, my little sister has fallen ill with a mysterious disease that is already too far along to be cured. . . .

But some people tell it differently. They say that, while my mother and the young Dayak were up in the tree house immersed in their affection, my little sister had the bad luck to fall from the tree house and shatter her spine against a huge tree root.

People also say that my mother, when she was saying good-bye to the Dayak youth, knelt on the floor of the tree house, wailed, sobbed, and begged him not to leave her. But the young man was unmoved. She embraced and kissed his legs, but he just kicked her away. Then he stepped over my little sister's rigid corpse, climbed a tree, and disappeared into the jungle like a cloud leopard, silently and leaving no trace behind him.

Whatever else is true, it's definitely a fact that my mother, who had been a botany major in college, wouldn't let anyone bury my baby sister. She let my sister keep sleeping in her tiny bed, and every day she sang nursery songs and lullabies to her. Most likely she thought that my sister was only languishing temporarily, the way plants do in the winter, and that she would be restored to health as soon as springtime came.

At first, I smelled the foul odor only when I passed by my mother's room. But after several days the smell had begun to spread swiftly through the entire parlor. I shut myself up inside my own room. I stuffed up the cracks around the door with my clothes and turned my face toward the window to breathe in the fresh garden air. At that time, the garden was certainly healthy, but it was nowhere near the extravagantly vibrant place it would be several years later.

When my father and a couple of hired workers wrested my baby sister from my mother's arms and headed out the door with her, my mother attacked them. I saw her break off one of my sister's arms in the struggle. Six months after that, I would still stuff clothes in the cracks around my door before I went to sleep. I didn't want to smell anything like that smell ever again.

As I was growing up, every time a ripe durian dropped from a tall tree to land on the ground with a plunking sound, every time a large jackfruit leaf came floating down from a tree, I would think about the image of my infant sister drifting through the air. People say that the tree house she fell from was over ten meters off the ground. If I had had the gift of clairvoyance, if I had known that my mother would forget herself entirely in the throes of her passion, if I had kept a firm vigil beneath the tree house, then maybe I could have caught and saved my sister, brought her home alive and well.

My sister's death really was like the tumbling to earth of a ripe fruit or a withered leaf; it seemed, in the end, like a perfectly natural occurrence. The obscured face of that baby girl grew more unreal each time I thought about her, until finally she came to feel like a false memory.

After my sister died, my mother's stomach began to swell, and nine months later she gave birth to a baby boy. The baby had thick eyebrows, big eyes, a prominent nose, and full lips, and his skin was the color of dates. One look at him, and you knew that he was not my father's child. On the early morning of the second day after he was born, my father put on his hunting clothes. Shouldering a knap-sack, with his rifle in his hand, he picked up the baby while my mother was sound asleep and went off into the jungle. My father spent seven straight days hunting in the forest, killing a number of vicious animals while he was out there. When he came home again after those seven days, he did not have the baby with him.

I watched my father go into my mother's bedroom wearing an in-different expression. But then, as he bent down over my mother where she lay, neither asleep nor quite awake, on her daybed, he put a look of consternation on his face. He spoke to her in quiet tones, looking like a repentant troublemaker. My mother's hands lay flat on her chest, clutching a pitch-black crucifix. Her eyes, detached and terrified at the same time, had been filled with tears for days. My father finished talking, and then he kissed the crucifix in my mother's hand. But she abruptly raised her other hand and clawed at his face, and then she beat him on the forehead with the crucifix. My father pushed her away and left the bedroom.

My father walked by me. His blood had trickled down his forehead into his eyes. Staring ferociously at me through his own blood, he said: It was a bastard.

I don't know what kind of lie my father told my mother that day, but my guess is that, at that time, my mother did not know what had really happened to the baby who had been my half-brother. If she had, her reaction would not have been that mild.

Chapter 2

In the mid-1950s, my father graduated from college in Taiwan and brought his Taiwanese girlfriend back to his hometown, in an area of northern Borneo with a large overseas Chinese population, to get married and start a family. My father was a Borneo Chinese, born and raised. He had gone to high school in Borneo and had been among the first generation of students to go to Taiwan for their higher educations. I was born in 1958, one year after he returned to Borneo and five years before my sister who was destined to die early was born.

My father was eccentric. I truly hated him when I was growing up. He was as smart as they come; in high school, he had won a national mathematics championship, and then in an international competition he had defeated the best math students from universities all over the world. In those days, the nearby country of Singapore was promoting the study of eugenics, and the medical school of the National University of Singapore had been trying to persuade my father to agree to donate his exceptional brain to them after he died, so that they could use it for research purposes. After my father declined this honor, several minor periodicals reported that in fact the university's real plan had been to preserve my father's brain in formaldehyde and display it in a public place next to a preserved brain of only average intelligence, so that visitors could compare the two brains and admire my father's. An English-language daily went so far as to report that Singapore's Department of Education had recruited the aborigines of Borneo to try to hunt down my father's head right away, at the point in his life when his brain was most mature, his faculties were sharpest, and he himself was at his most arrogant.

That rumor may very well have been the reason why the thieving Dayak who broke into our house was described as a valiant headhunter. In fact, though, what interested the Dayak was not my father's head but my family's fortune. And after he broke into our house, he discovered that my family's so-called fortune was overshadowed by my mother's beauty and kindness.

Because of his outstanding academic record, my father naturally had his pick of scholarships to foreign universities when he graduated from high school. But at the urging of my grandmother and in defiance of public opinion, he ended up going to Taiwan, the motherland, for college. The university there didn't provide him with a cent in scholarship money, nor did anyone there understand that he had a mind of such perfection that it might have been considered a work of art.

It had never occurred to me to ask my father why he decided to study civil engineering, but his later decision to marry my mother, a botany major, struck me as a perfect match.

After my father graduated from university, he sold his inherited property and purchased an undeveloped parcel of land just a few kilometers away from the jungle. He designed and oversaw the construction of our house there himself, tailoring his design to the parcel's topography and the arrangement of the ten or so giant trees that were the jungle's little outposts on our land. After my sister died, my mother, in addition to maintaining the trees that were already there, began to plant hundreds and then thousands of bizarre and exotic plants all around our house, with the near-mad fervor to tame frontiers that has characterized Chinese migrants to this place for centuries. It took her more than a decade to get the garden to look good enough to satisfy her.

Our land was vast and fertile. Weeds grew there with a powerful vigor, and the tropical plants were vicious fighters by nature, just like a brood of sisters and sisters-in-law all competing with each other. My mother certainly had her work cut out for her.

My mother must have suffered a great deal when she first began to tame her garden. A few days after she had leveled an area with her shovel, she would find that it was already overrun again by wild grass. Weeds would cover her newly sprouted plants before they had had a chance to grow. Those flowers that did emerge in any quantity were choked to death by creeping vines and parasitic plants. The vitality, the fighting spirit, and the rate of growth of the native weeds far exceeded those of the tropical plants that my mother introduced to the land. I must have been seven or eight years old at that time, and I remember seeing my mother sitting on a bench and crying as she looked at the surging and untamable waves of greenery that were inundating and scouring away the young plants she had cultivated with such care. I would walk up to her and try to lift a shovel, "helping" her with motions more symbolic than truly helpful. Sometimes my mother would ignore me, and other times she would lift up her blouse and yank me toward her sweat-soaked chest. Then I would suck greedily at the milk from her breasts, which were sunken and sagging but still harbored surprising force.

My mother observed and analyzed the conditions in the garden, and eventually she realized that the native South Seas people were able to cultivate this land only by burning away the wild weeds throughout the year. The natives called this the "burning of blossoms." The weeds were tenacious and wide-ranging enough that no one could ever burn them all, and as soon as the first spring breeze blew they would start spreading again, so one or two burnings were never enough, and the "burning of blossoms" had to be repeated year after year. Only this way, it seemed, could the bad seeds and corrupt growth be rooted out entirely. My mother looked at the evil grasses taking over her garden and decided she had something to learn from the culture of burning blossoms. She broke the garden up into a number of parcels and burned them one at a time, one each day. When a portion that had already been burned began to put forth fast-growing weeds or young trees whose seeds had been sown there by the wind, my mother would burn that portion again immediately, leaving the intruding plants no opportunity to thrive. This was endless and dangerous work for her. Any mistake of any kind, and her fires could spread to the neighbors' houses or the nearby jungle. Because of this, my mother wouldn't let me come too close to the fires at first. But then, in the last year or two of the process, when I was nine or ten, she let me take a little plastic bucket full of river water and stand vigilant guard off to one side. It never did much good, but whenever a fire started to burn out of control I would douse it with my water, at my mother's command.

I have very sharp memories of the years when she was setting fire to the garden, because that was when I suffered from what I called my "fiery cock." Although my mother forbade me from going too close to the fire, I usually found an opportunity to drift into its vicinity, close enough that I could stomp on sparks with my small feet. When I got bored with that, I would unfasten my trousers and deliver a stream of hot piss onto the fire. Then my small penis would begin to swell and turn red, the glans growing to the size of a doorknob. There was no pain or irritation, and my urine flowed without any trouble. But the weeds were poisonous, the soil was hot and moist, and when the flames were extinguished a sickly miasma would evaporate into the air. A grown-up would have had enough masculine energy to be able to unfasten his pants around these fires with no adverse consequences, but the incipient masculinity of a child was easy prey for an attack of yin. The fiery heat entered my body and subjected my small cock to horrible calamities. In the rural areas of the South Seas, when the fires are raging, children get this illness frequently, so it's clear that I wasn't the only one who had ever thought of pissing on a fire. My penis and scrotum trembled ferociously. My red and swollen groin looked just like a male fowl putting on airs or flirting; hence my name for the syndrome: "fiery cock."

My mother would tug gently at my penis and massage my scrotum, and then she would pick up a black iron pipe. The local peasants light their cooking stoves by bringing an iron pipe to their lips and using it to blow on the fire, and it was said that the only antidote to the poison that caused "fiery cock" was for a woman who had already been through her first pregnancy to blow on the penis through this type of pipe. My mother puffed out her cheeks and brought the pipe close to my child's cock, swollen to a size that would rival a grown man's. When she exhaled, I felt a soothing, incomparable burst of cool air moving across my groin. It's a strange thing, but the next day the swelling would be gone, and my penis would have recovered its original innocence. Despite all this, though, I didn't stop pissing on the fire. I remember that my mother had to blow on my penis regularly right up until I was ten years old. From these memories, I can deduce that her garden fires must have gone on for three full years.

In fact, my mother's "burning of blossoms" never stopped entirely; she kept it up in fits and starts. Whenever she felt at all dissatisfied with any bed of flowers in the garden, she would fix it in the best way she knew: by setting fire to the area and planting it anew. When the area that needed to be burned was relatively large, she would hire workers to help keep the fire under control. When the fierce southwest monsoon winds were blowing, they would fan the flames out of control, and often the workers would barely escape with their lives from the garden, which was, by then, already a labyrinth of immeasurable intricacy.

The garden came to be an unsettled, liquid, surging, and murky place. Whenever I walked through it as a child, I would feel like a small boat drifting out of control on the azure sea. Ten minutes after entering the garden, I would be lost: I would be sure that I had only gone a few steps, yet when I would climb a tall tree to get my bearings, I would realize that I had somehow drifted into a remote corner of the garden, like a kite whose string has been severed. I always had to expend quite a bit of effort just to return to my original location: climbing tree after tree to get my bearings, advancing and then retreating, turning and turning again, like a fish swimming upstream.

Sometimes, if I tried very hard, I could make out a few paths through the garden, but within a few days, because of the rapid expansion of the vegetation or because of my mother's abrupt new plantings or cuttings, those paths would have become just more of the many undertows and whirlpools that threatened to swallow me whole.

My mother, the fanatical gardener, was forever chipping restlessly away at her garden, as if it were her artistic masterpiece. Under the influence of her tempestuous and unintelligible moods, it had become a shape-shifting enigma. She nurtured her plants with the tenderness of a nursing mother, and she dug them up and destroyed them with the mercilessness of an assassin.

When I stood in the garden, or up in the tree house that I would eventually build, and watched my mother busily and nervously working on her garden, it would suddenly occur to me that I was in the presence of a grand and desolate tragedy, equal to the stories of the goddess Nüwa repairing the heavens or the bird Jing Wei trying in vain to fill up the sea.

When I turned eighteen, I faced the fire and pissed on it with all my might, and I found out that the swelling and redness could not affect me anymore. Maybe there was some truth to the native superstitions. Maybe I was already a grown man.

Chapter 3

Because of my father's reputation as a child prodigy, all sorts of local businesses and government bureaus wanted to hire him after he graduated from college. I still don't know how many jobs he held at once. But my father usually did not seem all that busy. He understood perfectly well how smart he was, and he knew that he could live a good life without working too hard, that only mediocre individuals needed to struggle to make a living. My father was such a distinguished architect that regional and state governors chose him, over architects who had studied in the West, to design their official residences, despite the fact that his degree wasn't even recognized in our country. He told me himself that his compensation for designing a golf course for the sultan of Brunei had been enough money to buy a Rolls-Royce and still have enough left over for our family to take a monthlong holiday on Bali. In fact, the sultan had originally wanted to pay my father by giving him one of the more than eighty Rolls-Royces in his garage.

But the sultan hadn't given my father a Rolls, and that was because of the hood-ornament goddesses. On the hood of each of the sultan's Rolls-Royces, there was a statue of a comely goddess kneeling in a posture of servile humility that contrasted markedly with the pose—wings spread, head held high—of the normal Rolls-Royce goddess and illustrated quite clearly the subordinate image of women in that Muslim country.

"These statues might seem to your Chinese women to be less than respectful," the sultan had said to my father, in a voice at once solicitous and haughty. "For us, it is fine to be legally married to four different women, but for you that would not be allowed. You Chinese are so old-fashioned."

My father wouldn't state an opinion one way or the other. I suspect that His Majesty was worrying unnecessarily. Once I finally came to understand my father, I realized that women in his eyes were even lower beings than those eighty cowering hood-ornament slave girls. If my father had ordered a custom-made Rolls from the factory in England, he would have probably asked them to put a statute of a female donkey on the hood.

My father let his professional achievements go to his head, and his personal life reflected this. His friends included princes and aristocrats, VIPs in politics and business, celebrities and prominent characters of all ethnicities. They were members of the local Lions' and Rotary clubs, and they formed all sorts of private recreational clubs—hunting, scuba diving, golf, tennis, flying, yachting, and cricket. All of them were wildly arrogant men, every bit as despicable as my father.

Our house was one of their favorite gathering places, so even though I had no interest whatsoever in these people, I also had no shortage of opportunities to interact with them. On Friday and Saturday nights, my father would make me get dressed up and greet every single guest. After that was done, he would say to me coldly, "Now get out of here. I don't want to see you again for the rest of the night."

Once, at a party that had gone on until very late at night, a confused owl ended up in our parlor, where it flew back and forth just beneath the ceiling. My father closed all the doors and retrieved four hunting rifles from his private arsenal. Then he invited the guests to have a go at the owl. Altogether, the heavily intoxicated men at the party fired thirty-some bullets. The one who finally killed the owl was a soccer star who eventually joined the Communist rebels. A little more than a year later, he was living in the jungle with a large Communist gang, fighting off the government troops and lending the party his skills as a sniper and assassin. Eventually, at a National Day parade, he shot and killed, from a distance of over a hundred meters, a Chinese businessman who had refused to give money to the cause of Communist "liberation." It's no surprise, then, that his aim had been eerily perfect even on that drunken night.

On the night when the owl was killed, I had been sitting in the study, gazing out the window in the direction of Chunxi's bedroom. When I heard the gunshots, I went out onto the balcony adjacent to the study to look down into the parlor. There, beneath the flickering lamplight, I had seen a woman climb onto the dining table and immerse the lower half of her body in an enormous glass bowl filled with punch as men fought to get ahead of one another in the line to ladle out a drink. Some of them even stuck their whole heads into the bowl.

They're crazy, all of them, I thought.

Before the next party, I caught around a hundred bats, and once the party began I set them loose in the parlor. The guests used up all the ammunition in my father's arsenal and still only managed to kill ten of them. A policeman who happened to be passing by our house in his patrol car thought that a shoot-out was going on inside. A state governor who was among the guests used the six bullets the policeman had with him to shoot down three more of the bats. Most of the guests were drunk that night, and one city council member was almost killed when a stray bullet hit his shoulder. A dozen women were throwing up until sunrise, and one young girl who had drunk herself nearly into a stupor and whose breasts were half-exposed kept knocking lightly on the door of my room.

When my father found out that I was responsible for the bats, he told me that from then on we could dispense with the formality of having me greet the guests at his parties.

I couldn't tell whether this was a punishment or a reward. In any case, my father soon lifted his prohibition on my presence and demanded that I start coming out again, all dressed up, to bow and scrape to the guests, because it had dawned on him that my mischief had actually injected new life into his parties, which had been growing tiresome. He drew inspiration from me. From then on, his parties descended even further into a carnivalesque atmosphere of absurdity, commotion, degradation, and salacity. At one party, my father staged a performance in which a python he had found someplace swallowed a bearded pig whole; then he cut the python open, extracted the pig, and had both cooked and made into a meal on the spot. At another party, he set loose twenty wild long-tailed macaques and pig-tailed macaques. After the ladies and gentleman in attendance had teased the monkeys shamelessly, a Dayak hunter used a blow pipe and arrows smeared with a virulent poison to kill them, slowly and one by one. For the grand finale, my father invited the guests to pick up knives and experience for themselves the ruthlessness and efficiency of the hunting tools used by the Borneo natives. Those guests would never forget the sight of the poisoned macaques dying in agony.

My father asked me over and over again, "Well, boy? What new tricks have you thought of?"

Sometimes I would keep my ideas to myself, but other times I would answer him, with as much scorn in my voice as he had in his.

Putting leeches in the swimming pool was the last trick I thought of for my father.

He accepted my proposal enthusiastically. On that night, I stood on the balcony and looked down at the radiant lamps alongside the swimming pool, at the indistinct black dots slowly forming clusters in the aquamarine water, at my father and ten other men wearing nothing but swimming trunks plunging into the pool to the raucous applause of the ladies and gentlemen surrounding it, at those men mustering all their strength to fight off the attacking leeches. When the first man climbed out, amid sighs of admiration from the crowd, it finally became clear to everyone what the rules of this game were. The last to climb out was a white man, who had stayed in almost an hour. He fainted while the others were picking the leeches off his body and shouting hurrahs for the conquering hero, and he had to be rushed to the hospital for a blood transfusion. During his life-or-death performance, his left hand had shriveled up until it was the shape of a dog's leg, and it was left permanently half-paralyzed.

The second-to-last man to climb out of the pool had been my father. Later, my father told Lin Yuan that he easily could have held on longer and been the last man out and that *he* would certainly never have been gauche enough to faint from loss of blood. "But if I hadn't climbed out first, that white devil would have killed himself to save his honor."

Chapter 4

It was a few years after my sister's death when my father developed his mania for holding extravagant all-night parties. And now I suppose I have to bring up a very unpleasant event from my childhood, one that I will never forget, try as I might. No matter how many times I look back on it, I still can't bring myself to admit that it might be the reason why my father was going to hate me for the rest of his life.

But I still maintain that I did nothing wrong. I was only six years old when it happened, and what does a six-year-old know?

The Sarawak Communists were at their most active in the sixties. The insurgents used the jungle as a natural screen. From behind it, they waged guerilla warfare against the government, under the banner of the Red ideals of Marx and Mao Tse-tung, for more than ten years. If the British government had not brought in its vicious but valiant Kashmir mercenary troops to help drive them out, then Malaysia, this former British colony incapable of defending itself, might have gone Red before anyone knew what was happening. Like nocturnal animals, the Communists laid low by day and came out at night to wreak havoc, to destroy, to subvert, intimidate, and murder. The military distributed weapons that ordinary people were to use for self-defense. After the Communists' decline in the seventies, my father supposedly paid inflated prices for everyone else's guns so that he could establish his own private arsenal. All he got were decrepit, old-fashioned rifles and shotguns, but they served his purposes well enough. Often he would tell people that he had bought the guns more for self-defense than for fun, that he hadn't forgotten the rumors about the price that had been placed on his head, and that now was precisely the time when his brain was most mature, his faculties sharpest, and he himself at his most arrogant. This sounded like a joke, but the money he spent on those guns was certainly no joke.

The story I have to tell happened in 1964, when my little sister was not yet a year old, when my mother, on her swing, was radiant like a falling star, when that Dayak youth had not yet broken into our house. At that time, my father, just like a good paternal provider, would go hunting in the jungle regularly, even though by doing so he was risking being accused of joining the Communists. I was six years old, getting ready to start school, ignorant, guileless, drawn to the natural world, fond of wandering by myself through the garden—which at the time was still half-fallow—picking wild fruit, hunting for eggs, catching crickets, and thinking longingly about my mother's rouge-red bosom, so flush with hints of mysterious insight and good fortune, as proud, damp, and swollen as two divine peaches. . . . One day, past the lush vegetation of the garden and the small stream, full of floating weeds, that ran through it, past the airborne dances of the dragonflies and butterflies, past the white clouds, whose translucent, gleaming, overflowing delicacy reminded me of my mother's breasts, I saw a long-haired woman dressed all in white moving quickly across the open fields. She bent down in front of the stream and took off her shoes and then crossed the stream barefoot and stood on the near bank gazing at my family's garden. My father emerged from behind a flowering shrub and went respectfully forth to meet her. His carriage and expression both suggested that he had been waiting a long time for her. My father was afraid to look directly at this woman in white, and his hands were trembling as he handed her a package. The woman took the package, turned around, walked back across the stream, put her shoes on, and disappeared. My father stood straight as a rail on that same spot while she vanished into the field.

My father stood there for a long time, staring dotingly at the field. Then, all of a sudden, as if he were emerging from a dream, he took off his shoes, forded the stream, and knelt, barefoot, on the grass that the woman had walked upon. He kissed the faint, dubious-looking footprints she had left behind her.

I witnessed this same scene at least seven or eight times. When the woman came striding barefoot across the stream into our garden, the bottom of her skirt would get thoroughly soaked. There would be grass stains and dew stains scattered sparsely over her white clothes. Her hair would be damp, her forehead sweaty. She usually came around one in the afternoon. After she left, black clouds would gather in the sky, a northeast monsoon wind would begin to blow, and then an afternoon thunderstorm would stupefy the world. This happened every time, without fail, so that I found myself thinking of that woman as a rain goddess or maybe, given her grace, her other-worldly, lotuslike manner as she crossed the stream, some kind of river goddess. She was something bound inextricably to water, whether it was rain from the heavens or rivers on earth.

One time, my father handed her a red flower along with the usual package. The woman stared at the flower for a while. Without taking it, she turned around to go back across the stream. But halfway across she suddenly turned back again and, with lowered head and muted smile, plucked the red flower out of my father's hand.

The last time I saw my father give the woman a package, he knelt down and kissed the palm of her hand. She stretched out her other hand to caress his hair and pressed his head tight against her lower abdomen.

I would see my father strolling all alone in the garden, sometimes singing softly to himself, sometimes raising his voice and belting his songs heartily. I had never seen my father so happy before, and neither had I seen my mother as despondent as she was while she was nursing my sister.

One February afternoon, I was sitting on the terrace at the front of our house, trying to make myself a paper kite, when an army truck pulled up in front of our door and ten or so British soldiers jumped out, wearing camouflage uniforms and carrying loaded rifles. They arranged themselves methodically into two perfect rows. The soldier at the head of one row, who had a small beard and was smoking a cigar, patted my sweat-drenched head and asked, "Is your daddy home?"

"Yeah," I said.

The soldiers filed into the house, rousing my mother and sister from their afternoon nap, but they didn't find my father there. I don't know what my mother said to the soldiers or if she said anything at all, but the one who had originally patted my sweat-drenched head came back and patted it again. "Where is your daddy?"

I hesitated.

"Your mom said that you probably know where your daddy is." The soldier took off his steel helmet, and the hair he brushed down with his hand was blond and as soaked with sweat as mine was. His movements were graceful, and the sight of him smoking his cigar reminded me of the people in imperial dress on postage stamps.

I thought of that little stream and the butterflies, dragonflies, wildflowers, and verdant grasses that grew so thickly around it, and then I reluctantly put down my half-finished kite. I led the soldiers across the vast and half-fallow garden, toward the stream that divided the garden from the open fields. I was not completely certain that my father was there waiting for the woman in white. But once I saw those dark clouds gathering in the sky and felt that moisture filling the air, once the northeast monsoon wind came gusting through the withered vegetation in the garden and brought to my nose the damp scent of the woman in white's sweat, I suddenly knew that my father and the woman were there by the stream immersed in their affection, clinging tightly to one another. I was the first one to spot the woman in white as she extricated herself from the arms of my father, who was kneeling on the ground, still trying to cling to her lower body. She turned around, crossed the stream, and was on her way. I could sense that her eyes just then were as damp as her feet. My father stood up and followed her with his eyes. If what happened next had not happened, I bet my father, that time, would have gone after her.

The soldier with the cigar saw my father and the woman first. He gave a signal, and the rest of the soldiers went charging swiftly toward the stream. Then he tapped his cigar, only to discover that it had already burned down to the end, so he flung it to the ground and stamped it out. He took a new cigar from his pocket, held this one in his mouth, and lit it languorously, unhurriedly, with his lighter. After his first, violent puff, he summoned up all his energy to shout something. I couldn't make out what he shouted, because his voice was as sharp and deafening as the roar of a wild animal.

My father and the woman in white turned around at the same moment, and the same expression of shock and panic appeared on both their faces. The cigar-smoking soldier pressed his hand against my chest to keep me from running forward; then he himself went striding toward the stream, still shouting.

The woman had no time to put on her shoes, and she went dashing barefoot into the open field. My father stood still. He kept moving his head back and forth, looking now at the oncoming tide of soldiers, now at the woman who was fleeing in the other direction.

The sky and the earth were fading into one unbroken stretch of darkness, as the dense, suffocating storm clouds covered the garden. Their guns at the ready, the soldiers broke into two groups and went careening past my father to cross the stream. The cigar smoker stopped in front of the stream and gazed off into the endless field, then turned around and looked at my father, then finally spat into the water. I guessed that the reason he hadn't crossed the stream was that he didn't want to get his tall boots wet. When the sound of gunshots rang out, my father began to shudder violently.

A raindrop landed on the tip of my nose, and this made me think that the woman must have gotten away. The rain always fell only after she was gone. This time it rained harder and longer than it ever had before. The cigar smoker used his helmet to keep his cigar dry. My father kept looking off at the field and didn't say a word, and he refused the cigar the soldier offered him. Suddenly my mother was there, coming toward me, and she grabbed my hand and brought me back to the house.

The rain was falling heavily; visibility must have been no more than a meter. Despite everything that my mother did to keep me from seeing, I still saw through the window, fuzzily, two soldiers, one in front and one in back, carrying a woman dressed in white past our house. I saw that the ends of the woman's hair were dragging in the mud. A huge red flower fell from her hair, and I was reminded of the red flower I had seen my father give her. Then I finally understood that this time the woman had not gone away as she always did. Or maybe I should say that she had gone away more perfectly this time than she ever had before: I never saw the woman cross the stream into our garden again, though I often saw my father walking by himself beside the water.

After the soldiers finished their protracted inquiries and left, my father came over to me and slapped me on the face with all his might. My mother pulled me to her chest and took the second blow for me.

For almost six months after that, I was afraid to go in the garden because my father was so often there, pacing like a madman on the bank of the stream that bordered the open field, his hair a mess, his face consumed with longing. Once in a while he would take out his hunting rifle and fire it at random. All in that same year, the young Dayak broke into our house, my sister's short life ended, my mother got pregnant again, and my father wrested my day-old half-brother, that thing he called a "bastard," from my mother's arms. Then, over a year after all that, when I must have been around eight, my father finally stopped his walks by the stream and began inviting his friends to our house for his all-night parties. His extravagant passion for entertaining and his determination to inject some kind of stimulant into the stale life of local society all predate my mother's obsession with her labyrinthine garden, but not by very long.

By the time I was in high school, I finally understood the chain of events that had led up to the incident by the stream. The Communists, whose bases were deep in the jungle and who desperately lacked support and equipment, got a substantial portion of their resources by extorting money, from rich people and ordinary people alike. My father was one of their prime targets. The person they had sent to wheedle money out of him was none other than that woman in white. Everyone said that she had been extraordinarily beautiful, so much so that it was hard to associate her with the Communists; that is quite possibly why they chose her for this mission. The English soldiers who killed her supposedly had no idea what the true relationship between her and my father was. Afterward, though, a number of soldiers were bivouacked at our house for a while, allegedly to keep my father safe from further harassment. It is possible that they were there less to protect him than to keep an eye on him, because the government suspected him of secretly donating money to the Communists. After the soldiers questioned my father several times, though, they satisfied themselves that he was merely a victim, like all the other bourgeois Chinese who had been threatened by the Communists. My mother's depression, my father's despondency, and all the different things that eventually came to pass would show me just how strong my father's infatuation with that woman had been and why he hated me as much as he did. But I stand by what I said before: I was only six years old when all that happened; what did I know about the world?

Chapter 5

One afternoon in October 1965, Lin Yuan, thirty-five years old at the time, took a pair of binoculars and a camera and followed a giant lizard around the fields near our house. On his route he encountered all sorts of marvelous flora and beasts and birds. Then, just like a macaque that had eaten wild loquat seeds or drunk the narcotic water from the pitchers of a carnivorous nepenthes plant, he disappeared without a trace. My father hired several native guides and took two of his friends from the hunting league deep into the jungle to search for him. For a while, everyone was convinced that Lin Yuan had died in the jungle. A month later, though, Lin Yuan showed up at our house in very high spirits. The next day, before he flew home to Taiwan to begin immigration procedures, he told my father that he was going to buy some land near ours and build a lair for himself there. He wanted to live out the remainder of his life here, with my father and the wild birds and animals as his neighbors.

There were several stories about what had happened to Lin Yuan during his time in the jungle, just as there were about my sister's death. Some people said that he had actually drunk the water from the pitchers of a nepenthes and gone wandering in a daze through the forest, living on fruit he picked himself and building a house high in a tree, where he lived for two full days before a group of Dayak hunters pointed their poison-daubed arrows at him, at which time he abruptly recovered his sanity and came down from the tree in a rage. One local Chinese swore up and down that Lin Yuan had had a spell cast on him by a Malay village shaman. Any time he wanted, the shaman could send poisonous insects spewing out of Lin Yuan's orifices or cause horrible hemorrhaging in his internal organs, and therefore Lin Yuan had no choice but to abandon his comfortable life in prosperous Taiwan and lower himself to the level of Borneo, its desolation and savage heat, so that he could live out the rest of his life, like a zombie, under the shaman's supervision.

Like most people who know Lin Yuan well, I find both these stories laughable. Not only do they reflect the silly superstition that prevails in the lower strata of the local society, but they also reveal how much the people who invented them envied and detested people like my father and Lin Yuan. This is not to say that I'm taking the side of Lin Yuan and his ilk. It's just that I know full well that Lin Yuan was too intelligent to do the kinds of irrational things people said he had done. I also understood better than anyone how much of a gift he had for dealing with other people and how impressive his social skills were. He was the kind of man who could arrange the beheading of an enemy who was a thousand miles away without any real effort. He handled everything meticulously and left no vulnerabilities for his enemies to exploit. There was no way he would ever have submitted to a village shaman.

So the only story I believed is this last one: that Lin Yuan had gone on one of the "sexpeditions" that had been popular among white men in Borneo years ago. He had ventured into the jungle by himself, visited the Dayak longhouses, and enjoyed an endless succession of one-night stands with young Dayak girls. For a little paper money and some jewelry, it was said, a beautiful, gentle Dayak girl would look upon any strange man as her husband for a night and would indulge his every desire. Especially given how Lin Yuan lived in his later years, I'm inclined to believe that this is what happened. I would also be willing to believe that Lin Yuan and my father went into the jungle on what they called their "sex safaris" more than once, thereby continuing the unfinished sexual adventures of their college days.

"The jungle's a mysterious place." Whenever he was supposed to be accounting for his whereabouts during his month in the jungle, Lin Yuan would find a way to stray from the subject. He would talk like a newly enlightened Zen master. "You were right, old friend. Returning to simple things, primal things—that's the best way to purify and elevate the soul. I want to be like the last rays of the sun as it sets. I'm going to spend the rest of my life here."

"To me, you look like an old lion," my father said to his friend, who was suddenly as full of health and swagger as a twenty-year-old; the haze of cares and tribulations that had shrouded the first half of his life seemed to have dissipated completely. "Our lives will be over soon enough. Remember to keep your feet on solid ground."

This conversation took place at a party, amid the smells of cigarettes and wine, in front of an attentive audience of distinguished ladies and gentlemen. My father was casual and unruffled, and Lin

Yuan was being lighthearted and cryptic. The guests returned to their desultory conversations, and I was the only one there who took what the two men had just said seriously. The odd nonchalance with which my father had overseen the search for Lin Yuan was proof enough for me that he had known all along what Lin Yuan was doing for that month. My father also hadn't been at all surprised when Lin Yuan decided to immigrate to Borneo. Before my father had moved home from Taipei to start his own family, he had done his best to try to convince Lin Yuan, his best friend from college, to give up his comfortable Taipei life and join him in founding a private kingdom in the South Seas. Eventually Lin Yuan, the scion of a wealthy family from central Taiwan, had succeeded, with my father's help, in becoming an authentic Borneo Chinese, and he was quickly absorbed into my father's high-society social circles. Lin Yuan turned into a decadent philistine, every bit as despicable as my father and his friends. He had bought an enormous piece of land that was even closer to the jungle than my family's house. Tycoons and other dignitaries liked to stay at the Lin mansion when they were in the area for business or pleasure. The exterior of the Lin mansion alone probably made it the single most impressive private residence in the entire region.

If my family's house was a forbidding and lifeless fortress, then the Lins' house was more like an inviting mountain villa or an idyllic resort, with doors open and lights blazing for guests at all hours of the day and night. The Lins kept a full menagerie of native birds and animals, which added exotic appeal and a sense of fun to the place. The atmosphere at their house was vibrant and pleasant.

An overnight guest at the Lins' could wake up at dawn and walk out onto a balcony to pick round red rambutan fruit for breakfast. He might see a peacock spreading his tail beneath the foliage or a barking deer munching languorously on a hibiscus flower. He would be enfolded by a sense of well-being not unlike that of a Buddhist believer treading barefoot on sacred ground.

The guest might then look out at the vista that extended before him and see that, even though dawn was already breaking, bats and owls were still out and about, circling around our house under the last rays of moonlight. My father would be lounging on his own balcony, and my mother would be fussing about in her kaleidoscopic garden like a professional watchmaker. At the only open window in the house, I would be drinking my morning *bak kut teh*, the herbal pork-rib soup that was the only thing with meat in it that I would consume all day. My face would be turning pale, and my tongue would be glistening, since my mother had raised me as a resolute and almost-perfect vegetarian, like herself.

Driven by curiosity, this guest might try to walk the long path that connected one house to the other. If he did so, he would discover that my mother's labyrinthine garden served the function of a watchdog for us—it was so easy for an outsider to get lost in it, even with the path to guide him. In the end, there would be nothing for him to do but gaze at my house and heave a deep sigh before beating a disappointed retreat back to Lin Yuan's.

This so-called path connecting the two houses was actually a walkway more than five hundred meters long, which Lin Yuan had asked my father to design. It stretched from the Lins' house to our backyard, so that the two families could come and go freely between each other's homes. The walkway had been designed to blend in with the topography and natural landscape, so it was actually quite hard to distinguish from its surroundings. Near our house it was almost entirely overgrown by greenery and seemed to lead only to murky and desolate places, whereas once it reached the Lins' property it led into great clearings, places awash with sunlight, where a person could take in everything around him with a single glance. The path traced a route like that a wounded elephant might follow as it fled from hunters: at first, the elephant would have the deep jungle for camouflage; eventually, though, there would be no place to hide any longer, and it would start racing maniacally, aimlessly, toward the most open place it could find; finally, it would fall with a terrible crash to the ground near Lin Yuan's expansive patio. That was where Lin Yuan liked to serve hors d'oeuvres and wine and entertain his guests with cockfights, dogfights, trained monkeys, trained hawks, and the like.

Sometimes Chunxi and I would take walks along this path, letting ourselves drift into hypnotic states at its farthest reaches, getting turned around, finding ourselves coming back to the same place more than once. It was just like the time we got lost in the jungle.

Chapter 6

Lin Yuan wasn't just an animal lover; he was a proper amateur biologist as well. After he moved to Borneo, he spent three solid years researching the giant lizard and the monkey-eating Philippine eagle, long enough to earn him the nicknames "Lizard Man" and "Eagle Man." Soon the fame and achievements of Lin Yuan the biologist had far surpassed those of Lin Yuan the veterinarian. His original vocation also had to do with animals, but it had been a different matter altogether from his hobby. In the animal hospital he had castrated animals, while in the jungle he was doing everything he could to ensure that their future generations would flourish and their species would endure.

The creatures that were allowed to wander around the Lins' yard were all mild and timid herbivores. The more ferocious carnivores were confined to a miniature zoo on the property, and this zoo was the cause of many arguments between Lin Yuan and his wife.

What happened to Chunxi is a good example of what could go wrong. One July morning, very early, both the wild birds and the birds in the Lins' aviaries were raising their usual racket, and the southwest monsoon wind rushing through Chunxi's bedroom was becoming a blasting vortex, piercingly dry and oppressively hot. But something was different from usual: in that vortex Chunxi could smell something moist and cloying, almost as if a ball of slick mud had been dumped onto her body, solid and hefty enough that she could barely breathe.

Chunxi's limbs were limp, and she felt listless all over. The ball of mud was sealing up her eyes, she could sense it. It was seeping in through her pores, invading her larynx and auricles; then, with a smacking sound, it had penetrated her female parts. It was squeezing through the gullies of her stomach and her thoracic cavity.

Chunxi spat out a huge mouthful of the mud and tried to scream, but then she realized that the ball of mud had already left her body and transformed into a hot current of air that resembled thousands of tiny flames leaping all around her.

Eventually the flames started to die out slowly, leaving behind wisps of white smoke that were about to disappear in the monsoon wind.

Actually, though, it's less accurate to say that the smoke disappeared than to say that it congealed to form a ball of lumpy matter that seemed to swim in the air like liquid that had escaped the pull of gravity. It mimicked, one after another, the internal organs of which it had just completed a tour. So Chunxi was able to watch the violent pulsing of the organs of her own body, her body that had been born prematurely. She could see her transparent ovaries producing eggs, a sight not unlike that of the transparent bellies of peacock fish, distended with a profusion of eggs.

This lumpy matter rode toward the window on the monsoon wind and then loitered around the window for a while before it finally wrapped itself around the windowsill, stretching and straining like a calf being born. In the forms it took, Chunxi said, she could make out her own hazy image, creeping prematurely out of her mother's body.

Only then did Chunxi recover consciousness completely. She opened her eyes all the way and saw the dazzling morning light in the vanity mirror. She saw a giant atlas moth fly away, as fast as a double-bladed razor slicing a sprig of flowers off a tree. Out of the corner of her eye, she saw an amphibious, carrion-eating lizard poised on the windowsill, about to exit through the window but still casting its eyes around the room. The lizard stuck out its tongue two times rapidly and lapped at the flavor in the air of Chunxi, waking up.

The second time the lizard's tongue came out, Chunxi turned her head and looked straight at the window. She saw that half the lizard's body had already disappeared into the morning light but that its tail was still dawdling inside, whipping back and forth on the windowsill. It was hard to imagine that such a huge tail belonged to a lizard. It made Chunxi feel like she was looking, from a fresh angle, at one more of the infinite faces of that ball of mud and that flying liquid.

After the lizard was gone, Chunxi took a look around her room. The floor was covered with scratches, as if a rake had been drawn across it. The desk was a mess. A tall vase that had stood against the wall was broken. The blankets were spotted with mud prints that looked as though they had been made by claws. The southwest monsoon wind was still coming in, still a blasting vortex, and was beginning to blow away the putrid odor that filled the room.

Chunxi ran a fever for the next three days. Lin Yuan and his wife argued about this incident for an entire month. From the mud prints on the blanket, Lin Yuan deduced that the intruder had been the largest of the giant lizards in his menagerie, an animal that had once swallowed a small dog whole. It had broken out of its cage, and it spent three days wandering between our house and theirs before it was caught. Lin Yuan decided that the lizard must have been lonely, and he empathized with it. So he made it a larger cage and then put in the cage two lovely, delicate female lizards, both of them virgins—I had heard Lin Yuan use that word when he described them to his guests. As far as his own daughter, Chunxi, was concerned, Lin Yuan just warned her mildly that she should be sure to turn on the air conditioner and close the window every night before she went to sleep. He also had bars installed on her window, as if the party whose movements had to be restricted was Chunxi and not the lizard.

"Every time I wake up from a dream, I always think I'm back in that incubator," Chunxi, who had been born two months premature, had told me. "I'm afraid I won't be able to survive outside my room. I want to shut myself up in there forever and never go out again."

After the incident with the lizard, Chunxi spent several afternoons in a row alone in the tree house I had built, napping and idling away the hours. Maybe she wanted to hide from that harem keeper of a lizard. (My father thought very highly of the lizard and trapped several more wild females to give to him; I still remember how rapacious that lizard looked as he set upon each of them.) Maybe that ball of mud, as murky as a birth canal, and that flying liquid, transparent like amniotic fluid, really did remind her of her own premature birth and her imperfectly developed infant body.

It seems to me that all of us were implicated in Chunxi's eventual, irrevocable sinking away from the world. I, Lin Yuan, my mother, my father, and even that dead little sister of mine whose name I've forgotten—we were five fingers forming a fist, fusing flesh and blood to become the instrument of Chunxi's destruction.

Chapter 7

At one of my father's parties, some time before the party where the lost owl was killed, I was talking with a few of the younger guests when I heard Lin Yuan describing, in that voice of his that reminded me of a hunter skinning his quarry, what he called the "object of his sexual fantasies." This wording is a bit forced, but so it goes. That night there were many members of prominent local families present. After everyone was sated with food and drink, a couple of distant relatives of the royal house of Brunei started discussing a rumor about the royal family that had been in circulation for a while but which the sultan's spokesmen had firmly denied. At that moment I was making small talk with two guys my own age who were about to go study in England. One of them was planning to pay a visit to Liverpool when he got there. At that time, John Lennon hadn't yet been assassinated, Paul hadn't yet been arrested for drugs, Ringo was hanging out in Hollywood, and George was promoting Indian mysticism. There was still hope that the group might reunite. Elvis Presley and Bruce Lee were still flush with testosterone, and both of them seemed destined to live forever. Everything was in its prime. We sang "Hey, Jude" softly to ourselves.

Pretty soon, ignoring the fact that some of us were underage, a man with a small beard grabbed a plump old man by the neck and warned him that he'd better not say the name of the member of the Brunei royal family who had chased the winner of the Miss Asia pageant around the palace swimming pool a week or so ago. But it was too late. The taboo royal name passed from guest to guest, traveling around the room just as the owl would later. I could tell, though, that everyone found the name of the Miss Asia pageant winner far more interesting.

Then a flock of ugly rumors about the royal family came spilling out of the mouths of those seemingly refined people, just like the bats I would someday set loose. Later, when I learned that the deaths of Bruce Lee and Elvis had been connected to their masculine swagger, their genital energy, what came to mind first was this scene. My idolization of the two stars was not changed a bit by the dishonorable circumstances of their deaths. The truth is that I had been ensconced in the warm circle of my father's salacious friends for so long that there was no part of me that they hadn't encroached upon—not even that little Cupid with broken wings that nurtured my relationship with Chunxi.

My father's hometown had been part of the Brunei empire a century before. By now, though, it was separated from that tiny Muslim country by a turgid, ink green river, long since polluted by Brunei oil. The traditions and souls of the people in that town had been polluted as well. This might sound a bit like a tale from *The Arabian Nights*—the idea that a strait-laced Muslim society could corrupt its immaculate neighbor. But in fact people who live under puritanical rules usually have an agenda different from that of the rule makers. After suffering through one more week of life beneath the crushing weight of the Mount of Five Fingers that was Islamic law, the followers of Allah who lived in Brunei would cross the international border every weekend to spend their nights out in my father's hometown.[1] Then, after three nights and two days of feasting and revelry, they would retreat to their own country and recite the Koran as penance.

My father's hometown supplied the whores, the gambling, and the liquor that the tiny Muslim country could not provide for itself, and there were significant profits to be made off the people on whom Allah had bestowed all that oil. It was a business opportunity too good to pass up, and so the town naturally devolved into a place where visitors were greeted by madams and chased out again by cuckolds.

My father's hometown—and mine, too, I suppose—existed solely to serve its wealthy neighbor. Prices there skyrocketed. The landscape turned weird, ruinous. Less than twenty years before, it had been a fishing village, a vista of masts and fluttering sails. The trees and open-air cafés that lined the roads had attracted wild monkeys;

---

1. In the sixteenth-century Chinese novel *Journey to the West*, the mischievous primate hero Sun Wukong rebels against earthly authority, and consequently the Buddha traps him under the Mount of Five Fingers.

hawks and crows had flown about. People had interacted with people, and animals with animals, and people with animals, in a pleasant, low-key fashion.

When common people set out to enjoy themselves, they do so with a noble dignity, so of course the royal family in the deepest reaches of the palace followed this principle in the opposite direction. The royal family used all sorts of pretexts to invite beauty queens of all nationalities to visit the palace as "goodwill ambassadors." By imperial edict, these so-called goodwill ambassadors had to spend the night with members of the family. Of course, the ambassadors were compensated very well for these visits, so the pageant winners and runners-up would generally capitulate in spite of themselves. The nights they spent in that extravagant South Seas palace were nights they would never forget.

There were, of course, a few who resisted. These women would have to be kept in the palace against their will, maybe given drugs. Rumor had it that a beauty from Venezuela who still refused to give in was stripped naked and locked inside a cage for seven days with only a randy young male dog as company.

The palace doctors subjected every beauty queen to a thorough medical inspection before each encounter, so that the noblemen, who placed a high premium on their own bodily purity, could keep their bodies, vessels of the imperial glory, clean and unmarred.

There was the occasional beauty queen who would try to expose the royal family's misdeeds to the United Nations, but the family knew that this tactic would never succeed. The authority of kings and sultans was untouchable. Everyone knew that America might at any time feign aggressive military maneuvers in order to preserve the illusion of peace between Communist China and Taiwan, and America was not about to alter its aircraft carrier routes or threaten to set off a nuclear bomb over the misadventures of some bimbo. So the royal family continued to flourish, and their gold-plated palace endured in all its auspicious glory.

It made a lot of sense to me that, between the sixteenth century and now, the once vast and influential Brunei empire had shrunk down to a tiny oil kingdom, only six thousand four hundred and seventy five square kilometers in size.

There is a point to all my blabbering about my hometown and Brunei. All this, as I myself would learn only much later, is relevant to what eventually happened to Chunxi. That night, when everyone else was busy being impressed by the fact that the young Miss Asia had powerful equestrian buttocks and a brilliant tongue that could speak eleven different languages (and surely it was because of her linguistic gifts and her knack with horses that she had been chosen as the winner), Lin Yuan was sitting by himself on the sofa, clutching a martini and staring at the reflections of the guests in the glass. Amid the racket of everyone else's conversation, he was mumbling to himself. I didn't know who he was hoping would come stir him from his melancholy reverie, but I knew that I, who had seen my father coming toward me and had just begun to plan my escape, was the only one listening to him.

"Her tongue is like a live coal. Her neck is slender, and her stomach is flat. Her whole body is feeble and yielding. A long club made out of flesh, as long as the rest of her body, grows behind her buttocks, a club of flesh that could slice a dog right in half. If I didn't have a club like that of my own, I'd have no way of controlling her. . . ." Then Lin Yuan turned his head and looked at me, and I saw that his arms and legs had gone rigid and that a bright red protrusion had erupted on his forehead. "Su Qi . . ."

"Take it easy, Uncle," I said. "You're still working on your research on the lizards' mating habits, is that it?"

I wasn't entirely sure that that was what was going on, though; maybe Lin Yuan was imagining that he was still roaming around the jungle or the menagerie, or maybe he was missing the Dayak longhouses. Maybe in his mind he had fused those scenes and the one in my father's parlor; the pursuit by the swimming pool, the randy male dog, the thoroughbred beauty queens, and everything else might have led him to confuse for a moment the roles of human being and of animal.

Lin Yuan looked like he was about to say more, and I suspected that what he was going to say might be a bit shocking. But then he spotted my father in the martini glass, standing very nearby talking to two female guests, and he quickly turned his head. In fact, the martini glass had created an optical illusion, and my father was still a good ten paces away. So Lin Yuan had to raise his voice to say to my father, "You're on pretty decent terms with the sultan. When are you going to bring the rest of us to the palace to experience all that for ourselves?"

"That'll be no problem," my father said, lowering his head as if he were telling a secret but speaking loudly and clearly. "The sultan loves visitors. The palace has twelve hundred guest rooms. Anyone who's interested is welcome to go pay court. Bring the whole family if you like."

The fathers of the two guys I had just met, the ones who were about to leave for England, asked me to take their sons on an evening stroll through the garden. What the two fathers both meant by that was that the sons had already fulfilled their social obligations to the older generation and that it was time to find a nice nursery to consign them to.

It didn't matter that my father never took his friends to visit the sultan's palace. The all-night parties, first at my father's house and then at the Lins' place, which didn't need to be approved by imperial edict and didn't require any medical examination for entrance, had already caught the attention of certain members of the royal family. I had heard that one of the sultan's sons had come "down the stream in quest" of something and had attended one of my father's parties dressed as a commoner. He was supposed to have sprained his ankle there and eaten so much he got sick. That night, Lin Yuan's peacocks and barking deer were wandering around just outside our gate. Parrots and birds of paradise were shuttling around my mother's garden. All the flowers were in bloom, and above all this the stars were very bright. By the time my father realized that something peculiar was going on, it was nearly dawn, and the prince was already gone. My father drove over to the river and learned that the prince had just boarded the boat that would take him across to Brunei. At that hour the white miscanthus grass was luxuriant, "and the white dew was not yet dry." My father made a deep bow toward the boat, as if the prince were there—lo! "on the islet in the midst of the water." I know all this only from my father's own account. I hadn't realized anything was going on that night, but not only had I apparently shaken the prince's hand, I may also have told him a few off-color jokes I had heard from the other guests. I hadn't noticed at all the propitious air he must have brought into the room with him or the odd reactions of the animals, all of whom seemed to know what I did not.[2]

2. The quotations are from the poem ""Jian Jia" (The reeds and rushes), one of the more than three hundred poems in the collection known as the *Book of Odes* (*Shi Jing*). The *Book of Odes* is supposedly a collection of folk songs assembled by Confucius and his followers in the fifth century B.C. The complete text of the poem, in James Legge's 1898 translation, is as follows:

> The reeds and rushes are deeply green,
> And the white dew is turned into hoarfrost.
> The man of whom I think,
> Is somewhere about the water.
> I go up the stream in quest of him,
> But the way is difficult and long.
> I go down the stream in quest of him,
> And lo! he is right in the midst of the water.
>
> The reeds and rushes are luxuriant,
> And the white dew is not yet dry.
> The man of whom I think,
> Is on the margin of the water.
> I go up the stream in quest of him,
> But the way is difficult and steep.
> I go down the stream in quest of him,
> And lo! he is on the islet in the midst of the water.
>
> The reeds and rushes are abundant,
> And the white dew is not yet ceased.
> The man of whom I think,
> Is on the bank of the river.
> I go up the stream in quest of him,
> But the way is difficult and turns to the right.
> I go down the stream in quest of him,
> And lo! he is on the island in the midst of the water.

Chapter 8

A return to simple and primal things, the elevation and purification of his soul—that was what Lin Yuan hoped to accomplish by moving to Borneo. Those were the missiles he fired into his personal fortifications, because he wanted to build something new amid the ruins. My father liked to say that Lin Yuan's ideas about all this were unrealistic. But then again there was little to criticize about the wish to change everything about oneself by making small adjustments to the hazel- and weed-cluttered Borneo landscape. I actually think that a very similar spirit of heroism drove both my father and Lin Yuan. My father must have understood how Lin Yuan felt, seen through Lin Yuan's goals in moving here. It was just that both of them liked to explain themselves very circuitously, and sometimes it was difficult to grasp the logic of the things they said. I myself never really understood what Lin Yuan meant by "return" and "elevation" and "purification." Nor did I have any real interest in understanding it. To me, words such as these were like the path that connected our two houses; they distorted things that should have been clear and clarified what should have been distorted, so that one thing at different times could look like something different from what it really was. No matter how hard you tried, you couldn't grasp the truth of it.

But I watched both men carefully, and I figured out that this talk about "elevation and purification" dated back to their college days. Before he moved to Borneo, Lin Yuan had come to visit us often, and after dinner the two men liked to sit on the patio, look up at the falling stars in the northern sky, and talk about their college days. My mother and I, sitting just behind them in the parlor, might as well have been a pair of potted plants for all they cared. These sessions occurred even more frequently after Lin Yuan moved to Borneo. Sometimes a friend of my father's who had studied abroad in England would join them, and his own memories of Oxbridge sophistication seemed largely similar to their college recollections.

The hot monsoon wind was like an endless river of blood, and it introduced a sense of arteriosclerosis into those sensuous, heady

South Seas nights. The South Seas, that fat beauty, shrouded our garden with her bodily greases. Our roof was trampled by her vein-laced calves and her preternaturally hairy feet. Owls and bats and centipedes and toads came rushing out of her. And I gradually came to realize that the sickly stagnation that afflicted all of us members of the Su family had something to do with the South Seas climate and its netherworld dampness. I think it affected my mother most of all.

My mother was a plant whose roots ran deep, with many branches but few leaves, that had not borne fruit for many years. Other, parasitic plants, chief among them my murderous banyan of a father, covered her. She had devoted herself to the cultivation of her labyrinthine garden and meanwhile had let her own life become a wasteland. Sitting in the parlor listening through the window to my father and Lin Yuan talking on the patio, she was as beautiful as a fig tree laden with fruit. But then she was also a tree ringed round by pythons, a forbidding figure for little monkeys and mice that may have wanted to approach her.

If you were to climb her, wriggling your way up on her branches, you would come to see that her heart was like an old anthill. You certainly did not want to do anything to disturb it, but it was also weak enough that you could destroy it with a single poke.

Oh, mother.

One time, when I was on the patio, looking inside at my mother through the curtains, her features disfigured by the dim lamplight, I suddenly thought of an empress dowager holding court from behind a screen, her spine twisted from osteoporosis but her hair and fingernails still done up in a fearsome fashion.

I must have been born at the wrong time, because I was never able to bask in the kind of youth that my father and Lin Yuan had enjoyed. I was stuck behind the window with my mother, watching as those two stood beside the lake of their youth and went fishing for memories.

Their memories clustered like fish in a calm pond, all kinds of fish, amid the waves and tiny ripples. I was often surprised at the size of the catch they could bring in without even seeming to try.

Usually the first load of fish would give them nothing but fodder for jokes and mockery. Once that load was dispensed with, they would start to fish in the deeper portions of the lake, the zones of subconscious memory. Depending on their fishing technique, the same fish might come out looking differently, or weighing more or less, than it had before. Sometimes it would be so different that I would mistakenly believe it was a different species of fish altogether.

I would have thought that my mother could have been found swimming in a fairly important place deep inside the lake. But my father must have been using a bitter, ineffective bait, because she came up on his hook very infrequently. My mother, who does so much to fatten up my memories, seemed to have been excised at some point from my father's. But then again, if I observed carefully enough, I would discover that my mother was there, acting like an amphibious creature that wanders from the lake onto the land and back again with an aloof and uninterested air.

She knew all about the fish in the deepest reaches of the lake, and she even knew the order in which my father would catch them.

They were beautiful, they were radiant. They were young and sentimental. They could be eaten, but they could also be admired solely for their beauty. They must have swum in the lakes of many men's memories. Most of them dated back to my father's and Lin Yuan's college days and had at some point been feverishly in love with one man or the other. The seeds of love that the two men scattered had been numerous and short-lived; most had died as soon as they started to sprout, by which point my father or Lin Yuan would already be looking for the next likely planting ground. In this respect they were like most other men: they saw that they were young and energetic and that there was no shortage of fertile fields in the world. They couldn't possibly limit themselves to tending one plant only.

I never got a clear sense of just how many tender young plants they had trampled on. But I understood vaguely that these were young women who had just broken free of the umbilical cord of high school and were experiencing independence for the first time. They had sucked greedily at the milk of first love that my father and Lin Yuan had offered them, but before long they had been cast down by one of the men into the quiet depths of his past. Now, all these years later, my father and Lin Yuan would cast hooks for these beautiful ghosts, now soaked to the bone, and pull them back onto dry land, to find that their former charms were unchanged. Given the high opinions my father and Lin Yuan had of themselves, one can only imagine how enchanting these women must have been.

The two men would strike immediately after they had identified their target, and they rarely failed in their attacks. They also never pursued the same girl at the same time. That way, if one of them failed in an initial pursuit, he could pass his prey, and his accumulated experience, on to the other. Never once did the second pursuer fail.

They were just like two hyenas chasing down a gazelle. If one got tired, the other one took over. Those girls, those tender human seedlings, were in the grip of first love, and they had no place to hide. The two men were cruel, and nothing could deter them. With their words they skinned the girls alive, and then with their sudden departures they delivered the mortal blow. The hearts of these girls must have been stripped bare by the shame they felt.

My father and Lin Yuan always got the better of their targets, because of their brilliant strategizing and their superhuman strength, just like champion athletes badly beating unknown challengers.

Once in a while, though, something did go wrong. One girl had come to their apartment with a knife and threatened to kill the father of the baby she was carrying. Another one slit her wrists three times, and Lin Yuan only managed to keep her from doing it a fourth time by paying an art student from another school to console her. There were too many stories like this for me to mention them all. I've seen pictures of my father and Lin Yuan when they were in college, and they look just like the male models in underwear ads.

The two of them were remarkable for their inexhaustible energy. They remained undisputed champions; their lead over their opponents just kept increasing. And they never lost their hyenalike ability to cooperate. After Lin Yuan moved to Borneo, all these traits continued to find expression in their social lives and on their sex safaris, or so I gathered from the evidence I had available.

Lin Yuan, the amateur biologist, often led my father on treks through the jungle. Over time, he convinced my father to give up his rifle in favor of a pair of binoculars, a video recorder, a camera, and a sketchbook and to look at the animals in ways other than down the barrel of a gun. One day I casually glanced through a sketchbook that my father had brought back with him from the jungle, and only then did I realize, with some surprise, how great an influence Lin Yuan had been having on him.

The book was filled with spontaneous sketches in pencil of birds and animals: the crocodiles and proboscis monkeys that lived in the swamps, the bearded pigs that gathered at the bases of durian trees, the enormous pitchers of the nepenthes, which looked as plump and well-fed as any carnivorous animal, the goats, honey bears, and various birds and insects that roamed through the thick weeds. They were all exquisitely drawn with delicate pen strokes, and this shocked me. I had had no idea that my father could draw anything besides blueprints, that he might have a talent that was related to real human feeling and did not stink of money.

This sketchbook let me see, through my father's eyes, what a series of sex safaris in the wilds of Borneo must have been like for two middle-aged men. Claiming that they were conducting field research, they would hire guides for long treks through the jungle. They would pitch tents and observe the fauna. But they would also go to the longhouses and seduce the Dayak women with jewelry, perfume, fine clothing, and money. More than half the sketches in my father's book had to do with this latter aspect of the expeditions.

Many of the drawings were of Dayak girls, naked from the waist up or naked entirely, cowering in forced poses in the corners of longhouses, trying to smile and not exactly succeeding. They looked like desolate ghosts on the verge of transforming into vapors and disappearing forever.

These drawings looked like photographs taken out of focus. The Dayak girls were fuzzy and difficult to distinguish from one another. Their bodies looked incomplete, and their breasts and faces were perfunctorily drawn lumps. Often the drawings contained some extra lines that made no sense, as if my father had drawn in the heads of snakes, dogs, lizards, or monkeys in place of the girls' actual heads.

My father also documented very scrupulously the details of life in the longhouses: decorations, household items, livestock (chickens, ducks, cats, dogs, cows, sheep), pets (monkeys, turtles, birds, snakes, martens, badgers), and so forth. These nonhuman creatures packed the drawings, made them crowded and lively, like spokes radiating out from the bodies of the naked girls. The girls' bodies, flimsy like cotton blankets and nearly transparent, were all clones of one another, exactly the same in every longhouse my father drew. Claws, teeth, and scales were everywhere among these girl clones; they were surrounded on all sides by threatening and hungry animals. There was something truly ghastly about the drawings.

I couldn't help being reminded of the witch Circe in Homer's *Odyssey*. Circe lives alone on an island, and she entertains travelers from afar with delicacies from land and sea. With a wave of her magic wand, she can turn these travelers into animals. Then she trains them to serve her, to stay by her side always. The white men who went in succession on sex safaris to the longhouses might have enslaved the Dayak women, or maybe it was the Dayak women who enslaved them. There is no way to tell for sure.

My father and Lin Yuan weren't like Odysseus, who was able to turn his followers from pigs back into men. As much as they longed to sail to the corners of the world, they always grew weary once they realized they could no longer see the shore.

If my father had only transferred the passion and care that went into his drawings to other members of the human race, I believe he could have been a real man, of real flesh and blood, capable of crying real tears. He might not have insisted on keeping my mother and me at an impossible distance. At the very least, I might have shed tears when he died or kissed his gifted hands, even though by the time I had that chance so much of the flesh had already rotted off his fingers that you could see the bones.

Or my mother might have embraced his dead body or spent more time trying to summon back the head that had mysteriously departed from the rest of him.

Even after the episode on the swing, I kept on believing for a while longer that my father must have actually loved my mother at one point. But after a little more fishing in my own memories, I finally found proof for the hypothesis that had been haunting me for a long time: in fact, my father had never loved my mother. And I realized, too, that Lin Yuan had never loved his wife—a girl who had majored in home economics in college, Chunxi's mother.

The incident I call "the episode on the swing" has nothing to do with my sister's death. It does, however, involve the tree house where Chunxi and I spent so many hours and which brought me so many mournful and horrifying memories, some of which have to do with my sister's fall from another tree house.

My father hated my tree house. One afternoon around teatime, he and a couple of English friends took a walk out to its base. The tree house was right in the middle of the labyrinthine garden, about a thirty-minute walk from the house. At that time, Chunxi and I had just met, and I was spending the afternoon up in the tree house by myself, wondering when I would see her again. An Englishwoman caught sight of me and my tree house and stopped at the base of the tree, obviously very impressed.

I'd been working on the tree house for over three months, but this was the first time my father had seen it.

"What's that up in the tree there? A monkey?" I heard him ask.

"It's your son!" The Englishwoman said.

"It's a monkey," my father insisted.

I sized them up through my binoculars, keeping my face expressionless. It was as if I were surveying a pack of reptiles.

Around ten minutes after they had left, I saw my father reappear beside a swing that was hung on a tropical willow tree, about thirty meters away.

He stood under the willow and squinted in my direction, and I continued to watch him through the binoculars. There was rage on his face at first, but after about ten seconds had passed I saw through the binoculars that icy smile I knew so well. The texture of my father's skin was unclear from that distance, but his teeth shone like the blade of a knife. I swear I could hear him laughing across the distance separating us. I understood why my father was angry, and why he was laughing that mocking laugh. On a Saturday afternoon about two weeks before, my father had had some friends over for tea as he always did. Around five o'clock, I had seen a woman sitting on that swing. Through my binoculars I could see that she was the wife of a local timber tycoon, a woman who had won a beauty pageant sponsored by the Young Entrepreneurs' Association before she was married. Five minutes later my father appeared beside the swing.

They just undid a few buttons, and the whole process was short and ugly, smoothly and expertly done, like an act they had been through countless times before. The branch that held the swing nearly snapped in two under their weight.

Not having seen it yourself, you couldn't imagine how savage it was. Maybe you've seen on television the simultaneously aggressive and defensive posture of an orangutan hanging from a tree branch. The way its rage radiates through the entire jungle, cast over it like a spider's web—if you've seen that, then you might come close to imagining the spectacular sexual encounter between my father and that woman, in my mother's labyrinthine garden.

Now, two weeks later, my father looked up at me from his position near the swing. He never asked me about it, but I think he could tell everything from the expression on my face. Later that afternoon, I thought he might have been acting more kindly toward me than usual, so that I would keep his secret from my mother. But eventually I realized that that hadn't been the case, that in fact my father didn't give a damn. Even if he had, though, he would have been wasting his time and effort, since I would never have bothered my poor mother with something as vile as that anyway.

Of course I never went near the swing after that.

One time, Chunxi and I were asleep up in the tree house, and I dreamed that my younger sister was swinging on the swing by herself. She was humming a nursery song that my mother had often sung to her. One of her arms was missing. Then I woke up and saw my mother sitting on the swing, cradling a bouquet of flowers. She was as radiant as a falling star, as dignified as the Blessed Virgin.

Some time after that, I saw an Englishwoman approach the swing, and I immediately climbed down from the tree house.

"I'm sorry, but I'll have to ask you to leave," I said to her. "This is private property. No one's allowed to use it."

The Englishwoman gave me an awkward smile. "Are you George's son?"

Just then my father—"George" to the Englishwoman—and some other people showed up.

"What's going on here?" George asked.

The Englishwoman explained.

"He's just fooling around," George said. "My apologies to all of you. Let's go."

After that, none of my father's friends ever went near my mother's swing. Another month passed, and then I took the swing apart and told my mother to hire some workers to build a new swing on a different tree. My mother didn't comment until the new, pure white swing was finished. Then she said to me, "That shade of white's too glaring. Why don't you paint it a nice green?"

Chapter 9

The first time I saw Chunxi was at a New Year's party thrown by my father. The year was 1975, and I was in my sophomore year of high school.

The rainy season wasn't over yet. There had been a thunderstorm around noon on New Year's Eve, and that afternoon the tropical night came on early. By four o'clock the sky was already filled with stars, and bats were hovering above our house. The brilliant lights shining around the house drew other nocturnal beasts out of the jungle, and I saw a huge owl swoop down from the eaves of our roof to catch a small snake, startling a group of people who had been chatting near a window. The owl's wing, which was as solid as a horse's hoof, knocked a wine glass out of a man's hand.

The first guests to arrive were mostly either white or Malay. After nine, the Chinese guests started trickling in. This night was different from most other nights in that a large number of guests who were not bachelors came, so that our normally moribund home was inundated with the noise of laughter and firecrackers. The rockets set off by the guests' children spread out over the night sky like spider webs and mingled with the stars to form a lonesome pattern of infinity.

That night the stars were resplendent, and the clamor of birds and insects was overpowering. A Borneo peacock fanned its tail in the direction of several heavily made-up women.

At that time Lin Yuan didn't yet have his menagerie. That peacock was wandering around our house all night, but I have no idea where it came from.

The man who had had his wineglass knocked out of his hand lowered his head to examine a cut between his fingers. Then he raised his head again and smiled at the girl standing beside him. He held out his wounded hand, with the palm open, and he held it there for a long time.

I could see the blood gradually filling up the deep crevices of the lines on his palm. It reminded me of three red baby snakes hatching. The man's tender, white, and delicate arm was like the mother snake about to crawl off slowly into the night.

My mother, who had been standing next to me, immediately went over to him, grabbed his wrist, and lifted his hand above his heart. Then she led him through the crowd to go tend to the wound.

"Su Qi, the air's bad in here," she said to me as they passed. "Take Chunxi out to the garden for a walk."

The girl who was standing by the window watched my mother and the man disappear into the crowd. She had, in the corner of one of her eyes, an opening through which my image could appear in her line of vision, blurred and in fragments. I could feel that opening gradually growing larger, until I appeared to her in my entirety, like a passerby who had stopped to ask directions and was destined to disappear again a moment later.

As I sensed her watching me out of the corner of her eye, I was so agitated that I felt like I had within me and was ready to release the gathered force of a thousand horses. I thought of the slow rise of a tidal wave.

Then the magnificent wave disappeared with a flourish, just like the owl had. And I was left behind like the shattered wineglass.

The ray of light that shone out of the corner of the girl's eye was very small, but it was as strong as the owl's wing, and it broke me into pieces.

I should admit that I didn't actually feel all that at that very moment. I imagined those feelings into being about a year later, once I started to fall in love with Chunxi. They have little to do with my real feelings that night. What actually happened was this: while my mother was leading the injured man away, I saw the owl come back and land on an orchid trellis just outside the window, where it swiveled its baseball-sized head around and clucked incessantly. It looked just like a Buddhist monk with a big, bald head chanting his sutras. The blazing decorative lights in the garden provided a bright enough backdrop for me to see the snake, still wriggling in the owl's claws.

Come to think of it, even more than the owl looked like a monk, the snake looked like a set of prayer beads twisting in a monk's hands.

Despite the sounds of fireworks, laughter, and the owl's cries that were reverberating through the house, I felt that the atmosphere in the room had all the desolate solemnity of an ancient, remote temple.

I suspect that the look I gave Chunxi just then was not entirely amiable. This probably had something to do with the pride I had inherited from my pampered Su ancestors. I blamed my mother for not introducing the two of us ahead of time and putting me in this awkward position; at that point I wasn't even sure if the girl by the window was Chunxi. The girl seemed to be a bit in shock from the sudden ambush by the owl, and she didn't notice me coming toward her.

The owl lowered its baseball-sized head and took the fatal bite out of the snake.

"This kind of thing happens all the time in our house," I said. "I'm Su Qi, Su Huan's son. My mother asked me to take you for a walk in the garden."

The girl cast a look in the direction of the garden.

"My mother's crazy about gardening," I said. "She wants everyone who comes to our house to be impressed by her garden."

After I finished saying this, the girl looked out the window again. She rested her hands on the sill and breathed in deeply the air from outside.

"I've been in that garden before, with my mother," she said. "There were a lot of mosquitoes there."

"Well, we don't have to go then." The snake was now nowhere to be seen, and the owl was still swiveling its head around while it paced back and forth along the trellis. Under the bright lights, it took on the hue and shape of a cast-off baseball glove. "My mother's worried that all the smoke in here might be bad for your health."

"What did you mean when you said, 'This kind of thing happens all the time'?" the girl asked.

"I was talking about the owl." I moved closer to the window and pointed at the nocturnal creature. "We're too close to the jungle here. We've had people get attacked by animals before, many times. Just a few weeks ago a swarm of bees built a hive up in the eaves. My father was having a birthday party for one of his friends, and a champagne cork flew up and hit the hive. Can you imagine what that must have been like, over a thousand bees attacking a couple hundred people in this room?"

"My father told me that your father aimed at the hive on purpose when he uncorked the champagne," she said.

"I think he did, too," I said. "But then for all I know it was your father's idea. They're quite a pair, those two. I wonder what they have planned for tonight."

"I like the sound of that owl's cries."

"This is your first trip to Southeast Asia, right? Who was that man you were talking to just now?"

"I don't know," the girl answered. "We were speaking English, and I was just stammering the whole time."

A stray rocket suddenly went rushing toward the trellis, but the owl didn't deign to move aside for it. After that, a couple more, not strays this time, exploded right around the trellis. In the glare of their fires, the owl finally spread its wings languorously and disappeared into the night. Then another rocket went off right near our window, and another, obviously startled owl came flying toward us out of the shrubbery. It flew into the parlor, passing right between the girl and me. After a couple of orbits beneath the chandelier, it exited through another window and headed back toward the garden. It landed on a tree branch with its back to us and then turned its head almost one hundred and eighty degrees to look straight at us. Its facial features were indistinct, and it had a centipede dangling from its mouth.

The man whose hand had been cut by the broken wineglass had returned with a bandage on his injured hand. He stood amid a group of guests with his hands behind his back, and he had raised his head to watch the owl circling just beneath the ceiling. This man had bright red lips, thick eyebrows, and narrow eyes—maybe they made an impression on me because I still had in mind the perfectly round eyes of the owl—and he had thin, wispy sideburns. His skin was as white as an albino beauty snake. As he followed the owl out the window with his eyes, an inscrutable smile suddenly appeared on his face. Maybe he thought that this was the same owl that had broken his glass. No one besides him, the girl, and me had noticed the owl fly through the room.

The girl watched the owl attentively as it devoured the centipede. The owl turned the rest of its body around to face us, and as it swallowed it stretched its entire body and partially closed its eyes. It looked cute, like a cat being petted. Then a gust of the northeast monsoon wind struck the owl, and its feathers bristled up like the fur on a rabbit. It emitted a series of gentle, almost feminine cries. This owl had a prudish, delicate personality; it was clearly not the same owl that had injured the man.

The owl was making that sound because another owl had started making the deeper cry of the male. The male and female pair went on singing together like that for a long time. My memory of those moments is very clear. Their cries went on until midnight, when my father set off all the fireworks.

"My mother told me you went to an American school. Your English ought to be good enough to get by." I was desperately searching for topics of conversation.

"That was for elementary school." The girl—maybe I should just go ahead and call her Chunxi—had been absorbed in the cries of the owls the whole time. The look on her face would in time become one of the memories that I cherished most and that haunted me the most. "Did you see the owl eating?"

I nodded. I didn't seem too enthusiastic, but I'd seen that sort of thing many times before. Obviously she was trying to find something more interesting to talk about. I can't say why, but at the time I just did not feel like giving her a real response.

"I'm a nocturnal animal, just like that owl," she said. "We both go flying around at night, getting into trouble."

Members of the Su family have never been good at witty repartee. I was temporarily at a loss for words. Chunxi started humming a song I didn't recognize.

"My mother's also told me that you and your twin sister go to different schools," I said. "Why is that?"

"Because no one can tell us apart." She pronounced this sentence as if it were part of the song she was humming. "We used to be in the same school, and the same class, but the teacher got confused all the time, and eventually it just got to be too much trouble. So they split us up. My sister—she's technically younger than I am—was always good at science, and I was good in the humanities, so we would take tests for each other. We did this for a whole semester before we got caught. It was so much fun. The math and physical sciences teachers could never figure out why I did so well sometimes and so badly other times. When I got sick, my sister would go stay in the hospital in my place, get my shots for me and all that. No one figured out what was going on until they gave her a blood test."

"How did they finally manage to catch you?"

"It was my fault. I was taking a Chinese test for my sister, and I wrote my own name and ID number on it by mistake." Chunxi was turning out to be quite talkative. "The teachers were furious. The next day, at the morning assembly, they had the two of us come up onstage and asked all the students and teachers to see if they could think of some way to tell us apart. But in the end all they could come up with was to have me wear a red armband on my left shoulder. Of course, we passed the armband back and forth! Finally they had no choice but to make one of us cut her hair short."

"Didn't you have your names and ID numbers on your uniforms?"

"That didn't stop my sister. She switched uniforms with me. We didn't do it just to be naughty, though. My health wasn't good, and I had to take off sick too often, so sometimes she would go to school as me to save my attendance record."

"My mother talks a lot about how pretty you two sisters are." My mouth was dry, and I thought my voice sounded unnatural.

"The very best trick we played, though, was at a school friend's birthday party. They'd invited a whole bunch of boys from another school." Chunxi stopped and imitated the gentle, feminine cries of the female owl. "One of the boys and I got along really well. After that he started walking me home from school every day. Then I had to take a month off because I was sick, and I asked my sister to fill in for me with the boy. He couldn't tell the difference. My sister told me that he said all kinds of nauseating things to her while she was filling in for me."

"And then what?" I asked.

"When I got better, my sister and I went to see him together, and we scared him half to death. After that he never came to see me again." Chunxi sighed. "How long are they going to keep on singing like that? Why don't they just get together already?"

Chunxi, who had been born prematurely, had spent the first two months of her life in an incubator. Her healthy younger twin, Chuntian, had been born two months after her. When she was sixteen, Chuntian had moved with their grandparents to California, but the invalid Chunxi had stayed with their parents. I wanted to keep talking about Chunxi's sister, but then my mother and Chunxi's mother suddenly appeared beside us, saving us from our somewhat dull conversation. Once midnight arrived, all the Chinese residents of the area, including us, set off fireworks. By then, though, I had already gone back to my own room and was sitting alone on the balcony looking out at the flowers and the uncommonly bright stars. My father, Lin Yuan, and their friends spent the rest of the night inside playing poker, and so during those hours the house was unusually quiet.

Chunxi was a sophomore in high school when we met that night, and at the time she did not leave that deep an impression on me. As it turned out, we had met before, but I had only one earlier memory of her. When I was still in middle school, a New Year's circus troupe had come to our house to perform and ask for donations, and Chunxi had been so frightened by the firecrackers that she had hid behind her mother. My father, ambitious as always, had insisted on setting off the loudest, longest-lasting firecrackers in town, and he had also given the most money to the circus troupe, so the dancers had performed for us with especial gusto.

"She's almost a freshman in high school, and she's scared of a few firecrackers!" I remember thinking.

Chapter 10

That summer, Lin Yuan came to visit again with his wife and daughter and stayed at our house for three weeks.

"Su Qi, I heard you were a little standoffish with Chunxi last time. This time they're going to be staying for a while. If you keep being so awkward, you're going to make her laugh at you," my father said to me at the dinner table, with Chunxi and her parents present. "After dinner you should take her out to the garden for a walk. Then when you have some free time you should take her to see more of the area, to let her get a sense of the local culture." Then he said, "The kid is nothing like me where personality is concerned. I think of myself as a strong presence, socially. Whereas he's a wallflower everywhere he goes."

Out in the garden, Chunxi kept asking me the names of various plants. I answered her as well as I could, but in the end I had no choice but to go into the study, dig up an English-Chinese dictionary and a few English botanical handbooks, and take these back out into the garden with Chunxi so that we could continue our research. Even then, we sometimes had to consult my mother, the botany graduate. With my mother's help, Chunxi and I were eventually able to write the scientific names of many of the plants on rectangular wooden boards, which we set up next to the plants they described. We made a point of doing this only after four in the afternoon, to avoid the worst of the heat, but even so that was too much exertion for Chunxi. On the fifth day of the project, with no warning whatsoever, she collapsed into my arms.

"You shouldn't tire her out, Su Qi," Lin Yuan said to me quietly as we were waiting for Chunxi to come around. "But this happens all the time. Don't worry too much about it."

The first time I saw Chunxi after her fainting spell was the next afternoon, on my mother's swing.

The sunlight on that South Seas summer afternoon was brilliant enough to turn a person's body transparent. The blue sky lay heavily on your scalp, and the clouds were like an extra layer of fat around your abdomen. The southwest monsoon wind went brushing along your body like a long-distance runner in a race with no finish line. Then there was the South Seas summer river, fleet and limpid sometimes, still and murky at other times, which seemed to pile hot, moist excess nerves onto your body.

The heat may have been one of the reasons I eventually took my mother's advice and built a tree house on a branch nine meters above the ground. The tree house allowed me to leave behind, for a while, the summer mire that covered the ground. It let me ascend to a drier, cleaner space far from that earth.

Chunxi and her mother, the former home economics student, were sitting on my mother's swing. Her mother was reading aloud from a small-print Bible. Chunxi's mother's interest in the Bible apparently had something to do with my mother's influence. After the Lins moved to Borneo, the two women would often light candles and read the scriptures together after nightfall like a couple of medieval nuns. In truth, though, neither of them was terribly pious; my mother had not been to church since my sister was born, and Chunxi's mother had never seen a minister in her life. Chunxi was staring straight ahead, and she seemed to be listening attentively to her mother's reading. With every casual movement either of them made, the crumpled, dilapidated image of my mother sitting there with my sister would peel off of their bodies like the shell of a molting cicada. When Chunxi started to hum a song, the dilapidated shell on which the mother-and-daughter image was engraved picked itself up from the ground and went floating around the swing like a lonesome ghost.

Chunxi's mother saw me first. She closed the Bible and said, still using the tone of voice she had used while reading scripture, "I'm glad to see you, Su Qi. Stay here and talk to Chunxi for a while. I'm going to go help your mother."

"Don't worry about my mother, Auntie," I replied. "She likes to fuss around in the garden all day. She refuses to take a rest. If she ever did take a rest, she'd likely get droopy, like a plant when you don't water it."

Chunxi's mother got up from the swing anyway and went a couple of steps before she stopped. "The garden's so big . . . where is your mother?"

I sniffed the air vigorously. From a place a hundred meters ahead and to the right, near a cluster of rose of Sharon, amid the myriad scents of mud and flowers that only my mother could distinguish, I smelled the scent of my mother, which to me was the strongest smell in the garden and which only I could distinguish. At that moment my mother was sitting on a wooden bench watching a hummingbird feed on sap. The foliage was thick in that place, and very little light or wind got through to her. Two hours earlier, a heavily perfumed friend of my father's had passed by that spot, and her lingering smell was still strong enough to choke a person, like a ball of phlegm stuck in the garden's throat. "Go straight ahead along this path, go past three forks, and then you should be able to yell to my mother."

Chunxi's mother went off in the direction I had indicated, the Bible in her hand. Chunxi and I watched her disappear among the flowers.

"Are you doing all right?" I walked over to Chunxi. "I'm sorry about yesterday. I shouldn't have tired you out like that."

"Not at all. I should be thanking you for doing all that boring stuff with me."

I could see my little sister, her features indistinct, crawling out from behind a tree, crawling right up to the swing.

"Let's take a walk somewhere," I said. The swing was making me think about how my sister had died and how the smell of her corpse had filled our parlor.

"I don't feel like walking. Let's stay here and talk." Chunxi brought both her feet up onto the swing. I noticed for the first time that her feet were bare.

"No, walking's better," I said.

My sister was trying to crawl up onto the swing. Her left hand was missing, and there was a gaping cavity at her spine.

Chunxi put her feet down and put on her sandals. "Okay, but not for too long."

I remembered Chunxi leaning against the windowsill watching the owl. "I should explain. There's a reason I don't want to stay here. I'll tell you later."

"It doesn't matter. There's nothing wrong with walking. I'm a nocturnal animal anyway. If I sat there too long, I'd have fallen asleep."

We went off along a different path. I turned around to look back at the swing. My sister was gone, but there were two spotted doves just beneath it. They always expected people to leave behind scraps of food. A Philippine eagle was floating across the deep blue South Seas summer sky, and the clouds were abnormally bloated, but it didn't look like it was going to rain. The blue sky emerged like a pool of water from the flowers and leaves at the horizon edge of the garden, and a black-and-white mottled stream of haze was charging up toward the clouds, gradually growing wider. Forest fires started easily in that kind of weather.

"As soon as my health improves . . ." Chunxi was caressing the plants whose names she did not know as she walked. ". . . I'll put up name placards for the rest of these plants. Right now they don't have any names. They're like dead souls no one takes care of. It's sad."

"I don't think my mother was happy that we did that. She gets bored with her plants pretty often, and when she does she digs them all up and plants new ones. Giving them name placards is like saying they're going to be there forever."

"Where did she find all these strange plants?"

"She spent a lot of money on them. She had people go gather some of them in the jungle. Others she bought from abroad."

"The jungle . . ." Chunxi stopped in front of a nepenthes plant and craned her neck to examine the contents of its insect-catching pitchers.

"There are all kinds of amazing things in the jungle." I pointed at the nepenthes. "Like this plant. In English it's called the saddle-leaved pitcher plant, but how do you say that in Chinese? It sounds silly if you translate it directly. I guess they call it that because the leaves on top of the pitchers look like saddles. It was first discovered by an Indonesian in 1899, and in 1924 the second one was seen by a German biologist, but after that no one ever spotted one again until now. My mother's the first person ever to get them to reproduce."

Chunxi sat down on a patch of grass she had selected. "I once read a novel written by an Englishman that was set in the Borneo jungle. In the story a young Chinese man, with a queue, because it's set in the Qing dynasty, goes traveling in Borneo by himself and falls in love with the daughter of a tribal chief. But the girl has already been promised to the son of another chief, so the two of them run off together, and the other chief's son leads a group out after them, to kill them. Along the way the girl drinks some water from the pitcher of a nepenthes plant and goes into a very deep sleep. The Chinese man stays with her, deep in the jungle, and the years go by, but she doesn't wake up. The strangest thing, though, is that she doesn't get any older. After fifty years, the Chinese man has grown old, over seventy, but the princess still looks exactly like a fifteen- or sixteen-year-old girl.

"One day, the old man finds the nepenthes plant that put the princess to sleep all those years ago. He pulls off one of the pitchers and makes her drink the water again, and then she wakes up. But the princess doesn't recognize the old man. She doesn't realize that she's been asleep for fifty years.

"'Ah Shan? Where is Ah Shan?' She keeps calling the name of her young lover.

"The old man is ashamed, and he doesn't dare tell her the truth. So he says that Ah Shan went out looking for food. They wait anxiously for a few days, but Ah Shan doesn't come back. The princess goes looking for him everywhere, and finally she comes to a village. She talks to the people there, and then she finally realizes what has happened.

"The princess goes back to the forest and finds the old man crying by himself. She throws herself into his arms. The old man covers his face and tries to push her away. He doesn't want her to recognize him. The princess touches the nepenthes that made her sleep and says, 'Ah Shan, my love. This water made me sleep for fifty years, and then it brought me back to life. If I drink it again, will it make me sleep for another fifty years? Would you watch over me for another fifty years?'

"The princess is about to drink the water, but the old man stops her. Then the two go on to live a peaceful life together. They grow older together, they have children and grandchildren. They live to be a hundred and fifty years old."

A large Oriental magpie flew past our heads with a piece of dry grass hanging from its mouth. Its wings stirred up a gust of hot air that lingered around us. It made me think of the owl that had broken the wineglass. The magpie, oblivious to our presence, on its way to build a nest for its mate, looked a little bit like Chunxi as she told her story. I had squatted down halfway through the story, beside a dipterocarp tree. Chunxi's voice was soft, and the various twists and turns of the plot of her story went radiating in all directions around us.

After that day, I only saw Chunxi two more times, at my father's parties, before she went back to Taiwan. The first time, she was standing in front of the window with the orchid trellis, the one the owl had flown through, listening to a group of middle-aged women moan about their troubles. The second time, she was again standing in front of the window with the trellis, the one the owl had flown through, chatting with the man whose glass had been broken and whose hand had been cut. When I passed them, a few other young men were trying to get that man to do some kind of ballroom dance that was popular at the time. The man grudgingly assented, and he ended up twisting his ankle. His friends did not look sorry in the least; in fact, they tried to get him to continue. He said that his ankle was hurt and that if he kept going he might end up crippled for life. My mother dragged another middle-aged woman over to him, and the two of them led him out of the crowd to attend to his injury. I took advantage of the commotion to leave the party.

And then, that October, Lin Yuan came back to my family's house by himself, and after spending a month lost in the Borneo wilderness that so intrigued him, he decided to move to Malaysia permanently and make our two families neighbors.

Chapter 11

The next time I saw Chunxi was the following year, on the day of the Lantern Festival. Lin Yuan had been staying at our house for a while after he had decided to immigrate. He had bought land and begun to build a mansion my father had designed for him. By the lunar New Year, the house was mostly finished, and Lin Yuan's wife and daughter flew in from Taiwan on the day when he was planning to move in. A week after that, they went back to Taiwan, since the winter school break was almost over and they intended to wait for Chunxi to graduate from high school and then return to live with Lin Yuan permanently. On the night of the Lins' housewarming party, I was on a camping trip in the jungle with a few friends from school, and after dusk we could look down from the higher elevations and see the fireworks lighting up a small piece of the horizon in the direction of the Lins' place. They went on for a full half hour.

I got home from the camping trip that Friday, the day of the Lantern Festival. My father had of course spared no expense in planning his party for that night. When I spotted Chunxi, standing as always in front of the window with the orchid trellis, the one the owl had flown through, it was just after nine in the evening, and the guests were still sparse and were mostly female. Later on, I found out that the men had all been in the backyard watching a dogfight that my father and Lin Yuan had arranged. The fight was almost too terrible to watch, but the men placed their bets with the serenity and piety of almsgivers at a church. These were people who would not be entertained for long at a party that offered nothing more exciting than good food and liquor; that was precisely the problem that so bedeviled my father.

I caught sight of a girl with long hair standing in front of the window with the orchid trellis, her back to me. It was a bright night, with only faint clouds visible through the dense clusters of tree branches, and the northeast monsoon wind was blowing through the wind chimes that my mother had made from seashells and hung in that window. All this made me think of the story Chunxi had told me about the sleeping princess in the jungle. That story dated back to the era of European imperialism, when Europeans were piloting their merchant vessels and warships in the direction of the savage Eastern isles, those lands of spices and milk and honey; an era when the martial trumpeting of the conch shell and the songs of whales echoed through the South China Sea; a time when the skulls of pirates and white men were submerged forever in the tidal waves of the Malacca Strait; an era when the trade in Chinese indentured coolies was starting to replace the declining African slave trade. The coolies were tied together by their queues and shut up inside the sunless bellies of boats, and they were taken across the sea to live out the rest of their lives like livestock in the frontier lands of the

New World or Southeast Asia. Meanwhile, white novelists followed the gunboats to the South Seas, where they drank wine in splendid estates and hotels, attended by legions of servants, and occasionally took up their pens to portray a bit of the sentimental flavor of these foreign lands. Oriental men and the sad fates of slave girls were some of the material they used to weave countless romantic tales like the one Chunxi had told me.

"Mark my words—there's a good chance all of us are the descendents of coolie beasts." I had said this once, in English, to a few of my father's Chinese friends at a party.

"But that doesn't mean we don't have the right to be romantic too," one older gentleman had said in reply.

Just as all these thoughts were rushing through my head, Chunxi left her orchid-trellis window all of a sudden, passed through the crowd, and went outside. She was looking around as she crossed the room, and at times she stopped to say a few words to another guest, but she stopped for good only once she reached my mother's garden. The light from the decorative lamps shone into the garden's many crannies. The paths through the garden were haphazard and defied all surmising, and the cries of birds and beasts created as great a commotion as that which came out of the parlor. Chunxi hesitated only a second before she set off on one of the small paths. I left the parlor and followed her into my mother's labyrinthine garden. Once I was inside the garden, though, I had to slacken my pace to keep a reasonable distance between us, because Chunxi kept stopping and starting again. After about ten minutes of walking, she stopped for a rest, took a good look around her, and then moved forward again. Before long she stopped yet again. It was clear that she had no particular destination in mind.

After seven or eight more minutes, I realized that Chunxi had unwittingly begun to go in circles. This happened to everyone who entered my mother's garden, even in the daytime. In fact, I considered it a more unhappy fate to get lost there during the day than at night. During the day there were enough visible distractions to weaken your judgment and intuition, whereas at night, with a little luck, the brilliant lights shining from either our house or the Lins' could guide you, and if you just walked steadily in the direction of one set of lights you would be okay.

The Lantern Festival light display at my house was especially extravagant, and from where I was standing the myriad rays seemed to penetrate right through me and through the entire garden. The denser the vegetation, the stronger this sense became. Nights in the labyrinthine garden had helped us members of the Su family cultivate senses of direction as accurate as those of homing pigeons.

By that point, Chunxi was obviously aware that she was lost, and after a few more minutes of aimless wandering she suddenly shouted, "Su Qi!"

Part of the sound of my name echoed endlessly through the garden, but another part instantly dissipated in it. I was not sure if I had heard her correctly.

"Su Qi," Chunxi called in another direction, "is that you?"

I walked toward her.

The mushroom-shaped lamps on the ground cast Chunxi's hair and features in a yolky yellowish light, and the visible world that shown out of her eyes seemed a limitless expanse there in the dark. Her features, as vague and pliant as those of a half-formed human fetus, grew gradually more distinct as I came nearer, and I even sensed that her chin, the tip of her nose, her eyelashes were all expanding exuberantly into the image of perfect beauty that I had been expecting. The womb of that garden had been impregnated with impish Cupids before, nurturing them to maturity with its dark umbilical cord. I realized only many years later that love tended to hit me like a giant asteroid, without any warning, sending convulsions through and then burying all living species in the land of my love's banishment.

"I knew it was you."

"How did you know it was me?"

"You snuck out of the parlor to follow me, and then when you saw I was lost you didn't bother saying anything," Chunxi said. "What remarkable self-restraint! Who else but a Su would be capable of that sort of thing?"

"You're the one who's been sneaking around," I said. "You snuck out of the parlor, and you snuck over here. What are you up to, anyway?"

"Your father's party is a bore. Just a bunch of white-haired old spinsters talking about the good old days." Chunxi's eyes reminded me of the mischievous stars above our heads, the ones that were constantly changing position and leading travelers astray. "It was selfish of your father to take all the men away to watch the dogfight and then ignore all the old women. Someone told me the dogfight was going on somewhere out here in garden. I just wanted to be part of the action."

I had a hard time reconciling my image of Chunxi with a dogfight. "You weren't scared of getting lost?"

"What's there to be scared of? I knew you were behind me, Su Qi," Chunxi said. "Take me to the dogfight."

"It's only been six months since I last saw you, but you seem like a completely different person." I was remembering the incident with the owl. "I thought you were the kind of girl who fainted at the sight of blood. I'm sorry, but I'm not going to take you there."

"Are *you* afraid of getting lost?"

"No, but I hate my father."

The lights in the garden went out suddenly, and we were plunged into darkness. I searched for the lights from my house, but all I could see were the fluttering shadows of the trees and the light from a couple of stars. No trace remained of the outline of the looming, solitary house, which had always seemed somehow to hang at the edge of a great cliff. I could only sense a few bats shuttling back and forth, owls rushing past us, dogs suddenly beginning to bark, sounding powerful and aggrieved.

"The power's out," I said, trying to get a look at Chunxi's face.

"I'm not afraid."

"There's no reason to be afraid of the dark," I said. "The dark sharpens our imaginations, it sharpens the animal instincts that we've lost. In the dark our ears are as sharp as dogs'. Our noses are as sharp as pigs'. We develop whiskers like cats, claws like panthers. In the dark we finally get to be free."

"Now you're just wasting my time. This is your territory, isn't it?" Chunxi was just as flirtatious as ever. "With you here, Su Qi, I'm not afraid of anything."

"So do you still want to see the dogfight?" I looked up to determine the position of the Big Dipper and Orion.

"But it's so dark. How are we going to get there?"

"With my animal instincts, I could get us there with my eyes closed," I said. "Besides, aren't you a nocturnal animal?"

Chunxi seemed to hesitate for a second. "Take me there, or else I'll keep standing right here and won't ever go back."

"I don't want to disappoint you, but I really do hate seeing my father."

"Who cares about your father?"

"It's so dark. I'll bet they've called off the dogfight." The truth was, though, that there was no way I was going to deny Chunxi anything she wanted. "Give me your hand."

Chunxi stuck her hand out in my direction. I grasped it. "Follow me, and keep talking to me," I said to her. "People say that there's a kind of ape-man in the Borneo jungle who likes to sneak into groups of travelers when it's dark. He'll take someone's hand and lead that person around the jungle until they're lost and exhausted. This garden's right next to the jungle, and we don't want the ape-man joining us. Tell me another story about the jungle. Who was the author of that story you told me last time, anyway?"

"I don't remember."

"Kipling? Maugham? Conrad? It wasn't Yu Dafu, was it? All of them spent time in Malaysia."

"I think it was a woman writer."

"What did the Chinese man do for the fifty years while the princess slept?"

"He was telling her stories the whole time."

My mother had told me that when she walked in the garden at night she could tell where she was just by paying attention to the scents of the flowers and the trees. And she had also said, proudly and piously, that if she ever lost her sense of smell, she would still be able to get around by listening to the cries of insects and birds and the sound of the wind in the labyrinthine garden she had created all on her own. She hadn't been trying to brag. She had simply been trying to express to me, in her own fashion, the extent of her loneliness and the many years of her life she had sunk into that garden. One time, she had imparted to me the secret formulae behind her sense of direction, showing me how to distinguish the scents of the different flowers and trees in different seasons and telling me where the different kinds of female birds built their nests and what the cries of the male birds sounded like. My mother had even organized the cries of different insects along the musical scale and had used this data to divide the garden into seven zones and seventy-two smaller districts, like a chessboard. Maybe you can't imagine it, but my mother just needed to pick up a piece of soil, sniff it, maybe taste it, and she would know which of the seventy-two districts it came from. I hadn't inherited my mother's gifts. All I could gather, from the chatter of the frogs, was that we were getting close to the edge of the only natural pond in the garden. So I led Chunxi by the hand for two or three more minutes until we saw the inky water ahead of us, selectively reflecting the skyscape above it, with the stars and the dark clouds and the far galaxies intensifying the complexity of the labyrinthine garden.

A slender black shadow went charging past us, emitting a bizarre laugh. A taller shadow followed close behind it, this one panting like a running bull, with the odor of cigarettes and alcohol coming off it like waves of heat. I watched the two people disappear into the garden and suddenly felt uncomfortable. Once again using my father as an excuse, I tried to persuade Chunxi to forget about the dogfight. But once we were halfway around the pond the fight came into view. Several cages full of dogs were arranged in a line on the grass. The dogs seemed listless and devoid of much fighting spirit. The glow from a cigarette or a laugh occasionally emerged from the area around them. So Chunxi and I returned to the parlor, to find that hundreds of candles had been lit and that the loss of power didn't seem to have affected the lively atmosphere. The only thing that put a damper on the festivities was Chunxi's mother, who had been anxiously searching for her daughter along the edge of the garden.

I eventually returned to the dogfight by myself, and on the way there I saw through the dark, among the flowers, a naked man and woman. They smiled at me and seemed completely unabashed by my presence. Later I found out that my father and Lin Yuan had been using the dogfight story as a ruse; they had brought a group of young native prostitutes to the party and then shut off the power deliberately, so that the men could take their pleasure undisturbed in the garden.

At the time, I had been shocked to learn that the garden, as dark and sacred a place as a womb, had been defiled in this way, made to serve as just one more labyrinthine vagina.

The next morning, Chunxi and her mother flew back to Taiwan.

Chapter 12

In July of that same year, while the devastating southwest monsoon winds were blowing, I climbed an enormous tree in the garden and built a tree house over two hundred square meters in area on a massive branch nine meters above the ground. I spent most of my days for the rest of that year in my tree house. Its construction was simple but solid; there was a railing on one side, but the other three sides were covered by tree branches that formed natural walls. When the monsoon winds were relatively strong, the house would shake and rattle like a boat on the light waves of a lake. When I napped in the afternoon, the greenery beneath my shoulders would feel like a load I had borne on my back through an arduous journey. The white clouds in the blue sky fluctuated gently as I lay looking up at them, so that it seemed as if the tree house were a flying carpet that moved according to my whims. And my mother, down beneath the beating wings that carried me, was like a roulette ball, leaping about and never coming to rest among the pattering fragments that made up the kaleidoscope of her garden. I was aware of my mother moving around below me, but I was never clear on where she was coming from or where she was going. When I looked down at her, I could see the two red silk ribbons on her broad straw hat flapping in the breeze, ascending and descending among the flowers. I would watch her until my vision got blurry or my interest waned, but I still could not figure out whether she tended her limitless garden according to some set of strict rules or without any guiding order whatsoever. Amid all the chaos down there, all I could guess was that my mother was working exactly according to her whims, taking care only to ensure that the plants were luxuriant and well spaced and that each got as much light as it needed. I observed and speculated, but I never could figure out why she would suddenly dig up a row of flowers in the prime of their lives and then spend hours planting a new row of another type of flower, no more beautiful than the first. I also never understood why she would take a green path that had offered a wonderful open vista and fill it with new plantings until it was an unrecognizable shadow of its earlier self. I fantasized about sketching the bird's-eye view of the labyrinthine garden and the tortuous, abundant paths that ran through it. But amid the thousands of threads and links stretching out in all directions I would soon loose my handle on whatever path I was trying to trace and would end up feeling more at sea than I had when I began.

Each time I gave up on the garden and tried to look up at the sky or concentrate on some point farther out in the distance instead, my mother would lurch into my line of sight like a retinal hallucination. But I could never focus clearly on her image, just as I could only capture in fragments the places where she hid in the garden.

The tree house had been my mother's idea. One day when I was helping her prune some of her flower bushes, she raised her head suddenly and looked off into the distance. Then she said, "Qi, do you have any idea how big our garden is?" I said I didn't know. She wouldn't give me a precise figure, but she said that it was big enough that even from a height of one hundred meters you wouldn't be able to see to the end of it. I told her that I liked to climb trees of different heights and survey the expanse of the garden, like a sailor at the top of a mast gazing out at the boundless ocean. I always looked hard, but each time my vista was more or less the same, as if I had been climbing the same tree all along. So then my mother looked at a tall tree nearby and asked me what the garden looked like from that height. A few days later, she and I were having afternoon tea next to the swing, and once again she raised her head to look at a tall tree and asked, "What does the garden look like from that height?" I said, "Mom, why don't I find the tallest tree we have and build a tree house in it? That way, when you have nothing else to do, you can climb up and see for yourself." My mother didn't reply. Over a month after I had finished the tree house, she still had not been up in it. Eventually, though, after I had grown bored with looking down at the garden, I found a muddy footprint up in the tree house that, judging from its size, had to be my mother's.

"Have you been up in the tree house, Mom?"

I had to ask her this twice, and the second time she just asked me, "What is it you do up there, anyway?"

So I told my mother about the things I had seen from the tree house. A high-school teacher who collected birds' eggs had been trespassing in the garden, and in the month or so I had been watching he had stolen more than ten birds' nests from us. One day he had gotten lost in the deep bowels of the garden and spent two hours trying to find his way out. Eventually I came down from the tree, led him to the nearest exit, and warned him that my dad might come after him with a shotgun if he ever entered my family's garden again. Another time, a pair of barking deer that had broken out of the Lins' menagerie had chased each other around a scholar tree. The male deer had been straining and eager, the female deer swollen and receptive, and it looked to me like the pair was about to mate somewhere nearby. I had also seen my father practicing his golf swing on the patio, using the nearby pond as his putting green. The little white balls would go flying past the camphor and fig trees, then past a row of coconut trees, to descend with a plunk into the water, with impressive speed and accuracy. I had also seen packs of some kind of downy animal that would come every evening at dusk, from all directions, to eat orchids and fruit; they looked to me like bearded pigs. The river that ran along the border between Malaysia and Brunei was as inky and turgid as ever, and the ferry and dock were sometimes cheerless and empty and sometimes crowded and lively. As always, every weekend, the followers of Allah who lived in Brunei brought their imported cars across the river for nights of debauchery. Some of them were coming to attend my father's parties. Up in the tree house, I would adjust the focus of my binoculars, and I would think that I could actually smell the savage odor of their makeup and their cologne, that it was rushing at me like the monsoon winds, moistening the lenses on the binoculars.

"Where did that man who was stealing the birds' eggs get lost?" my mother asked.

I told her. My mother went off in that direction with lowered head and a thoughtful air, looking like an elderly poet who had begun to spend more time dwelling on memories than writing poems. She dug around in the dirt there with simple, rhythmic motions, her features as placid and wise as the face of a bodhisattva. The garden was stamped with thousands of handprints, and the lines of fate were different on each one. Like a fortune-teller, my mother read all the ill omens on the palm of that place where the trespasser had gotten lost. She knew that no trespasser could ever escape from her own hand, no matter how hard he struggled, any more than he could from the hand of the Buddha.

My mother reacted very differently when I brought up the Brunei ferry. There was nothing Buddha-like about her face then. Instead, she looked like a supplicant still enduring the wait for enlightenment.

"I know everything that goes on in the garden anyway; I don't have to go climbing up and down trees like a monkey." This was all my mother said in reply to most of what I told her.

This sentence of hers was not something the Buddha would say, nor was it anything a supplicant on the verge of enlightenment would say. Rather, it was something that the stubborn and incorrigible Sun Wukong, the monkey king, would say. Under the dark shadow of my father's Tripitaka-like hypocrisy and the torments devised by the Zhu Bajies who were his friends, my mother had made that garden into the burial ground for the various skins that her schizophrenic soul was forced to shed.[1] Between the social graces and good cheer that she exhibited at my father's parties and the utter despondency that she expressed in her garden, I could never tell what was real and what was false with her.

When I urged my mother to build a new swing after I had seen my father coupling violently with that other woman on the old one, she wouldn't express an opinion either way. But then, when she took great care to select a location and color for the new swing that would practically camouflage it, make it a barely visible part of the back-

---

1. Sun Wukong, Tripitaka, and Zhu Bajie are three major characters in *Journey to the West*. Tripitaka, the ostensible hero, is a devout Buddhist pilgrim, but the more popular character by far is the clever and irreverent Sun Wukong, an anthropomorphic monkey who represents humanity's restless and rebellious mental faculties. Zhu Bajie, an anthropomorphic pig, is characterized by his lack of restraint in the face of fleshly desires.

drop of the garden, I thought I understood a little better how much truth and stubbornness lay behind that sentence of hers: "I know everything that goes on in the garden anyway."

El Niño was gaining strength; the rainy season was taking a long time in coming. By the middle of November, the maiden sun was burning the same gentle red as in earlier months. Clouds skated past looking like an array of tender buttocks, and the pristine blue sky was like a bed waiting to be wet by a baby. The season was in the thick of her adolescence, sprouting pimples and young breasts. The riverbeds were cracked, the earth was parched, and wildfires kept breaking out in the jungle. The only pond in our garden had dried up, and our running water stopped working once every day or so. The labyrinthine garden was in serious danger. A truck made multiple trips to our house throughout the day, delivering with each trip ten huge plastic jugs of river water for irrigating the garden. I kept careful count, and on the busiest day the truck came seventy-eight times. The water had been extracted directly from the river with a motorized instrument, and it arrived still full of fish. Sometimes there would be human or animal refuse mixed in. The garden acquired a foul odor, of dead fish and excrement, that reminded me of the smell of my sister's corpse.

"Imagine spending all that money to buy filthy water," I heard one of the deliverymen say from up in my tree house. "That woman's nuts."

Hundreds of golf balls, looking just like crocodile eggs, were now visible in the dried bed of the pond. My father retrieved them himself. He washed them thoroughly and then took them back to the patio and went on hitting them back into the pond.

My mother would pick up the balls that went astray and toss them gingerly into the desiccated pond bed. Eventually I saw one of the balls come soaring through the blue sky, past a willow tree, and land without a sound on my mother's shoulder. My father furrowed his brow, took a sip from his glass of white wine on ice, and then took another swing. This ball went flying past the camphor and fig trees, then past a row of coconut trees, and landed just as he had intended it to, in the roiling brown sand that had once been the pond. A woman who was sunbathing in a lounge chair beside him clapped her hands, and he leaned down to kiss her forehead. Coyly affecting the lassitude of a servant girl, she demanded that my father help her with her golf swing, so that she could dispel her lethargy and lose a little weight at the same time. My mother hadn't reacted at all when the golf ball hit her shoulder. If I hadn't seen the ball moving away from the edge of my father's club with my own eyes, I might have thought that it was a butterfly or a falling leaf that had struck her.

My mother stood in her garden and gazed off into the distance. She could sense that someone was lost over there. She shook the soil off her body, wiped the sweat off her face, and walked in that direction. Even from my tree house, I couldn't see what was going on until my mother reappeared with Chunxi right beneath me.

Chapter 13

Two weeks before that, just as the three of us were sitting down to dinner, Lin Yuan had showed up at our door with a bottle of Johnnie Walker. I had been reading a copy of *National Geographic*, my father had been reading the *Straits Times*, and my mother had just finished reading a page from the Bible and was thanking the Lord for his grace with lowered head. If we hadn't been interrupted, we would have kept on reading as we dined, turning the act of eating into something heftier and more refined, something more like the act of dreaming. Reading, or any activity other than chewing—one time my father had oiled his hunting rifle at dinner, sending the smell of lubricant wafting over the table—was for us a way of sleeping as we ate, and the eating itself was an elusive dreamland of poor digestion and numbed taste buds.

As soon as Lin Yuan sat down at the table, he told my father that the crocodile egg the two of them had smuggled out of the jungle a few days before had hatched. I was absorbed in one of the photographs in *National Geographic*, and my mother was gazing out the window at the garden. My father put down his paper and talked with Lin Yuan about how they had managed to evade the mother crocodile to steal the egg. The windowpane was covered with a thin layer of condensation from the air conditioner, and flower petals were dashing against the pane in a profusion of color reminiscent of a gaudy birthday cake. Thanks to my father's careful design, the dining room was always bathed in picturesque natural light, no matter what time of day it was and even when it was rainy. Still, everything that went on in that room was always heavily influenced by the weather outside. It was after six in the evening, and the pink sunset reminded me of the slaughtering yard at a fishing dock during crocodile season. The birds in my mother's labyrinthine garden sent up an awful cacophony that almost drowned out my father's and Lin Yuan's conversation. My mother, one time at dinner, had looked in the direction of the garden and said that she could pick out the cries of thirty-seven different species of birds. I had put down my chopsticks and listened through the sound of my father gnawing on a pork rib. I had been able to pick out three, and my mother had immediately named the other thirty-four for me.

My father had left the table, still gnawing on his rib. Just as my mother told me that the number of different kinds of cries had increased to forty-one, he emerged with his rifle and headed out into the labyrinthine garden, where he fired a single shot at the sky. The flocks of birds cast a pall of panic over our dinner table as they scattered in all directions. A moment later, my mother identified a forty-second and a forty-third cry.

I had told my mother the story from *The Water Margin*, about Lu Zhishen the outlaw monk pulling a willow tree out of the ground to drive away a bird whose cries had disturbed his drinking, but she had nothing to say in reply to that. By the time my father had come back from the garden, my mother had already carefully counted up to fifty-two species. The fifty-second was a variety of kingfisher that was as big as a human fist. Startled by the sound of my father's gunshot, it came flying at the speed of a meteor into the spotless pane of our dining room window. The kingfisher lay for a while, stunned, on the grille at the base of the window. My father's lower jaw worked over the pork rib, in search of any remaining tendon meat. The remaining portion of the rack of ribs sat in its platter, looking like something on the verge of being swallowed whole. While the kingfisher was lying unconscious, my mother cleared the table and washed the dishes, the birds regrouped in the garden, and my father got dressed up to look presentable for his guests. By the time my father's guests started to file into our house, the kingfisher had begun flapping its wings again. As it tried to fly away, though, it knocked its head against the windowpane a second time. This time it resolutely kept flapping its wings and righted itself again quickly. Before it fell to the ground a final time, it had already flown with its former meteoric speed back into the garden.

That was back in the days when my father only pointed guns at animals, never binoculars. But I suspect that the cathartic shot he had fired that night was actually directed not at the birds but at my mother's garden fortress, the expansion of which was beginning to obstruct his golf balls' route to the pond. While my mother was irrigating her plants with river water, my father and several friends trampled down the vegetation in one corner of the garden so that they could use it for cricket and lacrosse matches. This act reminded me of a cat or dog urinating to mark its territory.

My father had nothing but contempt for my mother's obsession with the garden, and he hated the private paths she had laid for herself within it. To him, those paths were like a series of bastards, things that bore no genetic trace of him, growing to behemoth proportions in my mother's womb and then creeping out one by one from between her legs. My mother, with the beauty she had been born with and the heavy burdens she had been forced to bear, was like a queen bee: her nether regions gave birth only with great difficulty and were forever forced to drag behind them the bloody form of a worthless male.

That night, the garden was as hungry and expectant as always, an eager land of milk and honey. My mother was thinking longingly about the new flower bed she had just planted, and suddenly I remembered how, right after my sister died, she had taken to walking barefoot out of the house and into the garden, where she would lift her shirt to reveal her swollen and erect breasts and then massage her upright nipples with her fingers and spill the deluge of her unused milk onto the grass.

One time, after my mother had walked away, I had gone to the spot where her milk had fallen, picked a blade of grass, and sucked crazily at the drop of milk that dangled precariously from its tip.

Two days later, my mother, sitting on her swing, had beckoned to me. As I approached her, she had lifted her shirt to reveal her swollen and erect breasts and then, with her hand stroking the back of my head, pushed my face against one of her upright nipples. I had sucked at it greedily.

I was six years old that year. Just as I was sucking anew at my mother's breast, that bastard baby that was not one of the Sus was growing inside her belly, a rapid and virulent revenge. When I lay against my mother's gradually swelling belly, I could sense him there, expanding into his own flesh as brazenly as the flowers in the labyrinthine garden expanded into new territory. He was baring his teeth and claws; he was kicking and slapping at me with his little feet, his little fists. I thought he was jealous of me because I had the good fortune to be able to suck at our mother's breast. One time, I couldn't restrain myself any longer and hit back, aiming for the place where his head would have been. I felt him lunging back at me, completely unharmed, with a self-satisfied swagger.

At the time I didn't know about the dubious origins of that baby. My mother's third pregnancy was a Su family secret. My father wouldn't let her go out or see his guests, and she did not see a doctor at any point in the pregnancy. What was odd was that my father did not insist that she have an abortion and in fact did not say so much as a harsh word to her the whole time. I learned only later that he had been making his own plans all along, from the moment he first noticed her belly growing bigger. On the day after he took the baby away from her, my mother had called me to her bedside, pinched my hair between her fingers, and pushed my face into her breast. Her breasts were heavy with milk, and tears were running violently down her face, so that I must have ingested equal amounts of both.

My mother's breasts kept me well nourished until I finished elementary school. By then I had sucked her milk dry. I remember when it happened: I had sucked with such vigor that my tongue and lips were numb and swollen, and my air passages and lungs were ready to split in half, but I still hadn't gotten a single drop of milk. So I bit down violently on her nipple. Then I felt her mammary channel, which had once led in its infinite fecundity to the farthest edges of the universe, rolling up and contracting forever, like an oversensitive plant. My mother had sucked in her breath sharply, and with her hands on the back of my head she had thrust my entire face tightly into her chest. I couldn't see; I couldn't open my mouth to yell; I couldn't breathe in through my nose. My arms and legs began to tremble. I felt as if I had been struck by the airbag of a car after an accident. When my mother finally released me, my face and ears were bright red, and my mouth was still locked in the position it had been in when I bit the strong breast that was now covered in my saliva. My mother gently pushed me away from her and refastened her bra. That was the last time I would ever see her breasts.

As I sat at the dinner table looking at one of the photographs in *National Geographic*, I was thinking nostalgically about the boundless flow of my mother's milk pouring into my throat.

"It's pretty fucking sad about that little monkey," my father said. "It was raised on human milk."

It was true that my father saw little difference between me and a monkey, but just then he was not talking about me. He and Lin Yuan were both experienced hunters, and they had a few unique tricks that they used to survive particularly dangerous hunting trips. One of these was to bring along a couple of small live animals to act as sacrificial lambs. According to them, this highly original formula had saved their miserable lives, or at least kept them safe from injury, at more than one life-or-death juncture, including the time they had stolen the crocodile egg. They had just finished paying a visit to a Dayak longhouse, and they had paid a good deal of money to buy a long-tailed macaque that one of the Dayaks had been keeping as a pet. The monkey had been raised since infancy by the Dayak women, who had breastfed it themselves—breastfeeding domestic animals like pigs or monkeys was common practice among the Dayaks—and it had grown up to be gentle and entirely tame. As it rode away from the longhouse on my father's shoulder, it had been as silent and melancholy as a human being leaving behind his family for a long journey. While Lin Yuan dug the crocodile egg out of the riverbank, my father kept watch on the river with his rifle ready. But he had been taken by surprise when the mother crocodile came charging at Lin Yuan from the riverbank, not the water. There was no time to escape; the mother crocodile was about to drive them both into the river. But my father had saved them by yanking the monkey off of his shoulder and throwing it to the mother crocodile. As she clamped down on the monkey with her knife-edged teeth, the two men were able to escape up the riverbank.

My father showed us the wounds on his neck, his shoulder, and his wrist. "That's how scared the monkey was. If I hadn't moved as fast as I did, it wouldn't have been so easy to get the thing off me. He was trying to glom onto me like glue."

"It's better to be bitten by a monkey than by a crocodile," Lin Yuan said with a wicked smile.

"So, buddy, if we hadn't had that monkey with us, who do you think the crocodile would have gone for first?"

"Well, she *was* closer to you than to me. . . ."

"I disagree," my father said. "You were the one stealing her egg. Crocs are smart rascals."

"If she were that smart, she wouldn't have eaten the monkey instead of us."

"Ah, well, because I made my move so quickly, she got confused. She couldn't tell the monkey from one of us. She was never any match for me."

"You moved quickly because that was your natural reaction. You were frightened. Whereas by that point I already had my knife out. I was getting ready to fight her myself."

"Yes, well. I'll remember that," my father said.

"That monkey gave his life for us, didn't he? You saw how he was, screaming and jumping around, trying to draw the croc's attention."

"Well, deliberately or not, he did save our lives." My father was gnawing on the flesh of some animal or another, and I couldn't hear what he said next over his loud chewing. I did, however, hear his final sentence clearly: ". . . Still, maybe it's because he was raised on human milk, but I can't help feeling a bit bad about the whole thing."

I kept on looking at the photographs in my *National Geographic*. The parched grasslands of the Congo, a line of green plants at the horizon, a deep blue sky, a gray rhinoceros resolutely striding along in his solitude or maybe just wavering there in hesitation.

"Su Qi, in another two months, Chunxi and her mother will be moving here, too," Lin Yuan said to me suddenly.

"Did you know that that kid was drinking his mother's milk right up until he was ten years old?" my father said.

My mother suddenly screamed, an acute and terrible sound. She swept her hand across the table and sent dishes crashing to the floor. My father gave her a cold, detached look, and Lin Yuan tried to calm her down. I said her name softly, called her "Mother." I didn't know what else to do.

Chapter 14

Around dusk on a night in October 1976, packs of bearded pigs came from all directions into our garden to eat flowers and fruit. I came down from my tree house and then climbed back up again, with Chunxi, whom I had not seen for over six months. We studied the fall of night all around us, with both the binoculars and our naked eyes. The paths of the labyrinthine garden were like the crisscrossing tunnels of an anthill. The garden was split up into thousands upon thousands of different flower beds that my mother had planted and nurtured. The dense concentration of flowers by the stream made me think that the woman in white was crossing the water and coming back again. Over by the river, the ferry crossing was as busy as always, and I thought of the Brunei prince on an islet in the midst of the water. The birds were raising such a racket that they could have drowned out the roar of a shot from my father's freshly oiled gun. The lights at my house were glowing, and the night's party guests were filing in. Chunxi and I lingered in the tree house. We didn't want to get back down. At that moment I suddenly remembered the image of the lonesome rhinoceros on the grasslands of the Congo. Chunxi asked me why I had gone through all that trouble to build the tree house, and I didn't tell her the truth. Instead, I said I liked being hidden and solitary, that it made me feel like a hawk, or a bear, or a lonesome rhinoceros. . . .

"Su Qi, have you seen the red mailbox in front of our door?" Chunxi said. I said, "I saw it the day your house was finished. Your dad likes to make everything big. Even your mailbox is the size of a coffin." Chunxi said, "I asked him to make it that way." I asked why. She said, "I'd had enough of the little mailboxes in Taipei, no bigger than a bird's nest." I said, "It's not as if mailboxes need to be the size of trash cans." She said, "No, but in Taipei they're full of junk mail. They might as well be trash cans." I said, "Well, that's useful, killing two birds with one stone." Chunxi said, "My father subscribes to a lot of magazines and newspapers from abroad, and a little mailbox would be full right away. A big mailbox has its advantages. You can get all kinds of letters and gifts. All the more so around holidays. If by chance someone sent you a really big gift, what would you do without a big mailbox?" I said, "But the mouth of your mailbox is still small. It's not a python, is it? You can't force big packages down its throat. Plus, if you don't get any mail, think how awful you'll feel." Chunxi said, "That's why you have to tell all your friends and relatives that you have a big mailbox, and then they'll keep sending you letters." I said, "Well, everything that goes around comes around, and so you'll end up spending all your time writing them letters back." She said, "You're always looking at the negative side of things." I said, "Well, you're just like an airplane stewardess who won't let the passengers watch movies about plane crashes." She said, "Well, you're like an insurance salesman who's always talking about all the bad things that can happen to a person." I said, "It's true that I'm hardly a good luck charm." She said, "What's that over there, where all the bright lights are?"

I looked in the direction in which she was pointing and said, "That's the ferry crossing. Brunei's on the other side."

I handed Chunxi the binoculars. She looked through them for a long time.

"Brunei's a boring little oil kingdom," I said. "The sultan is supposed to be the richest man in the world. It's a Muslim country, and they have more rules than there are hairs on a cow, so every weekend the people who live there come across the river in their cars to try to have some fun over here."

"That's a huge ferry," Chunxi said. "There must be twenty cars on it."

"The sultan and his family come over on the ferry all the time. The prince, too."

"Have you ever seen the prince?"

"Well, he's supposed to have come to our parties dressed as a commoner. I may have played chess with him."

"Does he come often?"

"I don't know. You'd have to ask my father. He says that the stars always get a little brighter when the prince comes and that the flowers come into bloom and the animals seem to know what's going on and there's a general sense of well-being in the air. He said this at one of his parties, loud enough for everyone to hear. My father knows how to suck up."

"I wonder what kinds of things are in the air tonight." Chunxi finally put down the binoculars.

"I heard that once one of the snow leopards in Uncle Lin's menagerie got loose and lay on a dead tree branch near the patio all night along. People shouted at it, but it wouldn't leave, and finally it just jumped down onto the patio, all of a sudden, and paced back and forth there for a long time. My father says that happened while the prince was in the parlor playing bridge."

"If the prince came over on the ferry, we'd be able to see him with the binoculars, right?"

"We could," I said. "But honestly I still don't know what he looks like."

Chunxi picked up the binoculars again and pointed them in the direction of the ferry.

"It's getting late. We should go back down." I had just realized that it was past seven. I turned on the flashlight.

We came down from the tree house, and after I had been leading Chunxi by the hand through the garden for about five minutes we ran into a white man carrying a hunting rifle. He looked like he was awfully anxious about something. He was covered in sweat, and he shone his flashlight in our direction.

"Are you George's son?" he said.

I recognized him as one of my father's old friends and a regular guest at the parties. One look at him, and I knew that my father was up to something that night.

"What are you doing out here?" He looked around. "Do you have a gun with you?"

"What would I want a gun for?"

"Stand still. Don't make any sudden moves," he said. "Your father bought two Malay tigers from a smuggler from the peninsula. He's letting us use them for target practice. Right now the beasts are somewhere in this garden."

Beneath that sky, crowded with stars, the garden seemed hospitable and peaceful. I figured he must be joking.

"We divided up into six groups, five people in each group, four men and one woman. The men all have guns, but the women went out empty-handed. One of the beasts charged our group, and we all ran off in different directions."

"Did you kill it?" I asked.

"I don't suspect it will be that easy. The beasts have been starved for several days, and now they're ravenous."

I started leading Chunxi back in the direction we had come from.

"Where are you two going?"

"This way will take us back to the house, too, and there's also a tree house on the way. We'll go hide up there for a while. We'll think about coming down once the rest of you have killed the tigers."

"Very good. Very good." The white man took a pack of cigarettes out of his pocket.

"Why don't you come up and hide with us?" I said.

"Only a coward would give up at a time like this." The white man extracted a cigarette from the pack and took out a lighter. "I've never hunted animals like these before in my whole fucking life."

"It looks to me like you're the one being hunted, Frank," I said.

"You're every bit as cruel as your father, kid. Want a smoke?" Frank tried to hand me a cigarette.

"I don't smoke. Thank you."

"Your father will try anything, but you're just like a little saint." Frank looked around again and then lit both cigarettes at once. "Get your girlfriend up that tree, quickly. The tigers are both males, and they're especially interested in women. That's why every group has a woman in it."

I didn't feel like continuing the conversation, so I got ready to lead Chunxi back toward the big tree that held the tree house.

But Frank kept on talking nervously. "Do you know why your father made a point of getting two male tigers? You Chinese are so fond of vicious animals. He plans to cook the tigers' unmentionable parts and then make a soup from their bones. Then we'll eat both, to enhance our 'vital forces.'"

"Good-bye, Frank," I said.

"No matter how tough the tigers think they are . . ." His words kept on coming as we left, in an unending succession, just like the cigarettes he was smoking.

I didn't say anything else to Frank. I could tell that Chunxi was stifling a laugh. Frank was typical of my father's friends: no matter what the topic of conversation was, he could always find a way to bring it around to sex.

"That mother of yours is strange, isn't she? She's made this garden as dark and creepy as a pharaoh's tomb," the white man shouted after us as we walked away.

Chunxi and I arrived back at the tree house. I had lost much of my interest in talking, but she apparently did not feel the same way.

"Su Qi, if you had your own gun, would you be brave enough to go hunt the tigers?"

"I've never held a gun before."

"Can tigers climb trees?"

"I doubt they'll be able to climb this one."

"Who do you think will kill the first tiger, your father or mine?"

"Why don't you ask me which one I think the tigers will kill first?"

A little more than an hour later, someone started shouting down below us. Chunxi and I climbed down from the tree house. A group of white hunters had killed one tiger, and the other one had run off into the jungle, with my father and some others in pursuit. None of the people who had gone on the hunt had been hurt, but the night had still been witness to the most tragic event that had ever taken place at one of my fathers' parties. Chunxi's mother, driven to distraction by worry, had been waiting just outside the labyrinthine garden for Chunxi to come back, and she had been badly mauled by one of the tigers. My mother and several other women had rushed her to the hospital. Meanwhile Lin Yuan, my father, and a group of white men had formed five new hunting parties and gone into the jungle after the tiger that had escaped, saying something about how it would wreak havoc with the ecosystem if it were allowed to run wild there. Chunxi's mother had lost a lot of blood, and her wounds became infected, which brought on a case of blood poisoning. She spent six days unconscious in the intensive care unit of the hospital, and finally, on the early morning of the seventh day, she departed from this world. By then, my father and the others had long since hunted down the poor endangered Malay tiger, and they had skinned and cooked it on the spot. After that, they had put up for the night at a Dayak longhouse and enjoyed a night of revelry with the native women. This had led to a small-scale battle with some of the native men, and at two in the morning my father and the others were forced to retreat from the longhouse and spend the rest of the night out in the jungle. Ten days after that, Lin Yuan came home with an urn containing Chunxi's mother's ashes. He was keening loudly and saying, "My wife, I've killed it. I killed the beast. You can rest in peace now."

A week after that, my mother disappeared into her labyrinthine garden once again, and my father resumed his parties, though he did ask his guests to wear black and white formalwear for the next month, as a gesture of mourning. At the first party, women surrounded Lin Yuan to offer their condolences. He kissed each of the many female hands that stroked his hair and his cheeks, and at one point he buried his head deep in the groin of one of those women. This brought to my mind the nightmarish, distorted memory of walking with my mother, who held my little sister, among the falling leaves, under the fig trees, while my father was secretly meeting with the woman in white by the stream. Me embracing my mother's leg and pointing at the stream, as if I had a secret to share, describing to her how my father would kneel and kiss the toes of that strange woman like a penitent kneeling to kiss the foot of a statue of a martyr. The look on my mother's face back then was as impassive as it had been recently, as she worked to restore the lovely virginal garden that had been trampled upon and mistreated by two tigers and a gang of madmen. My mother did not speak for several days after the tiger incident. She seemed distracted, and she had even mustered up the courage to climb up to the tree house. All this made me feel unsettled and afraid.

Both households quickly resumed their old daily patterns, but I had a new job: consoling Chunxi, the hardest job I would ever have. I took her on a few walks in the garden and along the walkway between our two houses, but my recollections of all the vile things that had taken place there, and the fact that there was always a chance that we would run into one of my father's friends there, made me uncomfortable and even filled me with rage. So I did my best to see to it that the two of us spent most of our time either safe in the tree house or exploring the jungle. At the time I didn't think about whether Chunxi could handle the sweltering air in the jungle. I just wanted to be as far away as possible from the Lins' house and from my house and even from my mother's garden.

My father kept on holding his spectacular parties every weekend. The governor of our state, the governors and cabinet members of every other state, and even the political leaders of West Malaysia and Singapore and a sultan or two all graced us with their presences. But my father still regretted sorely the fact that the most important politician in the state, the chief minister, hadn't yet bothered to make an appearance. Rumor had it that once, when the chief minister had gone to Taiwan to play golf, my father and Lin Yuan had made a point of being on the putting green at the same time he was and had held his umbrella for him and carried his golf bag for him; this story had become a joke among the local bigwigs. My father had collected dozens of bottles of wine that were supposed to be the chief minister's favorites, and they sat in our cellar waiting to be enjoyed by the minister. My father had also turned a bedroom that faced Mecca into a prayer room, so that the Muslim chief minister could sing the praises of Allah whenever the urge struck him.

To demonstrate his sincerity of purpose, for several months my father instructed the chef not to put pork on the menus for his parties. He would say proudly to the guests, "The Honorable Chief Minister could decide to grace us with his presence at any time. I would never dream of doing anything that might offend him."

My mother had said to me, "Chunxi's lost her mother. Do whatever makes her happy." Normally, I would have kept a comfortable distance from the parties unless my presence was specifically requested. But because Chunxi attended almost all of them, I had to go, too, to keep her company. Chunxi was always staring out the window near the orchid trellis. She seemed to have something on her mind. All the guests who approached her to make small talk were earnest and restrained and would choose their words carefully, trying hard to avoid the painful topic. When Chunxi saw me looking worn-out or irritated, she would say kindly, "Su Qi, you don't have to stay here with me. Go be a rhinoceros, or a lonesome hawk, or whatever you like."

So usually I would leave the parties halfway through and go by myself to the balcony off the study to look at the stars crowding the sky and the flowers crowding the garden. At that time of night, many of Lin Yuan's peacocks, parrots, young chickens, and barking deer would gather in the garden, drawn by the brilliant light of the outdoor lamps. They would circulate through the garden and around its perimeter, and occasionally one creature would go charging into the parlor and linger stubbornly underfoot. They made the garden at night into a singular sight indeed.

Chapter 15

At the end of December in my last year of high school, I went with my class on a senior trip to northern Borneo. Around the same time, Lin Yuan had made plans to take Chunxi's mother's ashes home to Taiwan. On the same day I left on my trip, he and Chunxi set out with the urn containing the ashes.

The itinerary for our senior trip encompassed all of northern Borneo, but we ended up spending the majority of our time trapped in the stuffy, noisy bus. When we climbed Mount Kinabalu, the highest peak in Southeast Asia, I suddenly felt that Chunxi was so far away from me that she and I might as well be in two different worlds. One of the guys on the trip said that the air was so thin up there that if you kissed a girl for a few minutes you could probably make her faint in your arms. Some of the others started teasing him, saying he should try this out on one of the girls, and this scared the girls enough to send them scattering like a flock of birds. Mount Kinabalu was known in Chinese as the Chinese Widow's Mountain; it was shaped like a woman gazing out to sea, waiting to see the sail on her lover's ship returning, waiting and suffering to no avail, until her body turned to hard stone. On the postcard I sent to Taiwan— and I don't know whether this qualifies as the sort of nonsense one is supposed to put in love letters—I wrote, "Love and oxygen are equally scarce in a place like this. Nothing but carbon dioxide and lost love wherever you go. It's enough to make you feel constantly dizzy, as if you're only half-alive. But even in a horrible place like this love can stand firm. It can survive."

Fierce rain arrived with the northeast monsoon wind, and the torrential downpour lasted for three weeks and completely ruined the trip. All highway traffic came to a standstill, the ferries stopped running, bridges were washed out, and we were confined to a hotel, where we played cards and listened to music all day, bored out of our minds. The senior trip was supposed to have lasted only ten days, but we returned home two months after we set out.

Chunxi had come back over a month before I did, and during that month she had spent a great deal of time in the tree house by herself. Then, one night around dusk, two weeks before I got back, she had fallen fast asleep up there and rolled off the edge, falling down the full nine meters. My mother had found her there before it was completely dark, lying unconscious at the base of the tree. The expression on her face had been peaceful, but her breathing was erratic. She still had our binoculars hung around her neck. Poor Chunxi had suffered serious head trauma and a long period of oxygen deprivation, and this had left her brain-dead. The doctors all agreed: barring a miracle, Chunxi was never going to wake up again.

At dusk, beneath the final rays of the sun, I went to see Chunxi. The cries of Oriental magpies and turtledoves came in through the window. Chunxi looked just like a baby lying in her bed. She made me think of the infant Chunxi, lying in an incubator, and of the Chunxi who had woken up one morning to find a giant lizard poised to leave her room through the window, turning its head to stare at her pubescent body. Chunxi's eyelids, her lips, and her nostrils were all fluttering, as if some kind of mood were animating those parts of her body, using them to satisfy her desire to move and to talk. These motions made me think of a tidal wave rising and falling, silent and slow. I was right next to Chunxi, but I had never felt farther from her. I was back on Mount Kinabalu, four thousand meters above sea level, where the air was thin enough that Chunxi would never have been able to climb it.

After Chunxi had been in her coma for three months, Lin Yuan took her to America for treatment, following the advice of his friends. Six months after that, the two of them returned to Borneo, with Chunxi still in her deep sleep. By that point I was in Taipei, coasting through a test preparation course and getting ready to take the college entrance exam. While Chunxi was in America, I had spent a lot of time wandering around outdoors, trying to shed the constrictions of my family and my home like a snake sheds its skin. I had suddenly developed an infinitely expanding hatred for my house, for the Lins' house, and for the labyrinthine garden, and I was anxious to leave all of it behind.

One day, while my mother was working in the garden, she suddenly stroked one of the plants and said, "Qi, little Qi, look how sweet these flowers are. They'll never leave you. They'll never change their minds about you. And they'll always grow up just the way you want them to. That's why I love them, because they have no future and no hope. They'll always need me."

In May of that year, after Chunxi had been brain-dead for almost six months, I boarded a plane bound for Taiwan and began my college life in Taipei.

Part 2

Chapter 16

I moved into a college dormitory in Taipei in September 1978. Before I started school, I had been living with some friends of my mother's while I took a test preparation course. I went to my test prep classes in an imbecilic daze, and I treated the entrance exam like it was an opinion survey and answered however I wanted. Then, after I was accepted into college, as I was packing my bags to move into the dorm, I came across the pristine handouts from my test prep course and looked them over, one by one; I felt like I'd seen them before only in a dream. One of my classmates from the course, who had started studying before I did but had failed the exam, thought that I had cheated and said I should take the test for him next year. I told him I would be happy to hand my college acceptance over to him if he would pay for me to spend another year in the preparation course.

The dormitory building had five stories and was divided into two wings, one for boys and one for girls. Architectural barriers divided the two wings, and we were strictly forbidden to enter the wing of the opposite sex. Supposedly the dorm had only been built a few years before, but it looked as old and rundown as if students had been inflicting their torments on the place for decades. Honestly, what I was doing in that university and that dormitory was something of a mystery to me. I had filled out my placement request based entirely on my scores on the various portions of the entrance exam. Even more absurd than that, though, is the fact that I didn't realize that I would be going to a normal university, for training teachers, until I arrived at the school to register. This of course meant that I would apparently be teaching school after I graduated. That was as absurd as anything

I could have imagined. And that was not the end of the absurdity of my situation. The dormitory regulations were pedantic to the point of being silly; we were treated like junior high kids. The idea was to mold all of us hotheaded young ruffians into proper, upright prigs within four years. I suppose that makes some sense, since in four years we would all be teaching a fresh gang of little reprobates.

The main gate to the dormitory was locked every night at eleven. Anyone who came back after that had to sign in and would have points deducted from his conduct record. Right after the gate was locked, the lights went off, so we couldn't even read after eleven, which didn't bode well for our future as teachers. Poker was forbidden in the dorm, as was mah-jongg. There were two morning assemblies held each week, at seven-thirty, and at these assemblies we had to sing the national anthem and the school song and listen to lectures by the dorm supervisors. Anyone who missed an assembly would have points deducted from his conduct record. Once a month we had our hair inspected, and anyone whose haircut wasn't up to standard would have points deducted from his conduct record. What they called the "conduct record" was probably something similar to the disciplinary records they keep on soldiers in the military, but I was never certain. I don't know how many times I was threatened with the deduction of points from my conduct record; still, in the end, I graduated like everyone else. Looking back on those days now, I am still amazed by how many ridiculous rules there were in that dorm. Logically, it would seem that the dorm's massive deployment of disciplinary tactics should have made students' lives a living hell, should have made every one of us either turn into a quivering ninny or else grow even more intransigent. In fact, though, neither of those things happened.

A week before classes began, an upperclassman from the foreign languages department who was serving as our residential advisor gave a talk to all of us first-years in the department, and what he had to say to us was a little shocking.

"My name is ____. I'm a junior, and I'm the foreign languages advisor for new residential students. If you guys are real men, you won't believe everything I'm about to tell you. The truth is I don't even know how many lounges there are in your dorm, or how many canteens, or how to get to the cafeteria, or where to find a public phone, or what time they turn on the hot water. That's how much of a mess I am. I feel sorta bad about that."

The upperclassman's hair covered one of his eyes. He wore a thick beard and had a cigarette hanging out of his mouth. He reminded me of a political activist on a hunger strike: extremely skinny, with a self-righteous air.

A guy from the south of Taiwan asked, in a simpering and deferential voice, "Sir, my hair's getting long, and I'm wondering where the nearest barbershop is?"

"A barbershop? I think there was one around here last year, but I don't know if it's still in business. And even if it is, I'm not sure exactly where. But why do you want some old man messing with your hair anyway? There are lots of salons around here. The stylists are all cute girls. For a couple hundred extra you can get a massage too."

"Sir, what exactly is a 'lounge'?"

"It's where you're supposed to go to hang out, have fun, watch TV. Delinquents like me spend a lot of time hanging out in the lounges. Or if your relatives or your girlfriends come to visit you can take them there. Yeah, that's right: girlfriends. I'm guessing you boys are all virgins, and I can tell you that over the next four years sex is going to be a major hassle. Girls in Taipei like to have fun, and they'll let *you* have fun, but you have to watch out. A pregnant girl is a big problem, you know?" The upperclassman pulled out a pack of Longevity cigarettes and held it out toward us, but we all shook our heads to decline. He lit a fresh cigarette and took several deep drags, as if to say, Yeah, a pregnant girl, now *that's* a problem. The upperclassman looked lonesome, smoking by himself, so I asked him for a cigarette. "Last year we had a guy in the department who got himself in a fix and then wouldn't own up to it. So the girl, she was from the Chinese department, three months pregnant, came after him with a knife right here in the dorm. He had to hide in the closet. Literally pissed himself. Pretty fucking humiliating for him, huh? Listen, you guys, if you're smart enough to get what you want from a girl, you'd better be smart enough to make sure you get *everything* you want. Don't forget that. If you absolutely can't control yourself, then jerk off."

"This is the dorm, it's not your house. Privacy's limited. So, guys, when you jerk off, pay attention to where you do it. Six hard dicks in one little room. If you're not discreet about things, you'll be bumping into each other all the time, and there's nothing fun about that. The showers won't do, since you can't lock the door. Plus the partitions between the stalls aren't high enough. They'll hide your bottom half, but the top half'll be completely exposed, and I'll bet none of you exactly look like you're reading scriptures when you do it. A few fuckheads like to go up to the roof and do it in full view of God himself. They call it 'setting off rockets.' That's no good either. There are tons of buildings taller than ours around here, and anyone on a higher floor could look down and see you. The only real option is in the toilets, and of course it's cramped in there and easy to get things dirty. So you've got to be respectful. After you've finished your business, remember to clean up. Listen, guys, you can't graduate still a virgin. If you can't find a girlfriend, then you can spend a little money, but then of course you have to worry about hygiene. No need to deprive yourselves because of that, though. I can tell you where to find clean girls."

"What else? Oh, yeah. There's suicide. Every year we have two or three fuckheads off themselves by jumping off the dorm roof. They all want to die for one of three main reasons: grades, girls, or boredom. The third one's kind of special. Guys who've read too many books often want to die, guys like us here in foreign languages. Jumping off a fifth-story roof isn't necessarily the best way to kill yourself, so if you decide you're going to do it you should think about how you want to jump. If you jump into the muddy yard between the girls' and boys' dorms, you'll die for sure, no question. Don't jump against the direction of the wind, because you don't want to hit your head on the building on your way down."

The upperclassman's doubts about the fifth-story roof were clearly genuine, because in the spring of the following year he jumped, naked, from the eleventh-story roof of the Student Activities Center. He never had a chance to tell us freshmen where we could find clean prostitutes.

The upperclassman was clasping a bouquet of flowers when he jumped. He had shaved his face as clean as a fresh-faced new recruit at the military academy, and his hair was done up in a magnificent pompadour. He had swaggered like a horny bridegroom on his way up the stairs to the eleventh story. When the supervisor at the Activities Center saw him at ten in the evening, his flowers were just about to bloom. When they found his body the next morning, they had bloomed into a bouquet more colorful than even the soft mess that had once been the upperclassman's skull.

Chapter 17

On my first day in the dorm, I opened my new tape recorder, sprawled out on my bed, and recorded myself reading aloud from an English translation of Yukio Mishima's *Confessions of a Mask*. Afterward, when I listened to the tape, I could clearly make out the sounds of other people, in and around my own room, lying down and sitting up, dressing and undressing and trying on the new clothes they'd bought at street stalls, blow-drying their hair, munching on snacks, killing mosquitoes, playing chess, snoring, singing Peking opera, playing the *erhu*, roaring in their infinite boredom. The place was full of youthful vigor and yet absolutely lifeless, like a nursing home and a playground at the same time. All these sounds surrounding *Confessions of a Mask* seemed to highlight the instability and monstrosity of Mishima's writing.

At first everyone thought I was practicing my English pronunciation, and they warned me that the English professors at this university all had terrible pronunciation and that I didn't need to work that hard. But soon enough they realized that I would turn on the tape recorder no matter what I was reading. It could be a martial arts novel or the political writings of Sun Yat-sen. Even if I was just killing time with my roommates, or going to class, or listening to the dorm supervisors' lectures, or watching TV, or walking around the night market, or going to morning assembly—I recorded everything that happened. Once, by mistake, I recorded some upperclassmen expressing very strong opinions about a certain violent Taiwanese political event in their dorm room, and they begged me to destroy the tape, but I refused. Then they tried to think of a way to steal it from me, but they never succeeded. After that they decided that I must be a spy planted by the Kuomintang.

I actually think I was pretty normal, compared to most of the guys I lived with. But during my first two years of college, it's fair to say that I spent much more time talking to the tape recorder than to real people, and I almost grew accustomed to talking to myself. I found that my words flowed on in a garrulous, unstoppable stream when I spoke to a machine or to an empty landscape but that I had nothing to say to real live people. I don't know what kind of lingering effects this might have had on me if I had let it go on too long. When I reached my junior year, I quit all that, not a moment too soon. But it wasn't as if I had been doing it for nothing. Back when I was still in the test preparation course, I had learned that Chunxi had been brought back to Borneo, her condition unchanged, and I had made up my mind not to go back home before I graduated unless she woke up. I was terrified of being steamrolled to an emotional pulp by the past, of having all my resolve destroyed by it. But I didn't want to break off all ties entirely; I wanted to maintain some kind of contact with the past, to demonstrate my concern and compunction. And one way of doing that was to record, in drips and drops, my daily life in Taipei and to send all of it home, to be played for my mother and for Chunxi. However, the huge stack of tapes I recorded stayed on my shelf for my first two years away. Not until my junior year did I begin to send them back in increments, two months of taped life at a time, and I did this because I felt that it was time for me to move on to something new, that there was nothing to be gained from spending all my time foundering in the past in a kind of deliberate dispirited indolence.

As I was mailing the tapes, I thought about the red mailbox in front of the Lins' door and about the story Chunxi had told me about the Postman Bear. I could almost see the Postman Bear in his green uniform, riding his bicycle, stopping in front of the Lins' door and dropping the package containing the tapes into the red mailbox.

The package would land inside the mailbox with a plunking sound.

The Postman Bear would ring the doorbell and then get back on his bicycle and ride away.

Just when I had finished mailing the last of the tapes, I got a phone call from my mother telling me that a week before Lin Yuan had sent Chunxi to an expensive nursing facility in America, where she could spend the rest of her life under the care of specialized medical personnel. I asked my mother for the address of the nursing facility, and she said, "You don't need to know that. Just concentrate on your studies." Several days after that, Lin Yuan called me. He urged me to forget about Chunxi; he hoped that that dark cloud could be cast out of our lives as soon as possible. He also said that he was very grateful for the tapes I had sent—he had already sent copies to America and asked the nurses there to play them for Chunxi sometime.

Chapter 18

College wasn't so different from high school for me. I went docilely to class every day; I took notes; I rarely missed a class no matter how boring; and I took as many courses as I could, including electives in other departments, so that I had eight periods of class a day and not much time to think about anything else. The campus and architecture of my prestigious university were reminiscent of the grounds of a Taoist temple, and the place made me feel like I had left the mundane world behind me. As I walked along those paths in my gray uniform I think I must have had the air of a monk at peace with the world. If it's fair of me to say that I now have the ability to change everything about myself and adapt to any kind of life, then the lethargic, conservative atmosphere of that school probably played no small role in developing that talent in me.

Life in the dorm just got worse after I got to my junior year. Rancid socks and underwear confronted me wherever I turned. Towels and clothes hung from every wall and every inch of the ceiling, and if you happened to bump into them they would drench you with their foul odor like a spraying skunk. There were shoes everywhere—

inside the room, just outside it, and all down the hallway. Books, magazines, newspapers, cups, plates, toothbrushes, washbasins, plastic buckets, fruit knives, teapots, guitars, basketballs, tennis rackets, dumbbells, curtain rods, cassette tapes, fishbowls, bottles, and jars cluttered the floor and made our dorm room look like a refugee camp. None of this junk served any purpose whatsoever—maybe it might have served as an alarm if a feral cat had ever decided to come sneaking into the room, attracted by the odors of rot. The facilities themselves often had problems as well: the washer and dryer were out of service as often as they were working, the drinking water tap was often dry, the hot water in the shower would come out only haltingly in the winter. In all honesty, I don't know how I managed to live there for two years and treat all this as if it were the most natural thing in the world. There were six of us, leading six very different lives, all living in one bedroom, and after a while we had no scruples about showing the ugliest sides of ourselves to one another. Because of this, conflicts broke out in the room every day. The dorm supervisors had all been in the military and held ranks of lieutenant colonel or higher, and they must have inspired awe and trembling when they drilled their troops, but they were at a loss with us college students. After a while they got too lazy to keep track of the cleanliness points that should have been deducted from our conduct records. It was all they could do to keep themselves from growing as slovenly as we were.

One of my roommates had drawn twelve columns on the wall above his desk. At the top of each column he had written the name of a month, and every so often he would use a red crayon to draw an eye-catching X in the column for that month. I counted sixteen Xs for June, thirteen for July, and twenty-one for August, but for September and October combined there was a total of only ten. Finally one of our roommates couldn't resist any longer and asked him what the Xs signified.

The guy had been hoping one of us would ask him this. He said in a depressed voice, "This calendar is sacred. It shows how many times I masturbate each month. One X for each time."

"Pretty good. It looks like you did it twenty-one times in August?"

"That's nothing. In high school my record was sixty-eight times in one month. I'm old now. I don't have as much product to unload. I'm doing well if I get an average of fifteen times a month."

He was so serious about it that the rest of us almost split our sides laughing.

"Don't despair. You're still young. You could still set a new record."

"That's what I've been hoping."

At the end of that October, I started to think about moving out after the next vacation. I didn't hate my roommates, but I was getting sick of the violent restlessness in the dorm, even though a part of me continued to enjoy the virile decadence of the place. My mother thought that two years in the dorm was enough to constitute a healthy epoch, and she compared my move to Jesus coming out of years of reclusion to spread the Gospels. That comparison baffled me, but I suppose that my accounts of dorm life on the phone must at times have made it sound like I was going through a monk's penitential rites, and, remembering that it wouldn't be long before I would be mired in all the difficulty and unpleasantness of a teacher's life, I guessed that my mother would be drawing similar comparisons and offering me similar encouragement in the years to come. Maybe my mother's overwrought worries, her view of life as one big crucifixion, had some basis: she had grown up in Taiwan, and the educational system there had been eating away at her spirit since she was a child. In any case, my mother wanted to ask her friends in Taipei to help me with the move, but I said, "Mom, this plant you've been watering since it was a tiny thing is all grown up now. I don't need you to worry about me." When vacation came around, I rented a twenty-square-meter apartment near campus, and a month after classes began I moved my things over to the new place and bade my farewells to the dormitory I had lived in for two years.

Life in my new apartment went on in much the same way. The only difference was that I didn't go to the library when I didn't have class. Instead, I holed up in my apartment and read or else went to a coffeehouse called the Study Hall. On weekend nights I wandered the streets aimlessly, and when I grew tired of that I'd find a Western-style bar that had live folk music. There, I would sit in a corner by myself, drinking drinks that cost fifty or sixty Taiwan dollars each, listening to the conversations of the young people and the pairs of lovers all around me. I discovered that most of the patrons of these places were just looking to chat or pass the time, like me, and that very few of them had come specifically to listen to the music. I liked that kind of relaxed atmosphere; I liked sitting alone like a rootless ghost with no more potent spirits to lead me astray. After two months of this, I settled on a bar called Fairy Tale, which was on the second floor of a building that overlooked a bustling night market. The facade of the bar was as dark as its interior, and its decor was no different from that of any other folk music venue: the walls were covered with wood panels and hung with exotic pieces of pottery, posters, prints of modern art, and foreign flags. All that was lacking was an ample supply of sunlight that would burnish the floor with a red glow during the day. Plastic plants, wooden wind chimes, cloth dolls, and fake currency from a variety of nations all hung from the ceiling, and busts of the heads of historical world leaders were also hung here and there: George Washington, Abraham Lincoln, Benjamin Franklin, the queen of England, the emperor of Japan, Sun Yat-sen, Chiang Kai-shek. The entire bar was maybe one hundred square meters, and the performances took place on a small semicircular stage by the bar that held stereo equipment, a microphone, a music stand, and a chair. Potted plants were set out on either side of the stage, and a trellis slightly larger than the stage itself, complete with plastic grapevines, had been placed over it. Two spotlights hung down among the vines. Posters for Disney animated movies were on the walls surrounding the stage: *Snow White and the Seven Dwarfs*, *Sleeping Beauty*, *Cinderella*, *Beauty and the Beast*. The bar was open every day from eleven in the morning until midnight, and the music began at five in the afternoon. A new singer would come onstage every fifty minutes. On Saturdays from eight to eight-fifty, the singer was a girl named Keyi who looked like a college student. Initially I thought that her name must be the Keyi that meant "delightful," or the one that meant "proper," or "refined," or "gift." But the program was handwritten, and there was no way they could have made a mistake: what was written was the Keyi that meant "dubious." Keyi had performed about twenty times, and I had only seen her wear two outfits: one a pair of white stonewashed jeans with a blouse and a long-sleeved sweater (she had two of these sweaters, one white and the other red) and the other a checked skirt with overalls and one of the sweaters. When the weather was relatively cold, she wouldn't even take off her jacket. For shoes, she always wore the same pair of gleaming white sneakers.

She would ascend the stage with her guitar in her hands and sing her heart out for fifty minutes without looking at any sheet music. The first half of the program would be folk songs that were popular among college students at that time, and the second half would be old songs from Europe and America. Customers who wanted to make requests would hand their written request form to her, and without lifting an eyebrow she would immediately start singing whatever it was they wanted. She could even handle the old Mandarin songs requested by forty-something patrons without making a single mistake. The confident expression on her face made it seem as if there weren't a song on earth that she couldn't sing.

Her guitar playing was no better than amateur level; her voice was good enough that you couldn't find fault with it. The look on her face while she sang was somewhat hesitant, and her enunciation was indifferent. But after a few minutes of listening to her, you might think you were listening to a carefree, illiterate peasant girl or milkmaid as she sang blithely in a breeze and slight drizzle, or along a sun-drenched ancient road, or amid rice fields and herding grounds. Even though the customers didn't listen to the music very attentively at all, she still threw her heart into everything she sang. Her favorite English-language songs were "The End of the World" and "The River of No Return," both of them songs with plaintive melodies and uncomplicated instrumental accompaniments, both of them sung without tormented theatricality, both of them sung with the bated breath of expectant young lovers together in the dark. When things weren't going well for me at school and I was especially dispirited, I would think about listening to Keyi sing that coming Saturday night, and I would feel better. Later on, I learned from the printed program that she was also slated to start performing every Tuesday and Thursday, also during the prime time at eight o'clock. So sometimes I would show up on those two days, too, if I didn't have too much schoolwork to do.

Around the end of December I figured out that Keyi often came to the Study Hall Coffeehouse, my favorite haunt, to study. One time I walked by her and saw that she had her head buried in a fat book, in English, on business or something along those lines and that "_____ University, Business Administration Department" was written on her notebook. I was disappointed to see that there was no name on the notebook, so I couldn't confirm whether Keyi was her real name or not.

She wore the same clothes at the Study Hall, that hangout for poor students, as she did onstage, and she usually had a cup of green tea on the table in front of her. She was as serious about her studying as she was about her singing: she kept her head buried studiously in her books and very rarely looked up, and as soon as she was finished she would leave without dawdling.

One Friday night in the middle of January, I got to the Study Hall a little later than usual and found that all the tables were already taken. The waiter asked me if I was willing to share a table with someone else, and I said that I didn't mind, so he led me to a seat at the same table as Keyi, directly across from her. Keyi pulled her books closer as I sat down, and I hastily told her that she didn't need to bother. I had brought only a novel and a dictionary; I didn't need much space. The waiter brought over a reading lamp for me, and I opened *The Heart of the Matter* and began to study.

The vast coffeehouse was laid out like a church. The counter where beverages were served was like a lectern, and the manager behind the counter performed his job with a preacher's zeal. The students studied like people engaged in silent prayer, and when they grew obviously tired of their reading they reminded me of penitents receiving the last rites. Probably these associations occurred to me because of all the times I had gone to church with my mother when I was a child. After half an hour, the couple sitting at the table beside me and Keyi began to fight. The girl had found an unsent love letter of uncertain origins in the boy's notebook, and she asked him to whom he planned to send such a nauseating letter. The boy said, "To you, of course." To this the girl replied, "You see me everyday, what would you need to do that for?"

He said, "Your birthday's next month, and I wanted to surprise you."

She said, "Nowhere in that whole sappy letter does it say anything about a birthday."

"I haven't finished it yet," the boy said.

She answered with, "How stupid do you think I am? Never once in all the time we've known each other have you written me anything even resembling a letter."

The boy said, "What's this, then? Didn't I just write you one?"

The girl tore the letter into two pieces.

"What are you doing that for?" he asked her.

She tore those two pieces, to make a total of four pieces.

He said, "Don't think I don't know about you going to the movies with that other guy last month."

"Not only are you a liar, you've got a wandering eye, too. You've been staring at that girl over there ever since we sat down!" And with this the girl pointed at Keyi, sitting across from me. I realized that Keyi was, like me, angling her head over in their direction and listening in on their argument. Now that she had been hit by a stray bullet, Keyi looked shocked and wronged.

The boy said, "It's perfectly natural for guys to look at girls. Especially pretty ones."

Keyi stifled a laugh.

The girl didn't say anything else. She just threw the scraps of the torn letter into the boy's face. The boy pointed at me and said, "Don't get all mad. There's a handsome guy here for you to look at if you want." I did my best to stifle a laugh, but in fact I couldn't do it, and I laughed out loud.

The girl seized a few more scraps of paper and threw them at the boy, too; then she gathered her books and stood up. The boy grabbed her hand, and she said, "Let me go, or I'll scream." He didn't let go of her hand, and she couldn't break free of his grip, so she banged him on the head with a book. He said, "Sit down, I'm begging you." The girl looked at me and Keyi, her face flushed up to her ears.

I couldn't help myself; I said to the boy, "Let her go."

He was floored by this, and he loosened his grip, looking dejected.

The girl stormed off. But in a minute she was back again. She sat down and said, "I'm not going to leave until you give me a full explanation." The boy was gathering up the shreds of the torn letter, and he said, "Why'd you have to take it out on my letter?"

"Did you really write it for me?" she said softly.

"Just forget it," he said.

"If you just read a couple sentences to me, I'll know if you're telling the truth," the girl said.

The boy said, "Well, it's all torn up. How can I read it now?"

"You must remember a couple of sentences," she said.

"Someone else wrote it for me," he said. "All I remember is, 'If I had all the seas of Paradise, with you as my simple gourd I'd be content.'"[1]

"Okay," said the girl. "I believe you."

"Yeah, but you still haven't told me about who you went to the movies with last month."

"You're bringing up *that* again?" The girl then pointed at me. "It was him! Okay?"

Then she stormed off a second time.

The boy sat dumbly for a while and then left, too.

Keyi and I and the other people sitting nearby all laughed as quietly as we could. I shook my head and said to Keyi, "That certainly came out of nowhere."

"You're quite a meddler, aren't you?" Keyi said. "Telling him to let go of her like that."

"Men have violent tendencies. Who knows what would have happened if things had gone on that way," I said. "Anyway, the real problem wasn't the letter. It was you. The guy was looking at you the whole time, and the girl saw and got upset."

"So I guess you weren't paying all that much attention to your studying. That doesn't make it my fault, does it? So I'm good-looking, so what? It's not a crime."

"No, it's not a crime. They were the ones with the problems."

Keyi took a sip of her tea. "I know who you are. You go to ____ University, and you come to Fairy Tale a lot. One time you came in

---

1. The boy's sentence is a slightly garbled version of a line, spoken by the hero to the heroine, from the eighteenth-century Chinese novel *The Story of the Stone*, by Cao Xueqin. The rendering here is a slightly garbled version of the translation provided by David Hawkes in *The Story of the Stone* (London: Penguin, 1973), 4:241.

wearing the ____ University uniform. Since when do people walk into bars wearing their school uniforms? Wearing the uniform on campus is a good thing, it's like wearing camouflage, but wearing it off campus makes you look like a dumb hick. You always come by yourself, and you always look so thoughtful. You don't say a word, and you sit by yourself in the corner by the British flag. Right? And you're a foreign languages major, right? I can tell from the cover of your notebook. Do you always go to Fairy Tale? I mean, even on the nights when I'm not performing, do you go?"

"At first I didn't go for any particular reason. I just went when I was bored. Eventually I started going on Tuesdays and Thursdays and Saturdays to hear you, because I like your singing. And I don't go every Tuesday, Thursday, and Saturday. I didn't go last night."

"Thank you. And are you coming tomorrow?"

"Saturday nights are when I'm most bored. I'll definitely go."

"If I'm not mistaken, you've never requested a song." She tore a sheet of paper out of her notebook and put it in front of me. "Write your favorite songs down here, and tomorrow night I'll sing them for you."

"I don't really care. Just sing whatever you want. I'm not very particular about the music I listen to."

"Do this for my benefit. Pick a few songs, okay?"

Without stopping to think, I wrote down, "Donna Donna," "Where Have All the Flowers Gone?" "Changing Partners," "Crying in the Rain," "Don't Cry for Me, Argentina" (which I thought was the greatest song I'd ever heard), "How Can You Mend a Broken Heart?" "The First Time Ever I Saw Your Face," and a couple more, for a total of nine songs.

"Looks like you're trying to get your money's worth," she said as she took the paper from me. "You know a lot of songs."

"Is that a problem?" I said with a smile. "Don't push yourself too hard. If you collapse, the bar will lose its biggest attraction."

"I'm just afraid I won't have time to do all nine songs. It'll be like I'm giving you a private performance."

"You don't have to sing them all. I wrote down nine songs so you could pick the ones you wanted to do."

She carefully folded the sheet of paper and stuck it inside her notebook. "Well, listen, I'll be able to sing them all. But because I'll be doing it for you, you should sit at the very front. Don't go hiding in the corner like a ghost."

"But I come by myself, and I only have one drink. Pretty shabby. I'd be ashamed to sit up in front."

"It's true. The boss just hates customers like you. It doesn't matter, though. Just buck up a little."

"If you're going to sing nine songs for me, I guess I should try to make a better showing," I said earnestly. "Tomorrow I'll go early and have dinner there and take over a table near the front. I can afford it."

In a voice like the twitter of a bird, she told me which dishes at Fairy Tale were the best deals. Then we spent another hour studying, and after that it occurred to me to ask about her bizarre stage name. "What's your name, anyway? Is 'Keyi' your real name?"

"You haven't told me your name." She lifted her head from her notebook, which seemed to have been causing her great consternation.

"My name's Su Qi. The Su is the same as the poet Su Dongpo, the Qi is the same Qi as in the word for 'other.'"

"That's a pretty old-fashioned name." She was writing my name down in a blank space in her notebook as she said this. "Is this right? My last name is Li, the same Li as the poet Li Bai, and my name is Keyi, but the Keyi that means 'delightful.' The 'Ke' is the same 'Ke' as in 'to be able,' the same 'Ke' as in 'Coca-Cola.' Then the 'Yi' is the one in 'pleased with yourself' and 'carefree.' My darned name. There's a whole bunch of Keyis in the phone book. You even see it a lot in lists of people killed in plane crashes. If you went up to the front of the room and called it out, I'll bet three different people in this coffeehouse would answer. All the girls these days have names like that. There's a bunch with Ke in them: Kexin, Keru, Kechun, Kewen, Keyu, Ke'ai. Then there are the ones with Yi: Xinyi, Jingyi, Meiyi, Fangyi, Lingyi, Zhenyi. Too many, and they're all basically the same name. Parents these days have no imagination."

I followed her example and wrote her name down in a blank space in my own notebook. "I like it. It rolls right off the tongue, and it's easy to remember. But why is your stage name the Keyi that means 'dubious'?"

"No reason. Anything that wasn't the 'delightful' Keyi was fine with me."

After that we each read our own books until the coffeehouse closed, at eleven. Keyi closed her textbook and yawned a deep yawn. It looked to me like studying was torture for her. "How are you doing?" I asked her. "Still okay? Is business administration that tough?"

"Oh, definitely not." She rubbed her eyes. "It's just that the damn professor likes to show off, and he's always assigning us these thick, heavy English books, all totally obscure ones that haven't been translated into Chinese. They make me feel like my head's going to explode."

We gathered up our things and left the coffeehouse.

"You're a foreign languages student. I'll bet your English isn't bad," she said.

"Good enough to get by."

"Do you think you could do a little translation for me?"

"No problem."

"I'm not kidding. I can give you my homework tomorrow."

"That's fine. I'd be happy to learn a little about business administration."

There was a small park with a playground next to the coffeehouse. A couple was sitting on the swings together, and another couple was playing on the seesaw. Seven or eight small alleyways formed the spokes of a wheel, the center of which was the park. The alleys seemed to split the nearby high-rise towers into fragments. A stray dog was sitting on its haunches in the grass and barking, soft and forlorn.

"I know this kind of dog," I said. "He probably started out as a loud, intense barker, but he's been beaten too many times by the people who live around here, and so his voice changed into the weird sort of thing we're hearing now."

"Looks to me like his barking days are almost over. I bet he'll be put to sleep soon."

"He was neutered back when he still had a home. That's why his barking doesn't sound very manly."

"A eunuch cast out of the palace! That's a much sadder fate than being put to sleep."

"There are robbers and perverts and delinquents and vagrants and psychos on the streets at this hour. Do you want me to walk you home?"

"Just take care of yourself," she said, as if she really couldn't care less. "There's nothing I hate more than people walking me home. A trip that should take two minutes ends up taking two light-years. Also, I have a test tomorrow, and I have to get to sleep early so I don't forget everything I just read. So I'll see you tomorrow."

It just so happened that we were going in opposite directions. After I got home, I took a hot shower and then lay on my bed listening to the Beatles. Amid the bars of "Yellow Submarine" I dropped down into a world both familiar and foreign, and soon I found myself half crawling and half leaping along the walkway that connected our house to the Lins'. The sounds of birds, bugs, the wind, and rustling leaves all converged to form a surging wave, and I was struggling to move toward a small, white Western-style house, a crystal palace. It was as if I were searching for a treasure that had been lost at the bottom of the sea for two hundred years.

I pushed gently at the door and entered the white house, and then I felt myself become a monstrous being in a scuba diver's costume, with the goggles and the flippers and an oxygen tank on my back. I needed all kinds of rigging and equipment if I wanted to enter that world.

I had to adapt slowly to the difference between the air pressure inside and outside. It was like the time I had climbed to the top of Mount Kinabalu and entered a stratum of the atmosphere that Chunxi was not designed to live in.

In the small, pitchy room, crammed with creeping vines, palms, and ferns, an only half-developed female fetus with shriveled arms and legs was lying amid the half-opened shells of mollusks. Plants of the psychotropic Araceae family had crept in through the window and had reached the foot of her bed; they were extending toward her parched lips and her sunken chest.

I tumbled into her lap like a boneless medusa, and with a smacking sound I bored my way into her vagina and up to her womb. Leaving no spot unpenetrated, as quickly as seeds sprout into young plants, I spread through her limbs and all her organs.

She began to tremble violently, and then suddenly her body rose from the bed. The tide was receding rapidly, and some kind of force was pulling me out of her body, distorting me the way a diver's body is distorted when he comes up from the depths too quickly.

The leisurely notes of "Hey, Jude" greeted me when I woke up. That night, for the first time, I thought about Chunxi, longingly but without any hope, and I concluded that Chunxi was getting worse by the day, sinking down into a world from which I could not pull her back up. A silicon memory chip was all that she had left behind, and it was lying at the bottom of the ocean, enormous with accumulated rust.

Chapter 19

At seven the next evening, I ordered a pork cutlet that cost one hundred and fifty Taiwan dollars at Fairy Tale and took the seat closest to the stage on the left. When I sat down, two girls were performing, both singing and playing guitar, and the expressions on their faces, their stage presence, and even their voices were virtually identical. By seven-thirty, the place was packed; Saturday nights were when sad and lonely people came out in force. The cutlet I was eating was not particularly good, and the recipe was fairly simple, but I didn't see the point in being picky. This was the only place in town where I could feed my soul; my stomach would just have to make do.

After the two girls finished singing, the audience got restless. I finished my pork cutlet and ordered a drink. My brain felt stripped of all thoughts. Two girl students were sitting on my right and were talking and laughing, their heads practically touching. Whenever I looked at them, they looked back at me. The upperclassman had given us lessons on how to pick up girls when I first moved into the dorm, and he had said that two girls were an easier target than one girl by herself.

Ten minutes is a painful expanse of time when you're waiting for something. I was studying the poster of the prince kissing Sleeping Beauty when Keyi came onto the stage. She sat down with her guitar to the applause of the audience, and by the time she was settled waiters were already coming over to hand her song requests. Keyi put the request forms on the music stand, her fingers started to dance over the strings, and she began to sing. First she sang "The First Time Ever I Saw Your Face," and after that her guitar moved into the melody of "Don't Cry for Me, Argentina." She performed all nine of my songs in one long string, serenely and effortlessly. After the last of them, "Changing Partners," she added a tenth song, "I'm Getting Sentimental over You." After that she had only a few minutes remaining in her set. Ignoring the request forms on the music stand, she took her bows early and then came down from the stage and walked straight over to me.

"You've been sitting so still. Are you asleep?" She made a fan out of her hand and waved it in front of my eyes. "Do you have anything else to do tonight?"

"Nothing. On Saturday nights I'm bored and have nothing to do. That's why I come here to listen to you."

"Would you go with me somewhere else to talk? It's too noisy in here."

I went up to the bar to settle my check, and she got her jacket and backpack from behind the bar. We walked out of Fairy Tale together.

"Did I do okay just now?"

"Too good for words," I said. "You're pretty impressive. You've got to know something about music theory to be able to string ten songs together like that."

"I spent the whole afternoon practicing. It's a good thing you came. It's a little cold out here; let me take you to a coffeehouse."

Parents had brought their children out to play in the nearby park. The same stray dog was there; he and another, pampered-looking black dog were sniffing at one another. One little kid fell off a swing and cried until his face was a mess of tears and snot. Keyi led me off into an alley, and after a few paces we turned into another, even smaller alley. Not long after that we turned into another alley, even smaller than the first two. Keyi was humming "Donna, Donna."

Just as we seemed about to reach a dead end, a street appeared at the far end of the alley. We crossed the street and entered another alley on the other side and then started the same game of twists and turns all over again. Finally we came to a halt in front of another park. There was a high-rise building beside the park, with a coffeehouse on the first floor. There was nothing particularly striking about the coffeehouse; in fact, as we walked in, I was tempted to think we were walking into the lobby of an ordinary apartment building by mistake.

We sat near the window, and a girl who looked like she could have been in junior high school brought us a menu that offered coffee, cocktails, soft drinks, and dessert. Most of the items were identified by the name of an author: the George Sand Coffee, the Hemingway Cocktail, the D. H. Lawrence Black Tea, the Pearl S. Buck Strawberry Cake, the Mark Twain Ice Cream.

"I know what you're thinking," Chunxi leaned toward me and said in a low voice. "You want to know what the difference is between the Yukio Mishima Coffee and the Ryunosuke Akutagawa Coffee, right?"

"Tell me," I said.

"Well, they say that every drink or dessert that has a writer's name was that writer's favorite drink or food," Keyi said, suppressing a giggle. "Come on, hurry up."

I ordered a cup of Yu Dafu Coffee. Keyi didn't want to drink coffee because she was worried about her voice, so she ordered a cup of the Henry James Black Tea. Before long the waitress brought the drinks, and we sipped them gingerly.

"You don't seem like you're from Taipei. Am I wrong?" Keyi asked.

I gave her the brief rundown on me and my family. "How could you tell I wasn't from Taipei?"

"You seem so all alone. I figured either you were five hundred miles from home or you didn't have a family at all." She hummed a few lines of "Five Hundred Miles." "I'm from Tainan. My dad's poor. He fixes plumbing and electrical wiring and things, but half the time he's out of work. Everyone says my mother was beautiful, but she ran off with another man when I was five. My father never told me about this. He and the neighbors all conspired to lie to me.

They said my mother was dead. But when I was ten my mother snuck back to our place to see me. At first I didn't believe it was really her, but finally she brought out a picture of her and me from when I was little, and I started to cry. She cried, too. She gave me a doll and a little money, and then she lied to me, said she was going to go see the neighbors. She never came back, and I haven't seen her since. When my dad came home, he burned the doll and then went to the department store and bought me a bigger, prettier doll. He said my mother was a she-devil and was out doing bad things with bad men. I never told him about the twenty dollars she'd given me, and I never spent it either. I still have it today. My dad got run over by a car when I was in sixth grade, and he broke both his legs. He's been in a wheelchair ever since.

"We have a neighbor whose last name is Xu. He's pretty young, but both his parents are dead, and they left him two furniture stores. He says that my father was very kind to him in the past, helped him out when he needed it, and so he started to help us out. Actually, it's more accurate to say he just out-and-out supported us. He paid for everything: all our expenses, my dad's medical bills, my school tuition. Then when I got into college I let him pay my tuition for one semester, but then during the second semester I started working in bars. I was singing at other bars before I came to Fairy Tale. I didn't make a lot at first, so I had to sing every day. After a while, though, I saved up some money and was able to relax a little. But now things have gotten tight again, so I'm singing three times a week. Now I pay for everything myself. I pay my own tuition and my own living expenses. The only thorn left in the bed of roses is that someone else is still supporting my dad. Well? Is my story sad and inspiring, or what?

"You're lucky. I've never talked about all this to anyone before. I'm not like you, I don't have the money to hang out at Western bars. This tea I'm drinking? As far as I can tell it's just Lipton with some kind of weird spice added."

"Maybe Henry James drank Lipton tea." I took a sip of my coffee. "You've told me a lot, so it's only fair that I try to tell you something about myself, too."

I gave her a brief account of my sister who had died, of my parents, and of Lin Yuan and his wife, and I mentioned in passing my father's and Lin Yuan's wild college days. I didn't talk about Chunxi. "When did you learn to play the guitar?" I asked her.

"There was a guitar club at my high school. I've been working at it for three years, but I still don't play all that well." She looked out the window at the bishopwood, maple, and banyan trees in the park. This was the first time I had seen her looking at all melancholy. It almost seemed as if not having a mother were a matter of much less importance to her than not being great at the guitar. "The little prince with the furniture stores gave me my first guitar."

"It sounds like he's helped you out a lot. Why are you making fun of him with this 'little prince' business?"

"Don't ask about him. There are some stories I shouldn't tell people."

I stared out at the park, too, and a touch of sadness overtook me. "You're amazing. I've never met a girl like you before."

"You're thinking about something sad, aren't you," she said, staring at me. "You drank the Yu Dafu coffee, and now you've started 'sinking.'"[1]

"This isn't the kind of coffee Yu Dafu drank. One of my father's older relatives was Yu Dafu's student in Singapore, and he knew his teacher never took sugar with his coffee, but, look, two packs of sugar came with this cup. Does that make any sense to you? So you've also read 'Sinking'?"

"Of course. My favorite part is when he spies on the Japanese girls taking a shower. You boys love to do things like that, right?"

I told her about some of the things that had gone on at school and in the dorm.

"Wow. Masturbating sixty-eight times in a month. That's more than twice a day!"

"That guy was not normal. I'm sorry, though. I shouldn't be talking about nasty things like that with you."

"I don't mind. I like to hear about it."

"You think that guy was obnoxious? There were guys in my dorm who were more obnoxious. There was one who would play his violin in our bedroom every day at lunchtime, and it sounded like pigs

1. Sinking" is the title of the Chinese writer Yu Dafu's most famous work of fiction. Yu Dafu was born in 1896 and died in Sumatra in 1945.

being slaughtered. You could argue that that was just another form of public masturbation."

"Well, if we look at things your way, all awful music and art and writing are just more forms of public masturbation."

"Pretty much. When I was a kid my mom wanted me to study piano, but my dad said no. He said it wasn't right for boys to play the piano, that I'd grow up to be a queer or a trophy husband if I did. Plus, Beethoven and Mozart didn't come to good ends—one was deaf, the other one died young—and I'd probably do even worse, since I wasn't going to be a genius like they were. My dad may be a math genius, but he's been way too sure of himself for way too long. He hasn't grown or developed; he's become a mediocrity. If you look at all the houses he's designed for rich people, you can tell right away—they're all so disgustingly vulgar. The old man has no imagination whatsoever."

"What's wrong between you and your dad?"

"There's just nothing between us. I don't think I'll shed a single tear the day he dies."

"Pretty heartless of you."

"When I was a kid I kept a tank of fish out on the roof. One day some seagulls flew up and ate every last one of them. I cried, and my dad said I wasn't acting like a man. He called me spineless. He said I wasn't heartless enough."

"It sounds to me like you care less about your father than you did about those fish."

I told her what had happened with my father and the woman in white when I was six years old.

"Well, now it sounds like it's your mother who's borne the brunt of it. What a depressing story. Tell me about your mother."

"My mother's beautiful. Men stare at her every time she leaves the house. When she was young she used to be a big talker. In junior high she represented her entire school in a public speaking competition. Her coach had some subversive political opinions, and so her speech criticized the government, but the school hadn't realized this in advance. After the speeches were over, she and her coach were both called in for questioning. They concluded that my mother wasn't to blame, but when she went back to school the principal and her teachers and her classmates all acted weird around her. She was completely ostracized. After that she spoke very little. When she was in high school she became a Catholic. It was her grandmother's influence. Whenever she had the time she'd act as a lay server at church. After my sister died there were times when I went a month without hearing her say a word."

"You seem very independent. Not like most of my classmates. They still smell like breast milk. They're all like, 'Goo goo ga ga, my dad says this, my mom says that.'"

"You're more independent than I am."

"I'm not as heartless about my father as you are about yours."

"Do you go home to see him often?"

"As much as a daughter's supposed to. Dad's not lonely. He plays cards and mah-jongg with the neighbors, or he wheels his chair over to the old folks' center to play chess and read the paper and chat with the others. Lately he's been learning how to sing Peking opera and play the *erhu*."

"That's great. Are you hungry? We could order some dessert. I'll treat."

"Nah. There's nothing good to eat here. Something called the Pearl S. Buck Strawberry Cake is probably old and stale. The Yasunari Kawabata Jam sounds like something you'd dig up out of the ground. All these names make me lose my appetite. We're better off eating at a street stall."

"We've been here long enough. Let's go eat something."

"Fine."

"I'm a big fan of Henry James. Let me pay for your tea."

The coffeehouse was doing a roaring business. As soon as we stood up, there were people there to take our seats. The customers were unusual types: men with long hair, women with short hair, elderly gentlemen with long beards, Buddhists with no hair. Keyi said they were all artists of some sort. It was ten-thirty by the time we left. "There's a night market near my old dorm. It should take us about ten minutes to walk there," I said.

"Okay. A dark night's passing." Keyi seemed thoughtful. "A long night's journey into day . . ."

I chuckled. "Is your backpack heavy? I can take it for you."

"It's not heavy."

"Are you afraid to have me carry it? Give it here. No need to be polite." I stretched out my hand to take her backpack.

"Your goodwill is a lot heavier than the bag itself." She wriggled nimbly out of the straps of the bag and gave it to me. "Poor people's bags are generally very heavy."

"Hey, I thought you said it wasn't heavy." I settled the bag onto my own back. "What's in there?"

"I'll tell you in a minute."

There were cars parked along both sides of the alley. Occasionally a car would come driving toward us, and we would have to stand still along the edge of the road while it went by. Some of the streetlights were very bright, some were dimmer, and some were dark altogether. A merchant selling lotus-wrapped rice cakes rode past us; his cries were no louder than the scraping and rattling from his bicycle.

"Do you like Shiga Naoya?"

"Who?"

"He wrote *A Dark Night's Passing*."

"Oh, him. I've never been able to remember his name." Keyi sighed. "I only read half that book, and I've forgotten it all."

"Have you read O'Neill's *A Long Day's Journey into Night*?"

"I read a bilingual version. For learning English, naturally."

We entered an alley where all the streetlights were extinguished and the houses were deathly silent. A black cat came jumping down from a wall and scurried across our path to the wall on the other side of the alley, giving us quite a scare. The cat then leapt from a tree to the roof of a one-story house, where it stretched luxuriously on the ridge of the roof.

"That makes me think of Tennessee Williams's cat on a hot tin roof," she said.

I turned my head to look at her. "Why are you studying business and not English?"

"Because I'm not interested in business."

"Explain."

"I wasn't so thrilled when I learned that the 'little prince' was going to pay for me to go to college." She stuck her hands in her jacket pockets and rotated her shoulders as she walked. "So I just said to hell with it and filled out my preferences for my major any old way. As long as my dad was fine with it, I was, too."

"Why do you dislike that man so much?"

"He's very pleased with himself about how much he's done for us." She kicked an empty cardboard box that was in our way, and it rolled over to the base of the wall like a balloon leaking air. "You wouldn't believe how trashy he is. He wears gold chains that are as big as an airplane seatbelt. He wears *cologne*."

"We're at the night market." We had reached an alley flush with lamplight and overflowing with people. The alley was lined with snack stalls on both sides. Most of the customers were students sitting on unsteady chairs in front of wobbly tables, tottering back and forth and presenting a very unrefined spectacle as they ate. The owners of the stalls were running around and sweating up a storm as usual. The entire scene reminded me of a class in session: a teacher peddling his learning in bursts of airborne saliva, the students subdivided into their own packs and cliques and not paying the slightest bit of attention to him.

People were crowded together shoulder to shoulder, and we had to turn sideways to get through the crowd. I was worried that someone would swipe the backpack, so I took it off and held it to my chest. In that instant I lost Keyi. I stood up on my tiptoes and looked behind me and saw her about two meters back, waving in my direction. I waved and shouted in acknowledgment, then turned my body sideways and headed her way through the crowd. It took me a full ten seconds to reach her.

"I'm so sorry. I wasn't paying any attention. I left you behind," I said.

"It wasn't your fault. There're a lot of people here, and they're all rude. I thought I was walking forward, but actually I just kept getting pushed back. I was going to yell for you, but I was too embarrassed."

The crowd was pressing us close together, with only the backpack dividing our two torsos.

"Let's not keep walking. We can just find something to eat here."

"Whatever you like. We're in your territory."

"This market is famous for stinky tofu and beef noodles."

"Okay. Let's have both."

"Come with me." I led Keyi off to one side, and we charged right through the crowd. I kept looking behind me, and suddenly I was overtaken by a powerful sense of nostalgia. I almost reached out and took Keyi's hand.

We emerged from the crowd, and I brought Keyi across another alley into a tiny restaurant. "You're not too hungry, right?" I asked after we sat down. "Let's get two small bowls of noodles and then one order of the tofu to share. If we're still hungry we'll order more."

I ordered two bowls of beef noodles and then swept back through the crowd to get a plate of stinky tofu from the stall across the way. When the tofu was ready, I paid, and then holding the plate high in one hand I swept through the crowd once again and returned to Keyi's side. Keyi took the tofu from me and set it down on the table; then she picked up two pairs of disposable chopsticks and handed one set to me.

"I got the stinky tofu especially for you," I said. "After you eat it I guarantee you'll smell like it for a week."

The owner of the restaurant came rushing over with our noodles. Once he had turned his back, Keyi whispered, "These are the *small* orders? The bowls are as big as washbasins."

"Maybe he heard me wrong." I leaned my head toward her and whispered, too. "His beef noodles are so good, he's got a real attitude. If he's wrong, just let him be wrong. It looks like I'll be feeding you well today."

Keyi formed a spool of noodles with her chopsticks, and just as she was leaning over the bowl to take a bite she smiled and said, "I feel like I'm about to wash my face and the noodles are a moldy old towel."

"When the owner comes back by here you should make a lot of noise eating. That'll make him happy."

We ate with lowered heads. I kept eating as I asked her, "You've been studying business for two years now. You must be a little interested in it by this point."

"Not at all." She didn't lift her head from her noodles. "If I were, I wouldn't be asking you to help me with my assignments. It's not that I'm lazy. It's just that I've been out working every night for a lot of the last two years. Sometimes I'd do three or four gigs a night. So I've just never had the time to really care about schoolwork, and that's the only reason why my English is so bad. This tofu's delicious."

"I can help you with your English whenever you have the time." I lowered my voice. "The owner's right over there. Start slurping."

We made a point of slurping loudly, but the place was too noisy, and we got no reaction from the owner.

"How about you? Why are you studying foreign languages?"

I gave her a rough explanation of my situation. "It worked out okay. I am sort of interested in it. But it makes my head hurt to think that I'm going to have to start student teaching soon."

"I wouldn't have guessed that you're even more confused than me. Are we supposed to eat all of this?"

"There's nothing the owner hates more than people who leave food uneaten."

"Oh, no. Help me eat some of this tofu."

"The owner's back. Drink your broth."

The owner came by and left again with no visible change in his expression.

"That owner's pretty cool," Keyi said, stifling a laugh. "I'll bet he heard us."

Less then ten minutes later, we could see the bottoms of our bowls and the plate. "I'm ready to burst." Keyi's face was bright red. She used a napkin to wipe sweat from her forehead and oil from her lips. "I'm going to have to fast for the next couple of days. If I gain weight I'm holding you responsible."

"It's late. Let's go," I said.

"Take it easy." Keyi pulled two English books out of her backpack. "This is my assignment for you. You ordered nine songs. You have to pay me back."

"So it was books all along," I said. "No wonder. Scholarship is heavier than poverty."

She opened the books and showed me the pages. "I want you to translate the places underlined in red, like here, and here, and here, and here, and here, okay? Then the places underlined in blue, like here, here, here, here, and here, I just want you to look at them and explain to me what they mean. Is this okay?"

"When do I have to hand in my work?"

"Next Saturday's fine." She closed the books and put them in front of me. "No need to look so sad. Next Saturday I'll let you request songs again. From now on Saturday night is your own private request hour."

"That makes sense, I guess." I paid for the noodles and picked up the books.

"You sure this isn't too much trouble?"

"It's nothing. Don't worry about it," I said. "It's after eleven. I hope you'll let me walk you home this time. According to you it'll take a few light-years."

I made a wide berth around the crowd and led Keyi to another small alley. It had gotten cold, and Keyi pulled on her jacket. She stuffed both hands in her jacket pockets and started humming something. I liked listening to her hum random tunes, with no lyrics; she seemed less restrained than she did when she was performing. We walked very slowly, and after five minutes of walking neither of us had said so much as a word. Eventually I spoke first.

"Are you renting an apartment?"

"I wanted to live in the dorm, but there wasn't enough space, and I lost out in the lottery. So I had to rent an apartment off campus with some classmates. Three bedrooms, two people per bedroom. You should come visit sometime."

"Okay. I'll definitely come. You can come to my place, too, when you have time."

We walked in silence. We passed the coffeehouse full of artists, and I spoke up again. "You haven't told me how I should give you my homework when I'm done with it."

"I almost forgot. Will you be at the Study Hall again next Friday night? Can you give it to me then?"

I nodded. Not long after that, she said, "Will you be at Fairy Tale on Tuesday?"

"I'm not sure. If I have time I'll probably go."

There was another period of silence, then she said, "There's no need for you to spend all that money. If you want to hear me sing, we'll find some other time, and I'll sing just for you." I said, "Thanks." She went on, "As far as getting together goes, you can come find me on Tuesday at Fairy Tale, at eight-fifty. Wait for me at the door. I'll come out when I'm done singing. Remember, though, if you're not there on time, I'll just leave."

"Okay," I said. As we were waiting for the light to change at a major street, she said, "Tomorrow's Sunday. You're all by yourself a long way from home. What will you do?"

"I'll do the homework you assigned me. How about you?"

"Oh, no. I feel bad making you hole up at home on a Sunday." The light turned green, and we crossed the street inside the crosswalk. A lone wide-body imported car came speeding by right in front of us. "Tomorrow our class is going on a field trip outside the city. Boring! But if I don't go people will call me antisocial. I skipped the last few trips, so I have to make up for it now."

On the other side of the road we ran into a pair of girls who greeted Keyi. "Will you look at that! These are my roommates." Keyi introduced us all. The two girls seemed like outgoing types. "I'll go on back with them," Keyi said. "You don't have to walk me the rest of the way. Thank you. Bye-bye."

I didn't go straight home. Instead I roamed around for a while with the two books in my hand. Most stores were already closed, and I made a point of walking through the covered arcades along major streets. I remembered that there was a used bookstall in the area, so I headed in that direction. The owner of the stall was sitting in the doorway reading the paper, with a plate of scallion pancakes and a cup of soy milk on the small table in front of him, as if it were already morning. I looked aimlessly through the books inside the stall and finally bought two back issues of magazines. After I was done with the bookstall, I decided to go home via the smaller alleys. In one alley I came upon a group of teenagers fighting. One of them had been pressed up against the wall by the others, and it looked like they were about to beat him up. Then another group of teenagers approached them to try to make peace. In the end everyone shook hands and laughed it off, and they all went off in different directions. I found myself back in the night market we had been at earlier. It hadn't been very long since we had left, but the crowds had thinned considerably, so that the stall owners now outnumbered the customers and now it felt open and expansive. As I walked through the night market, as the lights went out one by one, the image of Chunxi, sleeping fast and deep, drifted through my head.

Chaper 20

I spent about two days skimming Keyi's two books, and on the third day I began to translate the sections that were underlined in red. At eight forty-five on Tuesday night, I was standing outside Fairy Tale staring at passersby and the bustling night scene when I suddenly thought of that rhinoceros pacing across the African savanna.

"Hey, how long have you been waiting?"

Just as my heart was welling up with rhinocerine loneliness, Keyi appeared in front of me. Her face was practically pressed up against mine.

"Did I scare you? What were you thinking about?" Keyi, looking mischievous, seemed to be doing some kind of dance I couldn't name. "I had a premonition just now when I was singing. I thought you'd come see me."

I handed her the two books and a stack of paper. "I finished my homework early, so I came here to give it to you. What do you think? Pretty efficient, huh?"

"Wow, really?" Keyi took the books and papers with an exaggerated look of surprise. "Wow, thank you. If I were doing this myself, you know, I'd have to spend at least a week or two."

"It wasn't hard, but it was boring. I'd much rather have been translating Faulkner," I said. "Oh, there were a few specialized terms I wasn't sure about, so I put the original English words in parentheses in my translations. So let me consult a higher authority, and I'll get back to you on those in the next couple of days."

"No worries. I might know them." Keyi put the books and translations in her backpack. "If it's not too much trouble, I'll ask you to explain the parts underlined in blue to me on Friday at the Study Hall. It's already nine. Are you ready to go home?"

"I don't feel like going home," I said.

"Do you want to hang out for a while?"

"I was hoping we could."

"Why didn't you ask me if I was busy or not?"

"Are you busy?"

"Oh, you. If you wanted to hang out you should have just said so. I'm sorry, but I have to get home early tonight. I'm supposed to meet my roommates. It's still fairly early, though. Why don't you just come over?"

"I won't be bothering you?"

"Do I have any other choice? You're so pitiful. I can't just leave you on your own."

"Don't worry about me. I can go into Fairy Tale and listen to someone else sing."

"No way. I insist that you come with me."

I took her backpack from her, and we walked in the direction of her apartment. Keyi was wearing a white blouse and a yellow woolen sleeveless sweater decorated with a graphic of Snow White and the Seven Dwarfs. She also had on a very thin silver necklace.

"Did you have a good time on Sunday?" I asked.

"Not at all," she said without stopping to think about her answer first. "I had thought it was just going to be our class, but a bunch of boys from another school ended up coming along. The boys totally took over. There must have been three or four boys for every girl, and they waited on us hand and foot. The whole scene was kind of dodgy. The guys were fighting over us, and the girls were all acting coy. I won't lie to you: I had five Casanovas hanging around me the whole time."

"Did anyone tell them that you sing at Fairy Tale?"

"Of course! I don't know who it was. But today two of them were there watching, and they kept handing me request slips with sappy little notes written on them. But it's not my fault. It's not my fault I'm pretty or a good singer. Isn't that right, Su Qi?"

That was the first time I had heard her say my name. I nodded steadily and said "Right," six or seven times.

"You look like a woodpecker. Don't worry. I know what to do about those guys." Keyi put her hands on her hips and smiled a coquettish smile. "I'm a girl who's seen it all, and I've got some fool-proof tricks up my sleeve. There's no way I'm going to let a couple of little boys who don't even shave yet get the better of me."

"I'm impressed."

"You don't have to be afraid, though. I won't use my tricks on you."

"Thank you."

"Let me ask you something."

"Go ahead."

Keyi turned her back to me. "Did you notice that I'm wearing a new sweater?"

"Of course."

"What's the picture on the back?"

"Snow White and some dwarfs."

"How many dwarfs?"

"I'll give it to you straight: I've been trying hard to count them all this time, but I still haven't succeeded. It's not your fault. It's just too dark out here," I said earnestly. "Do you know about the Marco Polo Bridge outside Beijing? There are a few hundred stone lions along the railing, and people have tried to count them, but no one's ever done it. It's as if the lions that get counted one time hide the next time or new ones are born between the countings. So no one knows exactly how many lions there are."

"Okay, okay, I was just asking. No need to take it so seriously." Keyi turned back around and pointed at the sweater. "I'll tell you: there are five. One, two, three, four, five."

"And the other two?"

"I don't know. I guess whoever knitted this got tired and those two had to be culled."

"Why would you want to ask me a question like that?"

"No reason. Just that I'm wearing a new sweater and wanted to see if you'd noticed. This week three of my roommates all had birthdays, all three in one week, isn't that the craziest coincidence? Saturday night we're going to have a party for them at the apartment. We'll be inviting some friends and some classmates. Do you want to come?"

"Won't you be performing on Saturday?"

"The party won't start until nine. It may go all night. Are you coming or not? You can be my dancing partner."

"I don't know how to dance."

"So what? Just shake around a little, and you'll be fine. I can also help you cram a little before then."

"All right."

"All right. All right." She imitated me. "Doesn't sound very sincere."

"I'm still frustrated with myself over the dwarfs."

Keyi's apartment was on the third floor. The living room was only about ten square meters in size, and it looked like it wouldn't be easy to hold a party with dancing there. Two girls were sitting on an old sofa watching an old television. Images were leaping and flashing on the screen; sometimes the whole screen would turn to fuzz, and all you would see were floating strands in vivid, splashy colors. The sound, though, was extraordinarily clear. Two abstract paintings, as dazzling as the television images, were hung on the wall, as was a large study of a female nude. Four potted plants sat near the French window.

The two girls watching TV were the same two we had run into on the street the other night. One was majoring in Chinese, and the other in history; the two of them shared one bedroom. The girl who shared a room with Keyi was studying international trade, and two fine arts majors lived in the third room. Just as we entered, the international trade girl emerged from a bedroom. I chatted with the three girls in the living room while Keyi took a shower, and before long the two fine arts girls came home. Keyi emerged from her shower, and the six of them began to chatter on about the upcoming party, leaving me no room to get a word in edgewise.

The television was on the whole time. I was watching TV and appraising the paintings on the wall as I listened to the girls talk. The painting called "Lovers" portrayed a man and a woman looking like two octopi in the heat of battle. "The Internal Organs in the Act of Love" portrayed a variegated mush of wet, lumpy objects. "Woman Voyeur Spying on Man" was clearly imitating works from the European Renaissance. The naked woman in the painting had colossal breasts and buttocks and was squatting on a bench, looking like a circus elephant mounted on a stool. Crucial parts of her body had been replaced by pieces of fruit: her lips were two red peppers, her eyeballs were two grapes, her nipples were two tomatoes, and her private parts were represented by half a watermelon that had been cut in two.

Some of Keyi's classmates arrived after ten, bringing enough sweets and drinks with them to keep a street stall in business for two days. That was when I said good-bye to Keyi. She walked me down to the door, and we confirmed that we would meet on Friday night at the Study Hall.

Chapter 21

I forced myself not to go to Fairy Tale on Thursday night.

After dinner on Friday, at six-thirty, I arrived at the Study Hall Coffeehouse and found Keyi already there. She had two books on business administration open on the table in front of her, and she was reading them alongside my translations. Just after I sat down I realized that there was also a piece of paper on the table, on which was written in a neat hand: "Studying hard. No talking until eight." I suppressed a laugh and opened *Theory and Practice of English Language Education.* Even though she and I weren't allowed to talk, our eyes kept meeting, and each time it was as if we were saying words meant to eradicate the dull solemnity of what we were reading.

Before eight o'clock, Keyi began to look at her watch every couple of minutes, and soon after that she tore a fresh piece of paper out of her notebook, wrote something down, and gave it to me: "With but a single word, we will have loosed a horse that we can't call back. Let's talk on paper. Your translations aren't bad."

I wrote in hasty, flowery cursive just as she had. "I took an elective in translation. It met twice a week. So the work I did for it wasn't in vain?"

"I study things that stink of cold, dirty money. It looks like you study things untainted by the base world."

"How did your discussion go the other night? It was like you were planning a National Day party at the presidential palace."

"Everything's planned out. Now we just need to execute it. You didn't come to Fairy Tale yesterday."

"I've been working on your homework these last few days, so my own homework's backlogged a little. I'm kind of busy."

"It's a good thing you didn't come. One of the boys from the field trip last week tagged along with me part of the way home. But I sent him packing with one sentence."

"What kind of sentence is that scary?"

"I can't tell you."

"I trust I'll hear it when you finally get fed up with me."

"You know what? After you left the other night my roommates talked about you."

"What did they say?"

"I'd get too tired writing it all. I'll tell you later. But I can give you a hint now: the one who's a Chinese major said that you were staring at the painting of the nude the whole time, so you must be either an artist or a pervert."

"I choose pervert. What's an artist worth? Everyone from God to the devil, they're all 'artists.'"

"Those paintings are my fine arts roommates' masterpieces. The nude was painted from a live model."

"I thought it was a still life of fruit."

Keyi eyed her watch and then let out a breath and said, "It's eight."

I let out a deep breath myself. After a moment of silence, I said, "I like talking on paper." She pointed right away to her books and said, "All right, then you can write out your translation of the blue parts." I resolutely refused and launched into my rough oral translation of the sections underlined in blue. Keyi wrote down the major points in her notebook as she listened. Then we both returned to our books. At ten Keyi said, "If you don't mind, I'd like to leave. I can't stay here another minute."

As we passed the little park just outside the Study Hall, Keyi said, "Let's go in the park. I'll teach you a few dance moves for tomorrow."

On a path in the silent, depopulated, cool, and pitch-dark park, Keyi hummed a beat and moved her limbs in time with the rhythm. In half an hour she succeeded in teaching me six different steps, humming suitable music for each as she practiced them with me over and over again. My renditions of the steps were not much to look at, and I couldn't quite master the rhythm, but by the end I was doing well enough to get by at a party. Suddenly I was struck by a memory of Chunxi doing a skillful fox-trot at one of my father's parties. She had been dancing with the same man who had gotten his hand cut by the smashed wineglass.

"Pay attention," Keyi said. "Okay. We're done for now." She looked at her watch. It was already ten-thirty. She removed her jacket and sat down on the seesaw, and I sat on the other end. "Actually, you learn pretty quick. But now that you've learned the moves you don't need to be so serious about them. One of my roommates said you look like someone who's always sad. So I told her a little about your family and your background—I hope you don't mind. What songs do you want to request for tomorrow?"

I took a piece of paper out of my pocket and handed it to her. "These are all songs you like to sing. You can look at it when you get home. Do you want to eat something? Or go home?"

"We might be staying up all night tomorrow. It's probably best to go to sleep early." She grabbed her backpack and stood up. "You aren't afraid I'll corrupt you if you keep hanging out with me, are you?"

I took her bag from her and walked her home. At quarter to eight the next night I was ordering a drink at Fairy Tale, sitting in my usual corner, planning to leave with Keyi after her set was over. At five after eight, there was no sign of her. Instead a boy with a guitar came onstage. Ten minutes after that, I couldn't take it any longer and asked the waiter what was going on. The waiter disappeared for a few minutes, and when he returned he said that Keyi—I knew that when he said her name he meant the dubious "Keyi"—had asked for the day off. I left Fairy Tale and proceeded to Keyi's place. The party had just begun to gain momentum, and the living room was clamorous with music and voices. The girl who studied international trade told me that Keyi's father was seriously ill and that she had gone back to Tainan that day at noon. She had left in a hurry and hadn't had time to notify me; she also had not said when she would be back. I asked if they had her phone number in Tainan. "If you don't have it, we certainly wouldn't," was the roommate's answer. There wasn't a single other boy at the party, and I was afraid they were going to try to get me to stay, so after a few more minutes I said my good-byes and went out to the street, where I spent half an hour wandering around. Then I killed more time back at Fairy Tale, and I didn't go home until midnight.

I got a phone call from Keyi in Tainan the next afternoon.

"Su Qi, it's me."

"Is your father okay? What happened?"

"It was nothing. Just a little bug. He had to go to the hospital, but he's out now. But the people here overreacted and called me, so I had to come home. I'm so sorry. Did you go to the party last night?"

"Why would I go if you weren't there?"

"I left yesterday at noon. I'd tried calling you in the morning, but you were at class. I might have to be here a few more days, but I'll be in touch once I get back."

My next phone call from Keyi didn't come until the following Saturday afternoon. She told me that she would be performing at Fairy Tale that night and asked if I would meet her there.

Chapter 22

I sat in my dark corner watching Keyi under the fake grapevine, singing the songs I had requested the week before. As always, the bar was dense with human figures, and often my view of her was blocked. The sound of her singing sometimes almost disappeared in the sounds of conversations and laughter and eating and drinking, but despite all the commotion the magnifying effect of the microphone provided surer proof of Keyi's existence than did any visual stimuli. That night Keyi was wearing neither white nor red; instead, she had on a yellow blouse and a yellow knit sleeveless sweater, with a yellow skirt beneath and a rose-colored barrette in her hair. This time she didn't link together all the songs I had requested but instead paused after each one. It still felt as if she were releasing them all in one single breath.

After the last song she walked straight toward me, and I walked with her to the bar to settle my bill. We left Fairy Tale, and I asked her about her father's illness as we walked. Her answer was very vague; it almost seemed as if she wasn't sure exactly what kind of sickness he had had. She let drop a few unpleasant comments about their benefactor, the "little prince."

"He was the one who called me, and initially he refused to tell me exactly what was going on. He made it so that I had no choice but to go down there."

"It sounds to me like he really cares about you and your father. He's pretty young, right?"

"Let's not talk about him." Keyi yawned suddenly. "I just got back from Tainan today, and I'm exhausted. And I missed a whole week of class, so I'm only going to get more tired."

"You'd better go home and get to sleep. I can help you with your schoolwork."

"I was thinking the same thing. Are you free tomorrow?"

"As free as can be."

"Can I bring my work over to your place tomorrow and do it there? Then I can ask you for help if I need it. I'm sorry I have to bother you some more. But finals are coming up."

"I read those two business administration textbooks of yours. By this point I could probably even take your final for you if you needed me to."

"All right, then, I'll be at your place tomorrow bright and early. I can bring my guitar, and I'll play some songs for you when we're done working."

"All right by me. As long as I got to hear you sing, I'd be happy to perform the twelve labors of Hercules. Go to bed early, get up early. I'll walk you home."

"What are the twelve labors of Hercules?"

"Cleaning out a pigsty that hasn't been cleaned in thirty years. Capturing a magic bull with three heads . . ."

I got out of bed at six the next morning, had my breakfast, and went downstairs to buy a newspaper. When I returned, I found Keyi, with her backpack and guitar slung over her back, standing in front of the door to my building, facing away from me. I was considering sneaking up on her when she turned her head and saw me.

"I've been ringing the doorbell for ages. I thought you were still asleep." The expression on her face was perfectly calm, as if she had somehow known I was going to appear behind her.

"Please! And I thought *you* were still in bed."

My apartment was on the second floor. The living room was just shy of ten square meters; there were two couches and a coffee table near the door, and closer to the kitchen there were four chairs, a rectangular dining table, and a small cabinet. I had set up some bookshelves beside the dining table, and I generally read and did my homework there.

"You've got this place all to yourself? Spectacular." Keyi put the guitar down on one of the couches and bent down to inspect the tank full of tropical fish on the cabinet.

I put Keyi's backpack on the dining table. "Those fish are my only friends here."

She sat in one of the chairs and stretched out a finger toward the tank. "That's a peacock fish, right? How about that one?"

"A two-spot gourami. All my fish are species that live in the rivers around where I grew up. Fish like these were my best buddies when I was a kid, too. I think they and I have a lot in common: now that we've come to Taiwan, we all have to live in tiny containers, and we all need extra heating in the winter. If you set any of us loose on our own, we wouldn't survive for long."

"Is this your desk? I'll sit here. I like being close to water."

I made a pot of coffee and a pot of tea and set both on the "desk," then joined Keyi in her resolute studying. She had missed a whole week of class, and her schoolwork had piled up to frightening heights, but most of it had to do with those two English-language textbooks. I reviewed my history of European literature while fielding questions from Keyi about points she was unclear on. We worked until our heads were spinning, and then I went into the bedroom, brought out a cassette player, and put on a tape of foreign oldies. Buoyed up by the familiar melodies and rhythms, we sped seamlessly through our textbooks, and we did our written work with verve and gusto. Before we knew it, it was eleven. Keyi stretched and told me that today she was going to show off her culinary skills—she was going to make lunch.

In the kitchen, she rifled through the contents of the refrigerator. "You'd think this fridge was still in the appliance store. Are there any markets around here?"

The nearest market was about to shut down for the day, so the merchants were selling everything cheap. Keyi bargained with the stall keepers like a housewife of our grandmothers' generation, and the prices they settled on were likewise straight out of our grandparents' era. She shopped for fish with all the care and seriousness of a fisherman casting his nets for a live catch, but unfortunately at that hour the only seafood left was a bit rancid. Keyi also refused to consider the inferior fruits and vegetables that other customers had passed over. She rejected offhand goods and prices that seemed fine to me, but I had no choice but to follow her around and keep my mouth shut. Finally, when it was almost noon, she bought everything she still needed at one stall, even though I noticed that the food at that stall looked worse than a lot of the food she had spurned earlier. It was even starting to attract flies.

In the end, we went home with three huge bags of sundries.

"Don't you think you got a little impatient toward the end?" I said as we walked. "A lot of the stuff you bought is nothing to write home about."

"I know. I bought it because of the people running the stall. The man was dressed like a refugee, his wife was dressed like a man, and she had a little nursing baby on her back, and they had two dirty little kids lying there on the ground, wearing clothes that weren't as good as the paper wrappings on the pork buns over at the pork bun stand. Then there was another kid in a stroller, probably running a fever, because there was a medicine sachet on his chest. There's nothing wrong with me using your money to do a good deed, is there?"

"Funny, I didn't notice any of that," I said. "That's grand of you. Far be it from me to complain. Anyway, you seem to be quite the shopper, so I'm curious to see how your cooking is."

"Don't underestimate me. My mom left when I was six, so ever since then I've been doing a mom's job in the kitchen. I'll be the executive chef, and I want you to stand back and follow my instructions."

After over an hour of activity in the kitchen, we had, amazingly, produced four dishes and a soup. I cleared the books off the dining table and set the food out. Keyi talked like a great chef, and she ran a kitchen like a great chef, and her food certainly looked perfect, but in fact her actual achievements were disappointing. None of the dishes was completely unaccomplished. But they were all somehow indistinct and featureless, so that it was difficult to tell them apart. The onion-fried beef and the red-cooked fish with broad beans had a little bit of character, but the fish-flavored pork and the fermented bean curd with wood-ear fungus might as well have been the same dish divided onto two different plates. It made for kind of a heart-breaking spectacle. The ribs-and-bitter-melon soup was neither quite a soup nor quite a real dish, and I puzzled over whether to attack it with chopsticks or with a spoon. "I think maybe it needs more seasoning." I put on a tape of Western classical music.

Cradling a large bowl of rice in her hands, Keyi talked about her roommates while she ate. "Yunru's found herself a boyfriend. They haven't been going together very long, but now she's gone and moved out. Clearly the guy's quite the Casanova. An expert on how to handle the ladies. You want to know why she moved out after she got a boyfriend? I'll tell you later." Yunru was the roommate who was studying international trade. "When I first moved into that apartment, it wasn't Yunru I was sharing a room with, it was a girl named Wenxin. A geography major. For a while she and I were inseparable, but then a guy started pursuing her. He'd hang around our living room all the time and refuse to leave. One day Wenxin and I came home and found our bedroom door locked from the inside. We shouted and shouted, but no one answered. When we finally got the door open there he was, that boy, lying on the bed with a craftsman's knife in his right hand and a huge cut on his left wrist. All the bedding was stained red. Then what's even more absurd is, later, in the hospital, he told Wenxin he hadn't tried to kill himself over her. He'd tried to kill himself over me."

"What eventually happened to him?"

"Oh, he didn't die. When Wenxin moved out, I thought about moving out too. I didn't want to stay there any longer. I'd wake up in the middle of the night picturing that guy lying on the bed with a knife, and I wouldn't be able to get back to sleep. But then I had trouble finding a decent new place, plus I like the girls I'm living with. So I just stopped thinking about it and stayed."

"Don't you have some sort of trick for getting rid of boys? I remember you saying that you could scare off any suitor with one sentence."

"Yes, but I never had any clue that guy was interested in me." She took another helping of rice. "Why are you eating more slowly than me?"

"I'm trying to make a lot of noise while I eat, so naturally it takes longer."

"You suck-up. I don't really care about dressing up my cooking. When you first look at my food, it might not look so good, but the more you eat the better it tastes. Every man who's eaten my cooking wants to marry me."

"Isn't that the truth. Unpleasant women are usually bad cooks, and a person would only be making trouble for himself by marrying one. Has the 'little prince' ever eaten your cooking?"

"Why are you bringing him up?" Keyi's chopsticks stopped in midair with a few strings of julienne pork between them. "No talking crazy, little boy, okay?"

"So I'm a little boy then. Does that mean I won't offend you if I don't ask you to marry me?"

"I was just joking around when I said that." Keyi dumped half the plate of onion-fried beef into my bowl. "As penalty, you have to eat more."

"I know how you can get rid of guys who are after you." I stuffed a huge mouthful of food into my mouth. "Tell them you have a boyfriend already. Tell them it's me."

"That won't work on real Casanovas, but I'll give it a try." Keyi then moved the remaining fish-flavored pork into my bowl. "Look at you, talking nonsense. As penalty you have to eat more."

It was two o'clock by the time we finished doing the dishes. I made a pot of tea, and we drank it out on the balcony that faced the rear yard of my building. Behind my building there were a few Japanese-style low-rise houses and then a long, low housing project for military families. Clothes hung out to dry, flags flapping in the wind, and television antennas stretched on as far as the eye could see, blending with the grayish eaves, mottled brick walls, and the occasional mulberry, mango, or banyan tree. The clotheslines stretched across every courtyard in the complex seemed to form one enormous clothesline, a plaintive sight like a defeated dragon in hiding. A group of children were playing in the alleyways, running around like speeding bullets. A few old people were gathered in a circle in a small park, playing a game of chess and letting a long time elapse between each move. Beneath the trees in the park, some people were taking their pet birds out for air. Off in the distance, other people were training pigeons.

After a few sips of tea, I asked Keyi, "How much work do you have left?"

"Two or three hours' worth, probably."

"Do you want to take a nap?"

"I don't usually."

I said that probably it was better to get the schoolwork out of the way first, and we returned to the dining table. I hadn't wiped the table, and a slight odor of meat still lingered around it. I turned on the radio with the volume low and tuned it to a music station, which just happened to be playing an arrangement for strings of "Yesterday" by the Beatles. I asked Keyi if she could sing Beatles songs. She told me she could only really sing two or three; Beatles songs weren't written to be sung by girls. I said that my favorite songs to sing were all by the Beatles, and then I started humming along to "Yesterday." I said, "'Yesterday' is the most performed song on the planet, did you know that, Keyi?" Keyi said, "I didn't, but I can sing that one. I'll sing it for you once we're done our work."

"What others can you sing? Can you do, 'And I Love Her,' 'Let It Be,' 'The Long and Winding Road,' or 'Yellow Submarine'? I want you to sing all of them for me," I said.

"I won't do a very good job," she said.

"Don't be modest," I said.

"I really can't sing them well."

"Then we should sing them together."

"I'll play the guitar, and you sing," she said.

"Fine."

"Let's be good now and do our work."

"We can talk while we work," I said.

"If you don't take your work seriously, you'll never amount to anything."

"What do you want to amount to, anyway?"

"Let's not fight. There's a question here I need your help with."

We didn't talk again until five o'clock, when Keyi said, "That's enough for today. I'll sing for you before dinner." I carried her guitar out onto the balcony, and we sat together looking out over the expanse of low houses and little alleys. Keyi cradled her guitar and began to sing.

The old men playing chess eventually grew fidgety, like squirming insects, and they gave up on the chess to practice tai chi beneath the banyan trees. One old man sat on a stone bench languorously strumming an *erhu*, but unfortunately he was too far away for us to hear the music. The ranks of the children had increased. They were playing hide-and-seek; the children hiding were not moving, but the children seeking were like ants on top of a hot wok. The flags were fluttering in the wind just as before, but most of the clothes had been taken down from the clotheslines. A number of people had come out of their houses and were devoting themselves to various activities in their own courtyards. Some were repotting their plants or building protective structures for them; others were airing their birds or walking their dogs; others were washing their cars or fixing their garages; and some, with nothing else to do, were dropping in on their neighbors. The sound of Keyi's voice and guitar drifted nonconfrontationally, peaceably, down from the balcony into that world. It almost seemed as if the people down there could hear her music but no one was paying any attention to it, as if it were part of the natural backdrop to that scene, no different from the occasional barks of dogs, birdcalls, and human voices calling to their relatives.

Keyi sang one song after another. There was no microphone to weigh her down, no pernicious amplifier forcing a second set of man-made lungs on her, no eyes watching with anything but good intentions, no sounds of eating or cutlery, and no fake grapevine. I found myself thinking that there was no more magical experience in the world than listening to music like this with your homework done and all obligations cast away.

A young girl in a wheelchair wheeled herself out of her house into a nearby courtyard. She rolled her chair across the courtyard and toward the gate that led out into an alley. Her route was obstructed by a pile of bricks someone seemed to have placed there recently. She bent forward from her waist and picked up the bricks one by one to move them out of the way. Finally, once she had cleared a space big enough for a wheelchair to pass through, she wheeled herself up to the gate, pushed it open, and disappeared, slowly and clumsily, into the alley.

Since moving in, I had seen the young girl in the wheelchair perform the motions of going out over and over again. She never seemed to have any compelling reason for going out; all she ever did was gaze at the shabby scenery of the alleyways and watch the children at their games. She made me think of Chunxi.

"Do you want to sing some Beatles songs?" Keyi stopped playing and looked at me, leaning her upper body against her guitar.

She started playing again and made me sing ten Beatles songs in a row. The light was fading and night was coming to life by the time I finished. Lights were coming on in the houses, and the sounds of television were spreading through the neighborhood. The people who had been so vibrant and active not long ago were now holed up in their homes, languishing in front of their lit TV screens while they ate, did homework, napped, scratched their feet, and wasted the evening. Keyi was tired of playing, too, and she put down her guitar. I told her that I had a set of binoculars and that we could look down and see what everyone in the houses was doing. I went to get the binoculars even before I had finished telling her this. Keyi looked through them for a long time, but she didn't see anything remarkable.

"Nothing but a bunch of shirtless old men," she said as she looked. "Do you do this kind of thing a lot?"

"Back at home there's a jungle outside my house. When I had nothing else to do I would look out the window with binoculars," I said. "But here, of course, I only use them to look for naked girls."

"Freak."

"There's a man who does bodybuilding exercises under that palm tree over there. I think he's been entering competitions lately. He's always posing in front of a mirror." I stood up and demonstrated a few bodybuilding moves. Keyi laughed until her stomach ached.

During the months leading up to summer vacation, we spent almost every day together, doing schoolwork, passing the time. Then in the middle of June I got the news that my father had died. As soon as finals were finished, I started getting ready to go home for the funeral. Keyi told me that she would be in Taipei for most of summer vacation, maybe working in bars and saving money, and going back to Tainan once in a while to see her father. Before I went back to Borneo, I bought two English novels for Keyi. I thought of them as passbooks for her, which she could use to enter the world of English literature.

Chapter 23

In the Dayak longhouse, my father had caught sight of a fourteen-year-old Dayak girl. Her skin was fair, her hair hung down past her waist. As she walked on bare feet through the longhouse corridors and the paddy fields, she looked just like the woman in white who had forded the stream barefoot to accept the flowers my father had offered her. The corners of my father's mouth trembled. He asked the girl's name in a soft voice, but she only smiled and wouldn't answer him. The girl picked fruit, flowers, wild vegetables, and mushrooms. She fed the fruit and vegetables to the livestock, but the flowers and mushrooms she ate herself. Because of this she vomited constantly. After vomiting she would jump into the stream to wash herself, and after washing she would walk naked along the bank until the sun had dried her clothes and the monsoon winds had dried her body. When my father questioned her a second time, she merely picked a piece of fruit and offered it to him. He munched slowly on the wild fruit that she still held in her hand, and when only the smallest piece remained she still refused to let go, so he nibbled on her finger as he swallowed the last bite. This did not startle her. On the contrary, she pushed her finger deeper into my father's mouth and let him suck on it to his heart's content. She giggled. My father spit out her finger, grasped her hand in both of his, and begged her to tell him her name; but she just kept giggling. My father hung the sun-dried clothes over her body. She picked another piece of fruit and offered it to him, then she picked a red flower and put it in her own mouth. Only then did my father realize that this girl was not quite right in the head. But it didn't matter; by that point he was thoroughly infatuated. He got down on one knee and accepted with devotion the food she offered him.

When the girl's relatives saw how she and my father clung to one another, they initiated a carefully worded conversation with him. My father said that he was willing to convert to Islam and take the girl as a concubine through legal channels. Her relatives were somewhat incredulous, but the fiercest opposition came from her older brother. He said that my father was merely captivated by her youth and her flesh and that his younger sister was not an appropriate object for the sexual passions of a Chinese. My father was trying to explain himself as best he could, with tears sparkling in his eyes, when an eighteen-year-old boy approached him and, poking him in the chest, said that he and the young girl had been betrothed since they were children and were going to be married that year, after the harvest. He told my father to forget about having that girl.

A week later, at dawn, my father led the girl out of the longhouse and into the wild Borneo countryside. The two of them were not seen again. The chief of the longhouse sent out a search party of twenty young men, who searched for them for ten days. Policemen came to my family's house to ask questions and serve notice that my father would be indicted for the seduction of a minor. A week before all this occurred, my father had, with Lin Yuan's assistance, built a small wooden cabin high in the mist-shrouded mountains. He had put aside a month's worth of food, and now he and the girl were living as man and wife in the cabin. My father was convinced that his loving care and fatherly tutelage could restore the intelligence that the girl had lost to food poisoning ten years before. After another month, Lin Yuan set out with more provisions to pay a visit to his old friend, and he found my fortysomething father's face infused with the same glow it had had when he was twenty. The girl could now recite English poetry and do sums from a sixth-grade math text. Lin Yuan was dumbstruck. Ten days after that, the girl's betrothed found them. He used a blowpipe to fire two poisoned arrows at my father, who was teaching the girl to recite Neapolitan folk songs. My wounded father returned fire with his rifle, and the two of them struggled for some time before my father finally killed the young man. And two days later my father died himself, in agony, from the poison. When the police reached the cabin, they found the girl loudly declaiming English poetry from a book. Her voice was strong and clear, her face was streaked with tears. She kept pulling white flowers out of a basket and placing them one after another upon my father's blackened corpse, which lay beside her. Actually, at the time the police could not be sure that the corpse was my father's, because his head had disappeared.

I didn't get to see my father's body, let alone his face, when I returned home. By the time he was cremated, his body had already decomposed beyond recognition. When Lin Yuan was explaining to me how he had died, I asked about his sketchbook, and Lin Yuan looked a bit startled. There were in fact two sketchbooks among the items my father had left behind, containing forty-seven drawings in all, with a date written in the corner of each. There was one drawing for every day between April twenty-fifth and June tenth—the day my father had abducted the girl and the day he had died.

A beautiful long-haired girl is the main subject of every drawing. In some she is wearing a long robe, in others she is half-naked, and in still others she is entirely naked. There were drawings that showed her walking, kneeling, reclining, and even soaring through the forest fogs. Her face, its expressions, and the bearing of her body made me think of that beautiful barefoot lady beside the stream in the garden.

Two drawings in particular reinforced this association. One was of the girl in a long robe, standing beside a stream crowded all around with flowers and butterflies, reaching out her hand to take a flower offered to her by a man whose features are obscure.

The other was of the girl standing half-naked in a field. Her head is bowed, her eyes facing downward, as she strokes the head of a man whose face is pressed against her abdomen.

In every picture, the woman is surrounded by exotic plants and by bizarre birds and beasts. Some of these creatures are anthropomorphic, adopting the submissive posture of servants; others have the auspicious look of holiday symbols of good fortune. The shrinking humility of these faintly drawn creatures only emphasizes the girl's prominence and her noble look. These pictures were nothing like the ones my father had drawn before.

He drew in incredible detail every feature of the girl's face and body. In some places his pen strokes are lively and decisive, and in others they are hesitant and vague. A powerful attachment to the fragmented feelings of both the past and present reality is visible in every line; their alternating stagnation and fluency are indices of my father's suffering and his euphoria.

Chapter 24

My mother didn't leave the house for several days after my father's funeral. For the first time in years, she broke her routine of working every day in her garden. Then, one evening, she saw from the dining room a pack of Lin Yuan's party guests coming along the walkway and wandering around in the garden, and at that moment I saw in her eyes that powerful ferocity that kept dogged watch over the garden, one of the many layers of her schizophrenic character. She returned to her garden the next day.

I was with her all the time until she returned to the garden. By then it was already July. She was worried that the garden would be destroyed by the annual onslaught of El Niño, and she had hired an irrigation truck in advance, so the garden was redolent of its usual summer scent of putrescence and excrement. Laboring and sweating under my mother's command, the workmen hired to irrigate the garden stayed close to her, since most of them already knew what it was like to be lost in there. When they rested and took refreshments in the garden, they watched her pruning branches or burning flower patches or planting new seedlings, and they wondered where this impulse to destroy and rebuild came from. Their expressions were both baffled and reverent as they watched her moving around in the garden, radiant like a falling star, dignified like the Blessed Virgin. I came to realize that, even though they occasionally called her "the madwoman" (most of the time, of course, they referred to her as "the boss lady"), they treated her with the utmost respect when she was present, and they all fought to be the first in line to serve her. The fact that my mother was a generous employer cannot have been the only reason for this.

I heard conversations like this one on more than one occasion:

"The boss lady just lost her husband. She must be feeling lonely."

"I'd eat shit for the chance to put my arms around her, just once."

Working shirtless, they showed off their solid and hair-mottled muscles for my mother to see.

My mother wore a broad straw hat and sunglasses. She gestured with her gloved hands and used words sparingly. She was at once reserved and very kind as she directed like a shepherd her flock of manly men in their battle with the drought. One time she took off a glove and stroked a sunflower. The workmen's hearts raced as they looked at her white and tender fingers. They could not imagine how a woman who spent her days in flower patches could still have skin as liquid-soft as hers.

It was amusing to watch those twenty very masculine men, either out of fear of getting lost or out of loyalty and devotion, clustering around my mother as docilely and peacefully as a flock of sheep.

Toward the end of July, a new foreman arrived, a Chinese bachelor in his forties. He trailed behind my mother wherever she went, and even though he was supposed to be the foreman he carried out most of my mother's orders himself, no matter how large or how small. Once, when he was following my mother around with a parasol to shield her from the sun, he pulled out a fan to cool her sweat-soaked body. She waved him away, saying in a soft voice, "I'm not hot." He unfolded the fan and began to fan her anyway. She turned away from him, walked out from under the parasol, and went forth into the scorching, forty-one-degree sunlight.

Another time, the foreman brought two cups of hot coffee to the bench in the shade where my mother was sitting during the workmen's break. "Ma'am," he said. I happened to be passing through the crowd of workmen, and I had stopped, hoping to listen to them talk about interesting things I rarely got a chance to hear about. But they all fell silent when they heard the foreman call my mother this—he never had before. "It's true that there are some very unpleasant rumors going around about the death of your late husband. But the dead can't be brought back to life. You should cheer up."

When the foreman approached her, my mother had been wiping her face with a wet towel. Her straw hat, her sunglasses, a cup of iced tea, and a pocket Bible sat on the grass beside her. When she put down the towel and looked at the foreman, I was reminded of the look she had had on her face when, at the dinner table, gazing out at the garden, she had heard my father and Lin Yuan talk about stealing the crocodile egg.

"Your husband did wrong by you, but that's all in the past now. There's no need for you to suffer anymore." The foreman placed the coffee cups on top of the Bible and sat down beside my mother, on a large tree root. "Our lives are short, so you should be happy while you can. Would you like some coffee?"

My mother placed the wet towel over her knees and put on her hat and glasses. To everyone's surprise, she said, in a sweet voice, "Thank you."

The foreman contentedly settled his strong rear end against the tree branch.

"It's remarkable, ma'am, that you take care of this entire garden by yourself." The foreman took an affected sip of coffee, and the other workmen stifled their laughter. "If you ever feel overwhelmed, I can help you with the heavy work anytime."

My mother took a sip of iced tea.

"I know a little bit about plants." The surface of the tree branch was uneven, and sitting on it was awkward for the foreman. He kept adjusting the position of his legs and trying to brace his behind. The fabric of his jeans brushed against the tree bark, and a provocative scraping sound resulted. "I've heard that you shouldn't put too many sweet-smelling plants close together. Any one of their scents is no problem by itself, but if you mix them together, people will get confused and lose their sense of direction. If it gets bad enough, a person might lie right down on the ground and fall fast asleep. It's easy to get lost in this garden of yours, ma'am. It can't be because of all the different flower scents, can it?"

My mother lifted the wet towel off her knees and rubbed her neck with it, then went on drinking her iced tea.

"Hey, Ah Cheng, didn't you fall asleep in the garden the other day and sleep all afternoon?" The foreman looked at one of the workmen. "Did you smell anything funny before you fell asleep?"

"I don't remember," the workman said. "I just remember I had a bad dream. Some woman was chasing me."

Everyone laughed heartily.

"People also say that our plants have feelings, just like our pets do," the foreman said earnestly. "If you treat them with love, they'll give you love in return. Eventually they start to look and act like their masters."

My mother turned her head to look straight at the foreman. He drew encouragement from this and vigorously rubbed his buttocks around on the tree branch as if they were two inflatable balls.

"The plants in this garden come in a million varieties, but they're all warm, tender things. Like miniature replicas of their mistress." As the foreman said this, he tore a tiny flower off the creeping vine that was wrapped around the tree branch, brought it to his nose, and sniffed it. "Such a wonderful, irresistible perfume."

My mother got up to go. She had not even sipped the coffee, and she left the cup and the Bible behind on the grass.

At noon two days later, when all the workmen were napping in the garden, the foreman disappeared. After days of searching and waiting, everyone concluded that he must have gotten lost in the garden and wandered by accident into the jungle. A rescue party was assembled, and two weeks later they found the foreman inside a cave in the jungle. He was curled up in the darkness, sweating a cold sweat, with one of his legs broken and leeches crawling over it. He started trembling all over and screaming in plaintive tones when the rescue party arrived. After a week of rest and nourishment, he returned to our house with one lame leg. He approached my mother, who was still directing the workmen in the irrigation work, and said, "It was you, ma'am! It was you! It was you who led me away, you who got me lost, took me into the jungle . . ."

My mother furrowed her brow, removed her sunglasses, and stared at him.

"I suffered so much in the jungle. I almost died there." He pointed to his scars and his ruined leg. "Why, ma'am? Why did you want to lead me to my death?"

My mother put her sunglasses back on and told the workmen to be careful as they irrigated several young trees she had just planted with river water. Then she said to the foreman, "What are you talking about, Mr. Huang?"

"It was you, ma'am. You led me into the garden. You didn't say anything, but you had a look on your face like a harlot, like you wanted me. You tricked me. You led me around and around, and before I knew what was happening I was lost in the jungle . . ."

"Mr. Huang, do you want to keep your job?" she said in an amiable voice.

"This garden is haunted. It's haunted!" He pointed to the garden and then to my mother. "You're a witch, a witch . . ."

The workmen gathered around, trying to calm the foreman down and talk some sense into him. The foreman's accusations rang out, spreading out through the air so that even I, sitting on the swing with a book, could hear them perfectly. By the time I arrived on the scene, having followed the sound, his voice was already hoarse and exhausted.

"All I did was flirt with her a little, but that was enough to make this witch want to kill me . . ."

"You uncivilized piece of trash! I've never heard such brazen slander in my life."

Lin Yuan, dressed in his hunting clothes and smoking a pipe, parted the crowd of workmen and walked up to the foreman.

"Who are you?" the foreman asked.

"My name is Lin Yuan. I am this lady's neighbor, and I was a good friend of Su Huan."

"Ten years ago that witch cheated on her husband and had a bastard with a leper . . ." "Leper" was a derogatory term the Chinese in that region used to describe the Dayaks.

I tried to charge the foreman, but Lin Yuan held me back. "Get out of here, you uncivilized creature."

"You're no good either!" the foreman said. "I see you trailing along after this witch every day like a horny dog. A widow and a widower . . . dry wood always catches fire eventually . . ."

Lin Yuan seized a hard object he had brought with him and struck the foreman with it several times. The foreman's body began to twitch, and he collapsed into the arms of one of the workmen who had been trying to keep the peace. The hard object was the same electric prod Lin Yuan used on vicious animals.

Chapter 25

The days dragged on for me after my father's funeral. If my mother had not been so unstable, I might very well have boarded a plane for Taipei the instant the funeral was over and brought what grief I could muster to Taiwan with me, to display it for Keyi so that she couldn't accuse me of being a heartless, unfilial son. Once my mother returned to her garden, I started spending most of my time out on the swing, one of the few places in the garden that I knew well enough to feel certain I wouldn't get lost on my way there, reading or staring off into space, marveling over how much the garden had changed in the three years I had been away, into a strange and terrifying place of fecund enchantment. Nothing was the same as it had been three years before. My mother had linked her garden with Lin Yuan's, so that it was now hard to tell where one property ended and the other began. She had also closely surrounded both houses with trees and plants, so that now what may have been the two finest houses in the entire region had almost disappeared, fused with the profuse greenery of the jungle. In the mornings, when I woke up and saw the elephantine tree trunks and pythonlike giant vines outside my window, I would feel as if my body were drifting down into a deep abyss. Sometime after the incident with the foreman, I was walking through the garden, sniffing for the scents of every fruit and flower like a hunting dog, when I suddenly realized that the sense of discombobulation and discomfort I felt was not coming solely from the sweet odors but was also related to a vague foul smell whose source I couldn't discern. I studied the plants. All of them, young, old, or in their prime, in all their myriad shapes and sizes, had a certain coquettish quality, a fawning, debauched quality. All the birds in the garden, the pheasants, peacocks, and turtledoves, were unusually corpulent. The barking deer, squirrels, and mountain goats also had an overfed look. I felt as if I were at a noisy, ostentatious, and uninhibited party. The delicacies and wine were scrambling my senses and my insides. A bearded pig that darted across my line of vision was one of the treats of the evening, about to be butchered and cooked on the spot by the chef.

While my father and the young Dayak girl were living in their jungle retreat, Lin Yuan stepped into my father's role as the toast of their social scene, and once my father was dead his position as such was confirmed and made permanent. Lin Yuan carried on the tradition of holding parties every Friday and Saturday night. He would arrange musical performances, magic shows, gambling, and meals cooked by chefs from the finest restaurants, and he hired beautiful girls as hostesses. He let drunken guests spend the night. Lin Yuan was especially good at arranging practical jokes, so much so that even I, far away in my own house, often heard the startled cries of the guests and was duped into believing something really was happening. Once, Lin Yuan collaborated with a timber tycoon to have several of his employees enter the party dressed as robbers and hold up the guests. Then the "robbers" tied up the tycoon to take with them as a hostage, demanded that a very large sum be paid to ransom him within three days, and used some clever sleight of hand to pretend to cut off his ear. Lin Yuan fired rubber bullets from his hunting rifle at the "robbers," one of whom fell to the ground on cue. Another "robber" returned fire and hit Lin Yuan in the leg, then declared that he was going to cut off one ear of every guest as revenge. The Lin house erupted into total chaos.

One day in the middle of August, I was sitting on the swing with a book when Lin Yuan suddenly appeared. "Have you seen a girl come by here? About one and a half meters tall, with long hair, a half-breed who only speaks the native tongue?"

I said I had seen no such person.

"Can I trouble you to assist me?" Lin Yuan's face was drenched in sweat, and he took a deep breath as he put his hands on his hips. "The girl is one of my servants. She's made some trouble for me. She's saying she wants to go home. I don't know where she's gone."

I noticed that Lin Yuan had his electric prod hanging from his belt, as if he were hunting for a carnivorous animal that had escaped from its cage. I took my book, walked away from Lin Yuan, and proceeded through the garden until I found my mother, laboring over her orchids.

"Has anyone come by here, Mom?" I asked.

She shook her head and asked me, "What are you doing running around out in the hot sun?"

Since my father's death, both the way she spoke and the things she said had changed. Now she spoke with a gentle lilt, in a laborious, meticulous way that made me think of the voice of a stewardess on a world leader's private jet. On more than one occasion, I had woken up from a nap on the swing to find that someone had placed over me a light blanket, redolent with the smell of garments dried in the sun and with the smell of my mother's body that had inspired such a great hunger in me when I was still suckling at her breast. My mother's speech now seemed to communicate only indirectly.

I told her that one of Lin Yuan's maids had run away.

"Serves him right," my mother said. "Where are you going?"

"To look for the maid."

"You should stay out of his affairs. And you shouldn't be out in this hot sun. Where's your hat?"

"It's dark as a cave in here. What do I need a hat for?"

"This place isn't like it used to be. Be careful not to wander into the jungle by mistake."

Fifteen minutes later, I found a barefoot girl crouching by the side of the nearly dry pond, catching tadpoles. Her hair hung down to her waist, and she was wearing a batik shirt and a pair of shorts. She held in her mouth a transparent plastic bag full of pond water that was thick and inky green with tadpoles and algae, and she was reaching into the water to catch more tadpoles in her hands.

As I approached her, I noticed that her whole body was already soaking wet and that algae and squirming tadpoles were clinging to her dripping hair and back.

I said, "Where do you think you're going? Lin Yuan's looking for you."

She stopped fishing around for tadpoles and fixed me with eyes that were as inky green as her plastic bag and that rolled around fiercely in her head.

"Lin Yuan's looking for you," I said again.

She looked me up and down carefully, and then a smile appeared out of nowhere on her face.

The girl had thrown her shirt on carelessly, without fastening most of the buttons, and the sunlight glinted off of the moisture dotting her small breasts. She had strong features and ruddy skin and couldn't have been older than fifteen. Just as I was trying to figure out which half of this pretty half-breed's bloodlines was dominant and which language I should use with her, Lin Yuan showed up beside me and clapped me on the shoulder, saying, "Girls from the jungle hate wearing clothes. I've run myself ragged day after day telling them that they have to wear them. You can imagine how they are about my other rules."

The girl lowered her head and inspected a tadpole in her palm that she had just caught. Lin Yuan said, "You can go home now, Su Qi. Thank you."

Just as I turned to go, the girl flung herself into the pond. She floated in the water with her head and prominent buttocks sticking out and watched Lin Yuan moving toward her. When he reached her, he removed the plastic bag from her mouth and dumped the tadpoles inside it right onto her head. The girl screamed and seized his calf, and he, too, tumbled into the water. The girl wiped the algae and tadpoles from her face and then smeared a handful of mud on Lin Yuan's face.

As I passed my mother, she was muttering to herself, "Almost ready now. That ought to do it."

In the hopes of attracting the chief minister to his house, Lin Yuan had traveled into the wild interior country to select several young girls personally to work at his parties; he called them "maids." The male guests frequently made passes at them, but Lin Yuan wouldn't let anyone sully them. My understanding was that Lin Yuan had somehow managed to inform the minister, who had a penchant for underage girls, that these girls were patiently waiting for his attentions. I didn't go to any of Lin Yuan's parties while I was at home, but I would run into these girls in the garden occasionally, and the tadpole catcher was one of them. They were gorgeous, indolent creatures who reminded me of little pythons. Rumor had it that, on the day they had arrived at Lin Yuan's house, they had seen an electrician fixing one of the patio lights and one of them had accidentally touched a live wire with her finger. She experienced a surge of vague delight at the numbing soreness that spread through her arm, and she screamed in simultaneous pleasure and pain.

"You should try it, too," she told the others.

They touched the wire, one after the other. One girl wet her pants on the spot; another's eyes welled up with tears.

Lin Yuan, who had watched the entire proceedings, went ahead and ordered an electric prod that carried a charge equivalent to that produced by the live wire. He hung it on his belt next to the one he had long used on carnivorous animals and then began training his girls the same way he had trained his animals. One night two weeks before I was scheduled to go back to Taiwan, I saw Lin Yuan use his prod on a girl who had been flirting with one of the party guests. The prod skimmed lightly across the girl's body from the neck down, like a dragonfly skimming over water. She writhed like a serpent beneath it, her skin undulating ever so slightly, something like a smile and yet not a smile rippling across her face. Her screams were simultaneously sweet and pained, so that it was hard to tell whether this was supposed to be a punishment or a reward. After it was over, she rolled around on the ground at Lin Yuan's feet, grasped his calf, and gazed up at the man who had just assaulted her with electricity. Honestly, I could not tell whether she was happy or suffering.

The South Seas summer was brutally hot and dry, and the girls thirsted after some kind of release just as the plants were thirsting after a storm. One afternoon, Lin Yuan caught one of them meeting a boy secretly in the garden. He pulled out the prod he used on animals and waved it in front of the boy's face; I suspect that if he hadn't known the boy's father, he would have had no qualms about running it over his body. Once the boy had been driven off, Lin Yuan commanded the girl to remove her pants and lie down on the ground, and then he stuck one of his fingers into her vagina. The girl was docile and calm and acted as if this sort of thing were a regular occurrence. I suddenly recalled how Lin Yuan had once bragged at a party that he only needed to insert his finger into the vagina of a female of any species—cow, horse, pig, sheep, cat, dog, or human—to determine if she was a virgin. Other doctors had always responded to this claim with either unqualified admiration or a snort of contempt. I watched Lin Yuan extract his finger, bring it to his nose, and give it a sniff. Then he drew the prod in two arcs across the girl's buttocks, like a painter augmenting his work with the finishing touches that would make it a masterpiece. Her whole body twisted and writhed like a python that had just swallowed its prey whole. Her muscles stretched and contracted as if she were in unspeakable pain. But the look in her eyes was greedy; it betrayed a desire like the hunger for food, a desire as engulfing as a bottomless pit.

Rumors about the girls' bizarre reactions to electricity soon spread among the regular party guests. At one afternoon tea party in the garden, I heard a man telling someone about how he had grabbed the rear end of one of the virgins when no one else was looking and had felt a prickling numbness spread through his body. Another time, I heard an elderly man who was missing both legs say that when the girls rushed past him his electric wheelchair would shake violently. People also said that the virgins got especially rambunctious, especially electric, at nighttime parties when all of Lin Yuan's patio lights were turned on at once, that their laughter grew more sonorous as they walked by expensive stereo equipment, that their skirts blew up and their hair stood on end when they passed under the chandelier, that if they sat in front of the electric oven while a quail was roasting in it, the quail would turn out especially savory, every morsel both a pleasurable indulgence and a stimulant for the imagination.

I remember that another girl escaped into our garden a week before I went back to Taiwan. Lin Yuan and I spent a long time searching before we found her in the tree house. Lin Yuan took a rope up into the tree house and tied her up there. When he came back down, he said to me, "Ignore her. Let her starve up there for a night." After nightfall, though, I climbed up to the tree house with a flashlight and said, "I'm going to set you free. Go home now. Tell him I'm the one who did it."

She let me undo her bonds.

"I'm not going," she said. "He'll yell at me if I go back, and he'll dock my wages."

"You're going to spend the night up here?"

"What's wrong with that?"

"Aren't you afraid?"

"I slept outside a lot back when I used to go hunting with my father."

"Well, whatever you like."

"I'm so hungry," she said. "Bring a little food back here for me."

I went home and filled a basket with toast, butter, fruit, and two blankets and then returned to the tree house. I couldn't believe how quickly she ate the food I'd brought her.

"What's your name?" I asked.

"Amma."

"Why are you working here?"

"What's not to like about working here? I've got food, a place to stay, money. I get to have some fun."

"Why did Uncle Lin tie you up?"

"I was being bad." She suddenly looked straight at me with a pair of very large eyes. "Mr. Lin says he will get rid of us if any man ever has his way with us."

"Has that ever happened to you?" I couldn't resist asking.

"Of course not," she said. "One of the girls slept with a man, though, and she was sent away the very next day. Mr. Lin's really something. He just needs to touch us there, and he'll know. But he's not always right. There's one girl he still doesn't know about."

"Well, then, why did he say you were being bad?"

She bit her lip and didn't say anything.

"Enjoy your dinner. I'll go back down now."

"Can't you stay with me?"

"You should come down, too. At the very least you can spend the night at our house."

"I'm afraid to. Mr. Lin might come looking for me."

"You can't sleep here. You could roll out of the tree house in your sleep."

"I'm afraid to go down," she said. "There's somebody down there."

"Who?"

"A man," she said. "He's lame in one leg. He can't climb up here."

"There shouldn't be any men around here besides Uncle Lin. What'll that man do to you?"

"He wants me," she said. "He's come after two of the girls already."

"How? Did he force them?"

"Not exactly. He has an electric prod just like Mr. Lin's. I don't know why, but none of us can even stand to look at it."

"Have you told Uncle Lin?"

"I told him. He told me to stay up here."

I found out a few days later that Lin Yuan had been using Amma as bait to trap the man who had threatened the sanctity of his virgins. One afternoon before I returned to Taiwan, I was up in the tree house, bored out of my skull and looking around with the binoculars, when I saw Lin Yuan running between our garden and his own, carrying two electric prods. My mother was on the swing, reading her Bible. A girl who looked to me a great deal like Amma was napping under a tree. I let the binoculars drift back and forth among the three of them several times, and I was just about to look for a new target when I noticed that Amma had woken up. She raised her head with a broad smile to look at several white butterflies that were circling in the air above her head. One of the butterflies lingered just behind her, rising and falling there like an ocean wave. A few white flowers came drifting down from the tree and landed around Amma. Then one flower that was poised to land just behind her instead bounced wavelike up and down in the air, seemingly propelled by the motion of the butterfly, as if it were caught in a spider's web.

My curiosity got the better of me, and I adjusted the focus on the binoculars to get a better view of the area behind Amma. It was as if I were on a flying carpet, coasting rapidly in her direction until I had a view so good that I might have been sitting on the grass just behind her. I saw that a profusion of thin threads was being blown around in the air behind her, charging toward her like a giant tidal wave. The butterfly and white flower surged forward, the glistening crest on that gentle, transparent wave, and even the tree house seemed to rise and fall, and I felt again like a sailor at the top of a mast gazing out at the boundless ocean that was the labyrinthine garden. I adjusted the focus again to bring me even closer to Amma and discovered that the so-called tidal wave was actually twenty or more strands of Amma's hair, standing away from her body in a perfect horizontal line, as if they had escaped the pull of gravity. The strands mostly stood apart from and parallel to one another, but occasionally one would brush against another, and the friction between them would produce tiny green sparks. Then the bangs that covered Amma's forehead suddenly parted, as if they had just been brushed with an invisible comb charged with static electricity. As soon as this happened, Amma seemed to grow aware of the extraordinary situation. She turned her head to look behind her, and this brought her face "close" enough to me that I thought I could smell the hot sweat that had been drenching her body for a long time. Half the hair on her head was floating in the same horizontal lines behind her as she turned her head, and the strands rubbed against her cheeks with a sizzling sound, emitting more tiny sparks reminiscent of young flesh.

More butterflies began shuttling back and forth through the horizontal floating strands of her hair. In all honesty, I can't quite think of how to describe the beauty of that hair hanging in midair, motionless most of the time but occasionally bouncing up and down with a musical rhythm, like ocean waves or slender fingers manipulating the strings of a harp. The way Amma looked just then reminded me of the other young virgin who, the other day, had twisted and writhed at Lin Yuan's feet like a python that had just swallowed its prey whole.

I moved the binoculars again and saw that there was a man standing at the end of the tide's slow trajectory. In his hand was an electric prod that was emitting sparks and making a sizzling sound. He stood a short distance from Amma, and he was waving the prod in her direction, as if it were a remote control and she the mechanical doll it operated. Just then, some invisible force pulled all of Amma's hair toward the prod, and the look in her eyes evoked the hunger of an animal waking from a long hibernation, a hunger that could devour the whole of the universe, everything on land and in the sea and in the air.

The man was wearing jeans and a sleeveless shirt. He was dark and solidly built, and as he walked toward Amma I saw that one of his legs was lame.

I quickly adjusted my binoculars and rode my flying carpet toward my mother, only to find that she had already shut her Bible and left the swing and was just then disappearing into a flower patch. So I steered my carpet toward Lin Yuan, whose exact whereabouts I wasn't sure of, and after searching for a while I found him, still wandering through the labyrinthine garden with his electric prods. When I brought my carpet back to Amma, she was lying paralyzed at the man's feet like a ball of mud, looking up at him with eyes full of tears. Whenever he swung his prod around her or across her buttocks, she seemed to melt a little more, to flatten and spread further along the ground, and her mouth was forced open a little further, turning into a whirlpool that descended into an abyss. Her hair stood up on all sides, forming a chaotic ball, and the white flower had long since fallen to the ground and been crushed under her feet. The butterflies that had been hovering around her before were now nowhere to be seen.

The man put down the prod and crouched beside her. One of his hands was reaching under her shirt, after her breasts, which were heaving like a violent ocean current that assaults the bodies of hapless swimmers, and the other hand moved under her chin as he bent down to kiss her mouth, which had turned as soft as mush from all her trembling.

I went scouting through the garden, on my flying carpet once again. This time I didn't find my mother, but I soon found Lin Yuan, who was still wandering around. Then I went back to Amma and saw that she was still lying paralyzed beside the man. The man, though, had already stood up and had his eyes focused on something behind a nearby giant tree. He bent down, picked the electric prod up off the grass, and walked toward the tree. As he disappeared behind it, I caught sight of my mother on the other side of it, moving into another patch of flowers. The man followed her. She was languorous and composed, whereas he was fretful and nervous; sparks were shooting out from his prod.

I finally realized that this man was the same foreman who had made a pass at my mother and whom Lin Yuan had assaulted with his electric prod.

I climbed down from the tree house immediately and made my way at breakneck speed to Amma. She was sitting cross-legged on the grass when I arrived, and she looked at me with virtually vacant eyes. I went around the giant tree and headed into the flower patch I had seen my mother enter. I was worried about my mother's safety; the sparks that shot out from the lame foreman's electric prod illustrated his fury all too clearly. But I soon came across the prod lying abandoned on the grass beneath a giant cactus as tall as a city wall. I picked it up and looked around me. I saw that I was lost, amid the garden's intricate knot of paths.

Amma had been following me. When I stopped, she sank down at my feet, a ball of mud once again. I saw into her mouth, that bottomless wet crevice that had turned to mush and was reminiscent of a whirlpool and exposed her larynx and was growing deeper and darker by the minute. One of her hands grabbed my calf; the other hand groped for my genitals. In spite of myself, I remembered the time when I was little and had pissed on the wildfire and swelled up to the size of a doorknob.

I let Amma's hand grope at me for a while, but I broke free of her when I saw the top of Lin Yuan's head appear above a bed of flowers.

"What's going on, Su Qi?" Lin Yuan approached us, carrying his electric prods.

I told him about everything I had seen from the tree house.

"Don't worry," Lin Yuan said. "Your mother will have no problem handling that simpleton."

I didn't entirely believe him, but I handed the prod over to Lin Yuan. As I was leaving, he commanded Amma to lie down and reached for her vagina with his right hand.

I went back to the tree house. Not long after that, I saw my mother again, back on the swing, reading her Bible. I didn't hear anything else about the crippled foreman before I went back to Taiwan. After that incident, I often saw Amma in the garden, studying me from afar, looking at me so intently that I felt goose bumps rising on my flesh. But, then again, maybe the girl watching me wasn't Amma; she and the other virgins all looked so much alike. Every time I ran into Lin Yuan looking for them in the garden, I couldn't help making fun of him a little. "Hey, Uncle, has the chief minister's 'bait' run away again?"

Lin Yuan would grin and wipe the sweat from his face. "I'm getting old. Have you seen them?"

I told him I hadn't. "Those girls of yours are good runners. Once they get going, they're gone like a gust of wind."

"They're all so young," he said, eyeing me. "But they're also clever. Don't let yourself be taken in by them, Su Qi."

I smiled and didn't respond to that.

"When will that fucking chief minister finally get his ass over here?" I heard Lin Yuan say more than once.

"Soon now. Almost ready now." My mother would say this to herself, looking at the garden, every time I passed her.

Once again, I found myself wanting to escape from my home. This time it wasn't just disgust that was driving me away. There was also a vague terror that referenced nothing in particular.

Part 3

Chapter 26

I arrived back in Taipei on a Monday night in early September and immediately tried to contact Keyi. Her roommates told me that she had moved out and hadn't left a new phone number, so I called her number in Tainan. Keyi herself picked up the phone. She said that she would hurry back to Taipei the next afternoon. The weather service had predicted that a severe typhoon would hit Taipei on Tuesday night, and sure enough strong winds started up the next afternoon. For several hours after that, I had no way of contacting Keyi, but at nine at night, out of nowhere, my doorbell rang, and there she was, standing outside my door drenched to the bone, with a suitcase in her hand. She took a hot shower and changed into a set of dry clothes. The traffic had been awful, she told me, and since my place was close to the train station she had come here to hide out until the chaos was over. I took out a batik shirt and a tin letter opener I had brought back for her and then asked her, "Why did you move out of your apartment?"

"I'll tell you in a minute," she said.

"Did you finish the novels?"

"As a matter of fact, I did, but there were a lot of parts I didn't understand and had to just skim through. I've been hoping you'd explain them to me." Then she said, "These days I'm singing at a few different bars. From now on I'll only be free on Monday nights."

"What does a charming creature like you need all that money for?" I said.

"Well, I had a falling-out with that 'little prince,' and now I need to start pulling all my own weight again."

"Why? Does this have anything to do with me?"

"It has nothing to do with you. I should have done it a long time ago. I'll tell you the whole story later."

"So much grief for one so young!" Then I said, "I'm pretty impressed with you, rushing from show to show like a real star. Did you get your new jobs by answering ads?"

"Well, I've been performing for so long, it makes sense that I'd be a little famous by now. Plus, I'm good-looking, as you know. All the bars know a good deal when they see one, and they contacted me to ask me to work for them."

"So you'll be in class during the day and onstage at night. I guess we won't have much time to see each other," I said.

"No way. I'll still need your help on my homework, and whenever you're free you should come see me sing. I'll tell the managers you're my friend, so they won't charge you anything." Then she said, "A few of the bars are pretty close to each other, so I bought a bike to ride from one to the other. That way I can lose a little weight too. Hey, when you have time you should come along and be my chauffeur!"

"You look fine as you are. You don't need to lose weight."

"It was all your fault. Whenever I was with you we ate fatty food. I had to diet all summer, and I still haven't taken off all the weight you put on me," she said.

"Where did you get fat?" I asked her.

She showed me the palm of her right hand and said, "Look, my fingers are like sausages." I took her hand in mine and inspected it closely: the fingers were long and slender, a ruddy glow shone through her pale skin, and all in all it was very much like my mother's hand. I said, "Wow, your love line twists around an awful lot."

"Well, where do you think it leads?" And then she said, "Su Qi, you've lost weight! Maybe I was eating your portions all last year."

"There was a lot going on at home. I'll tell you about it later." I tightened my grip on her hand and felt her shiver. I said to her, "Are you cold?"

"No," she said. I grabbed her hand even tighter, and she shivered again. I said, "What's the matter?" She didn't say anything; she just bit her lip and closed her eyes. I was about to let go of her hand when I heard her say, "No, don't let go." So I clutched it tighter, and this time she reacted calmly. I took a step forward, dropped her hand, and then put my arms around her. I kissed her temples, her forehead, her eyebrows, her eyes, her nose, and her mouth. I was awkward and overeager, and she was intense and somewhat stiff. When she put her arms around me, the tips of her fingers danced up and down my spine. Her tongue darted in and out of my mouth. She was trembling so violently that at times I felt as if the body I was holding were being flogged. She buried her face in the left half of my chest, and when she spoke I could feel the tip of her tongue grazing the portion of my flesh that encased my heart. "Su Qi," she said, "I don't want to go home tonight, can I stay with you?" I said, "That's fine. You've been on the train all day, you must be tired, you should go to bed." I walked over to the bed with her, and we both lay down. Then I started kissing her again—I kissed her temples, her forehead, her eyebrows, her eyes, her nose, and her mouth. She was squirming the whole time and seemed to be trying to evade me, but then she was also clutching tightly at my hair and my shoulder blades, like a feline creature that had been given tranquilizers that were now on the verge of wearing off. She didn't seem to wake up fully again until I entered her, a little hastily and roughly. Then, after that was over, she began an agile, violent pursuit of what remained of my erection, and before long I was as swollen as I had been when I had pissed on the fire when I was a kid. She said in my ear, "Let's do it again, okay?" So I entered her a second time without giving it a second thought. I remembered wandering around amid the smoke and the flames after pissing in the fire and seeing my mother off in the distance, dodging and drifting here and there in the thick, visible heat. In the visual confusion of that moment, I had thought I was seeing the woman in white who brought a great and torrential rain with her every time she appeared.

At that point I suddenly became aware of the violent rainstorm outside and the complete darkness inside. "I wonder when the power went out," I said, and then I lit a candle that I kept at the head of the bed. The candle illuminated the tearstains on Keyi's face. I pressed down with one finger on a tear that was scurrying down her face. Her tears were flowing like a river through a dam that had burst. I held her and kissed her forehead. She pressed her cheek close against me, moistening my chest. We held each other without speaking for a long time.

"Thank you, Su Qi."

I didn't know what to say. "What are you thanking me for?"

"For making me feel like a woman."

"Silly girl."

"I lived next to a military housing project when I was a kid. My mother left when I was five, you know, and I got bored a lot, so I'd go over there to play. There were a lot of nice old men in the housing project. They said I was cute, and they'd give me candy and soda and ice cream. One time they took me over to an abandoned building and gave me some chocolate and an old doll, and then they started to touch me. I got scared and wanted to go home, but they wouldn't let me. They said, Don't be scared, we've got more chocolate here for you, just wait a few more minutes, and you can have it, but if you go home now you'll owe us for all the candy and soda we gave you. Then they started touching me again, and they took off my clothes. I don't know how many of them there were. Maybe three or four, maybe five or six. After it was over they told me not to tell anyone. They said if I did they'd tell my dad everything. I didn't want my dad to know. I thought he'd beat me. It was my own fault, for taking other people's candy. After that I was too afraid to go back to the housing project, but one day I ran into one of the men on the street, and he said, I bought lots more candy for you, come with me, if you don't I'll tell your dad what happened last time. This went on until I was twelve and my dad had his car accident. Then I got brave all of a sudden, and I said to them, Go ahead and tell my dad, I don't care, he's in a wheelchair and can't hurt me. I don't know if the old men started dying off or what, but after that they never came looking for me again. That was when I finally realized that they never would have told my father."

She turned over. Without the air conditioner and fans running, the room was muggy and stifling. Sweat was dripping down my forehead.

"I was afraid of all men after that. I didn't have any male friends in school. Then, my freshman year in college, a guy took me out on a date and tried to hold hands, but I freaked out the minute he touched me. After that I went out with another guy, and he tried to put his arm around me. At first I just didn't like the way it felt, then after a while I actually started feeling queasy. But he kept holding on to me and wouldn't let go. I lost my temper and stomped on his foot. After that I was afraid to go out on any more dates."

The light at the head of the bed suddenly went on again, and the air conditioner started up. I got a towel and gave it to Keyi, telling her to wipe away her sweat so she wouldn't catch a chill. I had just blown out the candle, and Keyi had just finished drying herself, when the power went off again. I lit the candle a second time.

"Then I moved into that apartment, the one you've been to. I hadn't been living there very long when I caught a little cold. One of the fine arts girls came to my room to see if I needed anything. We talked for a while, and then I told her I was having trouble sleeping. She said she could massage me, maybe that would help put me to sleep. So she told me to turn over. I didn't suspect a thing. At first she was very proper, just rubbed my back, but then she started getting a little out of line. I said, What are you doing? She didn't answer. She just lay down on top of me, so I couldn't move. I struggled for a while and then stopped and let her do what she wanted. After she left, I just cried and cried. I don't know why I didn't make her stop, Su Qi. A few days after that, the other fine arts major snuck into my room while I was asleep, and she started doing the same sorts of things, with her hands and her mouth. This time I really fought hard, but after a while I gave up and let her do what she wanted, too. From then on the two of them came into my room a lot. Sometimes I made them go away, other times I didn't."

The storm hadn't let up, and flashes of lightning came and went.

"Those two girls had the original lease on the apartment, and all the roommates they brought in were like them. They would test every roommate, and if she wasn't that type they'd make her move out. All my roommates were that kind of girl. Do you remember why Yunru moved out? Because she found a boyfriend. Because she turned normal. Once they found out I was seeing you, they all turned against me. I didn't mind, though. There was nothing they could do to me. Remember that party they had? It was a lesbian party."

"So that's why there were only girls there." This was the first comment I had made since Keyi started talking.

"They knew I wanted to invite you, and they fought with me about it. I got mad. And just then my dad happened to get sick, so I just said, Fine, to hell with all this, I won't be here for the party, and I went back to Tainan."

"It sounds like you cared about them a little, though."

"Yeah, I did. At the time I was pretty upset. I could have just hung out with you and avoided the party that way, but instead I went all the way to Tainan."

"Why didn't you move out earlier?"

"You've got me there. That's exactly what's been bothering me. I guess some part of me didn't want to leave them."

"Did they keep coming into your room at night?"

"Not for a year. It was the same thing that happened with the old men when I was twelve. I just stood up to them. I said, If you come after me again, I'll move out. The fine arts girl who had come in the first time said I couldn't leave. She said she'd die if she could never see me again."

"But now you've finally moved out."

"All because of you, Su Qi."

"I had no idea I was anyone's rival. They were okay with you leaving?"

"The rest of them were fine, but the original fine arts girl cried like the world was coming to an end. She got down on her knees and begged me to stay. I felt like we were married and I'd betrayed her."

"So you moved out because of me?"

"You could say that. But notice that I didn't say I'm in love with you. You're a very difficult person, you know. If you'd shown me some affection earlier, I might have moved out earlier. Su Qi, all this time we've been seeing each other, have you really never thought about even holding my hand? Even just as a silly little gesture, like if you thought I was about to slip and fall or something."

"Of course, I've thought about it. But I thought there'd be plenty of time for that later."

"You and your 'later.' Just now, if I hadn't taken the initiative, you would never have done this with me, would you?"

"That's not necessarily true. It's just that this was my first time. I didn't know what I was doing."

"Tell me you don't look down on me now."

"How could I ever look down on you? The very first time I heard you sing, I thought you were a goddess from heaven. Now, if anything, you've ascended to even higher heights in my mind. You're even more unreachable."

"Do you know how I got rid of the little prince?"

"You told him all your secrets?"

"Of course! At first he didn't believe me, but then we went to look for those old men. We looked for a long time, and it turned out that only one was still alive. Then he believed me. He'd been pursuing me for so long, he was really unhappy to hear about this, and he said he was going to press charges against the old man. I told him not to. Just to get him mad, I told him I'd been okay with it all along."

"You shouldn't say things like that! What if he told other people?"

"I could tell he'd never have the guts to. In any case, though, he's helped us out a lot. I told him I'd pay him back all the money bit by bit."

"So that's why you're trying to earn money like your life depended on it."

"Remember when I told you I had a sentence I could say to get rid of any boy who was after me?"

"I get it now. You tell them you're a lesbian. Do they believe you?"

"Even if they don't believe me, there's nothing they can do about it. All right, Su Qi. You just told me this was your first time, but still. You're usually so elegant and polished, but just now you were so rough and wild. You weren't like yourself at all. Why is that?"

I told her everything I had never told her about my home life, omitting only the parts about Chunxi. My account included all the recent events.

"No wonder you were such an animal. You've spent the whole summer watching girls run around half-naked."

"That has nothing to do with this!"

"Oh, so you won't admit it? You really hurt me tonight. Now it's time for a little retributive justice."

Keyi picked up the candle at the head of the bed and held it so that a drop of hot wax fell onto my chest.

"That's no big deal." I tried to ignore the pain.

"So you're a masochist, are you?" Keyi let another drop of wax drip onto my chest.

This time, I made a point of screaming.

"Are you done showing off now? You know, Su Qi, I've told you all those things about myself, but you haven't tried to comfort me at all."

"Everything you told me about is in the past. You might as well just forget about it. How am I supposed to comfort you?"

"Are you up for a third time? It looks like that hot wax got you excited."

"How many times will it take to make you feel like you're normal?"

"Shut up. Or else I'll let some wax fall on you right there." Keyi held the candle above my groin.

Chapter 27

Early in September, my mother told me that a gardening magazine was going to publish photographs of her labyrinthine garden. The photographer even went up in a hot-air balloon so that he could capture it in its entirety. My mother said that when she was showing the magazine reporters around the garden she had noticed that certain spots were overgrown with weeds and that in those places the garden looked as rank and wild as it used to. I told her I thought that was probably for the best and that she shouldn't bother trying to clean up those areas unless the growth was really out of control. She felt the same way: she said that the prime of the garden's life had already come and gone and that at this point it was a place more corrupt than comely, more sluggish than heroic, more lewd than dignified. It would never again bear any fruit or flowers more lovely than those weeds, and so the best thing to do was to let it return to its wild state, to the destruction that nature had arranged for it.

Only the garden's death could bring the possibility of a new life for it. My mother told me that I should try to make it back for another visit if I could, because the demise of our Garden of Eden was coming. I thought about my mother, seated on her swing, as radiant as a falling star, as dignified as the Blessed Virgin, flipping at will through her Bible. She was not a traditional religious believer by any means. When she was ten, she had gone with her grandmother to church, and the kindly face of the auburn-haired, blue-eyed Western missionary had made her think that he was Jesus' new incarnation. Every night, her grandmother used to sit by her bed and read her a section from the Bible, just like a Buddhist monk chanting his scriptures, and that would lull my mother to sleep quickly. Only after she moved to Borneo, and before she immersed herself in her labyrinthine garden, did my mother get interested in reading the Bible on her own, driven to it by loneliness and boredom. She had gone to church a few times with some other rich men's wives, but then she had stopped, because the priest had tried to force her to go to confession once a week and she was neither willing to lie nor used to exposing her deepest secrets to a stranger. Then, when I was four years old, my mother had begun going to church again, and she would always bring me with her. I remember seeing the illustrations of the stations of the cross from the book of Matthew on the church wall for the first time and thinking, as I leaned against my mother, that the eight-month-old little girl who was still growing in her belly was as pure a creature as the baby Jesus in the manger. I remember looking up at my mother and seeing her, with lowered head and eyes, staring at me while she listened to the sermon. That was the first time I realized that my mother's eyes, shining kindly down upon me, were as radiant as a falling star and that her full, solid, gypsum-like bosom was as dignified as the figure of the Blessed Virgin. In my memories, my mother at church is always either sporting a swollen belly or holding my infant sister; thus, even though my memories are cloudy, I have to figure that she stopped going to church for good after my sister died. As much as she enjoyed reading the Bible, she only ever discussed its content with me once in her entire life. That was after she had struck my father's face with the crucifix, when she had called me over to her bedside. After I had finished sucking at her breast, she had given me the bloodstained crucifix and told me to wash it for her. I saw that blood had stained half of the cross and half of Jesus' body, and the story told in the stations of the cross on the church wall flashed into my mind. When I looked at the blood on the palms of my own hands, I recalled with special clarity the image of Jesus' pierced hands and feet. I turned on the bath faucet and washed the cross; I scrubbed the body of the afflicted Christ and my own hands with soap until both were redolent of the sweet fragrance. My mother hung the crucifix on the window lattice to dry, then told me to sit down and started reading aloud from the Bible. I noticed that she had hung a new crucifix around her neck. At the time, I was only six; I don't remember anything about the content of what she read.

My mother's forty minutes of chatter on that international phone call made me remember all this. She told me that all her relentless burning of blossoms in the garden had been her attempt to create a swath of pure land, just as she had come to Borneo with my father in the hopes of finding a paradise on earth, never dreaming that her "pure land" would become the dominion of hedonism and debauchery or that her "paradise on earth" would turn out to be a land planted with the seeds of misery. We live in a savage world, a carnivorous world, my mother said. Creatures like us are frail in our kindness, beside the robust violence of arrogant lions, avaricious jackals, spiteful snakes, indolent hogs, gluttonous crocodiles, lascivious monkeys, acrimonious nepenthes. We are as nervous and naive as fawns as we tiptoe past their sharp teeth. We watch as those around us slowly make a habit of squabbling and betraying, as one or several among them succeeds in subjugating all the rest, because of arrogance or spite or indolence. Only when we are about to die do we finally realize that our own sweet fawns' faces also sport lions' teeth, that we, too, have claws like the jackals, that the seed of more hogs and snakes and monkeys and crocodiles has been sown in our blood. Then my mother's tone of voice changed entirely, and she said, "Since your father died, I haven't felt much like working in the garden. It was only because of him that I threw my heart and soul into the garden for ten whole years."

I didn't understand what she meant by that. I summoned up my courage and asked her, "Mom, are you sad that Dad died?"

"I am." She hesitated a little. "My life has lost all meaning now."

I didn't respond to that. I still didn't understand what she was trying to say.

"I'm angry," my mother said. "Why did he have to die so soon?"

She offered no further explanation. Before we hung up, I asked her, "Has the chief minister come to visit yet?"

"He hasn't. Your father waited his entire life for him to come."

"And how's Uncle Lin?"

"He's lost his mind. He treats those girls of his like animals."

I got another call from my mother three days later. She had started seeing my little sister crawling around in the tree house, she told me, but whenever she climbed up to the tree house my sister would disappear. One time, as soon as my mother got to the top of the ladder, my sister fell out of the tree house and drifted slowly through the air like an inflatable doll until she hit a tree branch that punctured her back and sent the air leaking out of her. Then she had shrunk until she was nothing but a semitransparent film that disappeared as soon as it hit the ground. My mother had also seen my sister in the dim reaches of the garden and in the house, coming toward her with her arms outstretched. My mother would lower her head and see that in her own hand she held my sister's detached hand, spotted with dark blood. Also, my mother said, she had seen the swing swinging back and forth on its own, going higher with each arc. No one was on the swing; there was nothing and no one around for miles. My mother knew that my sister was the one swinging, because she could smell the gushing breast milk that she remembered from the days when she had swung with my sister years ago.

"You miss her, Mom, that's all. Those are just hallucinations," I said. "I've had hallucinations like that, too."

My mother acted as if she hadn't heard me. She went on, saying that a tree made of human flesh was growing in the garden. She said that the red of real blood showed through its white skin, that its body was muscular, that it had hair that blew in the wind, and that in place of fruit it produced living, moving, laughing, crying babies. But my father had come and cut down the babies with an aboriginal dagger. He had cut into their bellies so that their guts came tumbling out.

My mother had also seen my father with a woman in white clothes. She had seen the two of them turn into a pair of swans and frolic in the river. Then she had seen my father and another young girl turn into white cranes and build themselves a nest high up in a tree.

"What's the matter with you, Mom?" I said. "You've got to stop letting your imagination run wild."

I got my third phone call from her another two days after that, on a Wednesday night. I been chauffeuring Keyi home on her bike from the bar where she had been performing. Halfway to her place, she had told me she didn't want to go home but wanted to spend the night with me instead. So I had brought her back to my place, and she had thrown herself into my arms as soon as we got through the door. The intensity of her passion took me by surprise. It had been more than a week since our first encounter; we had seen each other only twice in that interval, and both times I had been distracted by worry about my mother. I gave Keyi a frank account of everything my mother had been saying, and she replied that she wouldn't have expected that my father's death would be such a heavy blow for my mother. I said that it probably wasn't that simple and explained to her that since my sister died my parents had been like strangers, that my father had asked nothing of my mother except that she make herself look glamorous and show up on time for his parties, that my mother had asked nothing of my father except that he let her do whatever she wanted with the garden, that essentially neither had had any other use for the other. Keyi then asked if my parents had continued having sex after my sister died, and I said there was no way, that after my mother attacked my father with her crucifix he never set foot in her bedroom again. The two of them had eaten dinner together like two animals who had come together from their separate territories to water at the same pond. Of course, it didn't help matters much that my father had his fill of other women, so that my beautiful, gentle mother must have held as little appeal for him as a piece of fruit that hung high above the head of a sated carnivore.

Keyi asked me if I had seen my father with other women. I told her about the encounter on the swing that I had witnessed, in enough detail to make it clear that my father's ability to pull off such a feat so adeptly was the result of ample practice. My mother had known about this before I did, I said, so it was no wonder that she didn't hesitate in granting me permission to destroy that swing and build a new one.

Then the two of us analyzed my mother's recent behavior. Keyi said that I should have seen through my mother a long time ago, given that she was still breast-feeding me when I was ten. I told her that I was the person I was today precisely because I had been inundated with my mother's milk and the repressed bile it contained.

Later that night, as I was kissing in my routine order Keyi's ears, forehead, eyebrows, nose, and mouth, the telephone rang. Keyi told me to ignore it, but I said, "It might be my mother."

"Where have you been? I've been trying to call you." My mother's voice sounded a bit frantic.

"I've been out with a friend," I said. "Is everything all right, Mom?"

My mother said that it had all started when she found ten piles of animal bones in the garden. The skeletons of several large bearded pigs were among them, and she had begun to worry that a carnivore had built a lair somewhere in the garden. And these past few nights she had had dreams about Chunxi's mother, about the view of her back as she stared into the garden. She had been hearing ear-shattering roars coming from the garden. When she investigated, she found giant animal droppings and the prints of giant paws, muddled and yet somehow unmistakable, and then it finally dawned on her that one of the two Malay tigers my father had set loose in the garden years ago was still alive in there. They had never managed to hunt down the one that fled into the jungle. It must have come back to the garden after knocking about the wider world for a while, and it must have been living in the garden for some time already. That would explain why Lin Yuan rarely let his animals roam free in there anymore. Probably Lin Yuan knew about the tiger. And that was why he spent whole days patrolling the garden with his electric prod and his hunting rifle and why he got flustered and anxious every time his virgins went into the garden. My mother had examined the bones, droppings, and paw prints, and she had concluded that the tiger must have been living there for at least a year or two. Its roars were powerful and unfettered. Its paws made prints in the dirt that were firm and sharp. Its droppings were plump and hefty. Like the mythical dragon king, it would not appear to human eyes, but still the fullness of its existence was readily apparent. My mother knew the ecosystem of the garden as well as the back of her hand, and yet until now even she hadn't been aware of the presence of this ghoul in the place of her life's work. For the first time, she felt frightened by and estranged from the garden that she had always loved the way a mother loves her own child. To me, her son, she said over and over again that the time for its destruction had arrived. The droppings of that carnivorous beast, the rotting bones it had left behind from its feedings, and its influence on the entire ecological chain of the garden had confounded my mother's ability to understand the garden through smell and sound. She could no longer rely on her senses when she walked through it; nothing was left of the smells and sounds she knew from before. Still, though, her senses themselves were as keen as they had ever been, and toward dusk the day before she had smelled the reek of fresh blood emanating from the garden. She had made her way into the garden, following that smell, and eventually she had seen the tiger, munching on a barking deer against a backdrop of blood-red flowers and evening clouds. The fresh blood of its prey formed a necklace around its neck and dotted its entire body like tiny flames; its gorgeous striped coat was infused with the hues of sin. It stayed motionless when it saw my mother approaching and only stared at her. Its protective coloring allowed it to camouflage itself against the garden and the sunset. Sometimes my mother could see it, and then sometimes she couldn't. It adjusted its posture again with each step she took.

"The tigers both died a long time ago, Mom," I said. "One was shot in the garden, and Father and the rest of them skinned the other one out in the jungle."

"No, no," my mother said. "We only have one tiger skin hanging in our house."

"And the other one's at Uncle Lin's house. Go to his house, you can see it."

"That can't be. I saw the tiger. I heard it. I smelled it."

"You have to take it easy, Mom. You've worn yourself out."

"Why is Lin Yuan always carrying around his rifle, then?"

"He hasn't been carrying his rifle, Mom. He just has two electric prods, and sometimes he carries an aboriginal dagger or a club or that sort of thing."

"You don't believe me, Su Qi, do you?"

"I believe you, Mom; it's just that what you saw was an illusion. It's spooky in that garden. It makes people hallucinate."

"Well, it doesn't matter anyway." Suddenly my mother's tone of voice changed entirely. "This Saturday is Lin Yuan's forty-fifth birthday. He's going to have a party in the garden. It'll begin in the afternoon and go on until late at night."

"You see? If there were a tiger in the garden, would Lin Yuan feel comfortable doing that?"

"It was my idea. I suggested it to him about ten days ago."

I was floored by this for a moment. "You're fine with letting all those people make a mess of your garden?"

"It doesn't matter. The party will be a big affair. Lin Yuan's been planning it for over a month, and all kinds of people will be there. I've heard the chief minister will be coming."

I let out a deep breath after I hung up the phone. Keyi was as affectionate as before, but my mother's tiger had entrenched itself in my mind and was not about to leave my thoughts so easily.

Chapter 28

On Friday night, Keyi told me that after her Thursday performance the manager of one of her bars had introduced her to some representatives of a well-known recording company, one of whom happened to be a famous folksinger. Apparently they had been impressed by Keyi's singing and looks and were interested in promoting her. The folksinger wanted to write a song for her to perform at an upcoming annual competition. I congratulated Keyi and compared her to the proverbial classical scholar who enters the capital to take the official examination after a decade of study and privation. Keyi quipped that it was more like entering the mortal world after a hard decade in the realm of ghosts. There were only about two weeks remaining before the competition, and Keyi was as nervous as she was excited. The folksinger had assured her that the judges were all his friends and that they wouldn't dare let her slip through without winning something; still, though, he had told her that she would have to report to him every day to practice. That night Keyi was as affectionate as ever.

I got a phone call from Lin Yuan on Sunday afternoon. The birthday party the day before had proceeded as planned until a fire broke out at about four in the afternoon. The southwest monsoon wind had been blowing fiercely. El Niño was still affecting the area, so everything was parched, and the garden was particularly torrid and combustible. The fire extended in all directions and engulfed the labyrinthine garden like roll upon roll of a giant tidal wave. Half of the two hundred guests either suffocated amid the smoke or were immolated in the garden. The fire truck arrived in time to save my house and the Lins' house, but both our gardens had burned to the ground in less than an hour. The firemen weren't able to contain the fire, and it had spread into the jungle. By the time Lin Yuan phoned me, it had already split into multiple divisions, like a marauding army, and gone raging off into the inland countryside.

"Is Mom okay?" I asked.

"Your mother's fine, but she's not very stable emotionally. Everyone's very busy right now, Su Qi. You're going to have to come home to help me take care of your mother."

"I'll come back tomorrow. Hey, is the chief minister all right?"

"The old fellow wasn't scheduled to arrive until the evening." Lin Yuan's voice sounded a bit odd. "He escaped, the lucky devil."

Chapter 29

The firefighters had been able to save the houses from the fire only by cutting down all the trees around them and setting a few smaller diversion fires. The Su house stood like a glum fortress on the scorched earth, amid the hot dense vapors and billowing smoke, while the Lin house still looked like a splendid country villa; the two made for a striking contrast. All these years, the two houses had been covered by vegetation, and now, exhibited in their full nakedness, they seemed foreign to me. I couldn't quite believe that after living in that place for eighteen years I was only now, after a fire, seeing for the first time its air of desolation and destitution. I arrived at my own door at dusk on Monday and was greeted only by the flies circling enthusiastically overhead and lighting occasionally on the putrid animal corpses, the flesh of which they had already mostly stripped away. I guessed that the dutiful fire and rescue squads had already cleared away all the human corpses. The local press reported that the fire had taken ninety-six lives and that several dozen more were still fighting for their lives in the hospital, so the death toll might continue to rise. Since my father first built our house, it had been witness to only two deaths: the woman in white and Chunxi's mother (assuming one should not count my younger sister). Now there were too many wronged dead souls to keep track of, but it was hard to say who had wronged them. The pink sunset clouds, shrouded in hot vapors rising from the earth, made me think about my mother's tiger. A few black dogs were cavorting in the ashes, an owl was perched on a denuded tree branch, and bats had begun to set out on their group sorties from the eaves of our house. Normally, at this hour the house would have been surrounded by the happy sounds of birds and animals reuniting with their relatives at the end of the day, but now all was silent. My mother sat on the sofa in the parlor. She had a crucifix in her hand and her pocket Bible open on her knee. When she saw me, her brow furrowed into a kind expression, and she sat up straighter, which made her look all the more dignified. I half-knelt in front of my mother and let her look me up and down. She drew her index finger lightly across my lips and said, "Did you miss your mama?"

"I'll always miss my mama," I said. "When Uncle Lin told me the garden burned down, the first thing I thought of was you. Are you okay, Mom? You must have had quite a scare."

"Silly boy. Your mom's just fine," she said, winding her fingers through my hair. "Look, though. There's nothing left of the garden."

"That's not important. If you really can't live without your garden, I'll help you fix it up again, just like when I was little."

My mother looked at me and didn't say a word. Then her eyes moved to the window. "So many people died."

"Don't worry about them. You shouldn't dwell on this. It was an accident, that's what the newspapers said. Uncle Lin says he takes full responsibility."

"So many people died there. It's best that it stay a wasteland forever."

"Whatever you say."

"Qi, my little Qi, the tiger didn't die in the fire." My mother was still looking out the window. "I just saw him, from right here, walking around out there, and I saw him yesterday at sunset, too."

"I don't see any tiger." I followed with my eyes my mother's line of vision out the window. "You're mistaken."

"Every night at sunset he's there, out on that scorched land, looking at me. His coat is magnificent, just like a ball of fire."

"All I see out there are a few stray dogs."

"'Wildfires cannot consume the wild grasses; they grow tall when the next spring wind blows,'" my mother said abruptly, quoting the poem by Bai Juyi. "The fire couldn't kill it. The trees and the flowers are like that tiger. They'll come back to life again before too long, and they'll grow even thicker than before."

My mother spent all the next day inside with her crucifix in her hand, reading her Bible. I had to shout to get her attention. I said to her, "Mom, the print in that Bible is too small. It's got to be hard to read. I'll go buy you a new one." But when I put the new Bible down next to her, she kept her head buried in the old one. After that I said, "Mom, your hair's getting long. We should get it cut." My mother then sat there like a plant while the hairstylist tended to her hair with scissors and comb; her only reaction was to shake her head when the stylist suggested she get a perm for a more youthful look. Then the stylist said, "A lot of your hair has turned red, ma'am. Perhaps you'd like to dye it black." My mother furrowed her brow and shook her head again. When I looked at my mother's freshly cut hair, I noticed that in fact it was not jet-black any longer. As she looked at herself in the mirror, she seemed as severe as an empress dowager for a moment. At sunset I took her on a walk outside, hoping to cheer her up after all her days confined to the house and to rip out the roots of the terror that the idea of the tiger had planted in her heart. Her terror had grown into a tree; its leaves were lush and darkened half the Su house with their shade. My mother pointed to an artificial landscaped hill and said that the tiger had once made his home just behind it, like the sun as it encamps behind fleeting clouds at sunset, sending its radiance down to light up even the world's deepest, darkest crevices. She also pointed at a patch of greenery that had survived the fire but was now threatened by weeds and said that every time the tiger approached that place he would disappear as suddenly as a lantern is extinguished. By the fourth day of my visit, my mother refused even to go out walking with me anymore. That night, Lin Yuan finally found the time to come have dinner with us.

When the last rays of daylight shone on my mother's hair, I could see even more clearly how it was mottled with patches of red. Lin Yuan said that a visible red heat had surrounded and entered the house when the garden burned and that even those areas that weren't actually threatened by the fire still hadn't escaped the poisonous thermal vapors. "Look," Lin Yuan said, pointing to the orchids on the dining room table, "the petals are wilting, and the vase has started to crack. Your mother kept watch over those flames with courage and stamina for a whole afternoon, evening, and early morning, and that's why that beautiful head of hair of hers was scorched red in places. At the very least, we'll have to wait out the cool northeast monsoon winds and the rainy season before it will recover. As for that garden, though," Lin Yuan pointed out the window as he spoke, "people will be getting lost in there again before the month is out. In two or three months it will join up with the jungle, and in six it will be occupied by all the creatures that live in the jungle. The Dayaks and the Penan nomads will think it's part of the jungle, too, and will start hunting there. Biologists from all over the world will be doing ecological research there. Maybe that's why the authorities called this accident an act of God, because they saw it as just another one of the forest fires that break out here every summer. There's no way to contain that kind of fire once it starts. The fire that started in the labyrinthine garden is still burning, somewhere in the jungle." The sound of Lin Yuan's chewing dominated the dinner table and made me think of my father. My father used to talk to us only when his mouth was full of rich, fatty food; when his mouth was empty he never seemed to consider us worth a single sentence. Both men's voices had a structured firmness that came from a strong jawbone. Sometimes Lin Yuan looked at me, and sometimes he looked at my mother and the scorched earth outside the window. I could tell that he didn't particularly want us to respond.

The only thing the authorities could not understand was how high the number of casualties had been. Two more party guests had passed away in the ICU in the past two days. The guests who had managed to escape had explained that at the time everyone had been very drunk. The dead ones had completed their lives' journeys happy and confused, amid alcoholic revelry. When the southwest monsoon wind came rushing across the land and sky, carrying the fire and the smoke, the guests had raised thunderous shouts of appreciation, thinking that this was just another one of Lin Yuan's impromptu amusements. So they had raised their glasses and started singing and gone straight into the flames like moths. Before anyone knew it the flames were upon them, and still they didn't understand what was happening. The guests who were relatively alert saw the rot and sickness of the garden fuse with the perverse destructiveness of the fire, and just before they died they saw their own insubstantial souls drifting through a sea of flowers even as the ashes of their corporeal selves were scattering amid a sea of flame. Everyone who witnessed the chaos and terror knew that it was actually a miracle that half the guests had survived.

"Maybe you won't believe me, Su Qi," Lin Yuan said, looking suddenly at me, "but it was my virgins who led the survivors out of that inferno. They'd spent so much time in the garden that they knew their way around, so even when no one could see anything through all the smoke they were still able to find their way out, relying on their intuition alone. I don't understand it. They'd only been here a couple of weeks, but they knew their way around the garden better than me, and I've spent over a decade here."

"People raised in the jungle have that natural gift." I had finally found an opportunity to interrupt. "They're used to navigating by the stars."

"The police initially thought that they had started the fire as a prank," Lin Yuan said. "But they most certainly did not. Maybe because of the rumors that started, though, people have apparently given them a nickname: 'the little bolts of lightning who lit the Sus' dark garden on fire.'"

"Where are they now?"

"Two disappeared during the fire, and I still don't know what happened to them. I sent all the others home." Lin Yuan's expression as he gazed out the window was at times remarkably similar to my mother's. "What use do I have for them now? Now that this thing has happened, even the regular crowd will be scared to come around here, let alone the chief minister."

I was the first to leave the dinner table that night. Ten minutes later, when I passed through the dining room again, Lin Yuan was standing behind my mother and had put his hand on her shoulder. He had a pained expression on his face, and his lips kept moving. I had never seen him talk so softly or behave in such a guarded, gingerly manner before. My mother remained silent and kept looking out the window. Before long, Lin Yuan began to stroke her hair, and then he bent down and tried to kiss her on the forehead. But my mother stood up abruptly and began to clear the table, looking at me as she did so and saying, "Su Qi, entertain your Uncle Lin. I'll brew a pot of coffee for the two of you."

The sky full of stars was rich with some kind of meaning but held its accustomed silence; it seemed to me that in this respect it was very similar to the way I had been feeling recently. The experience of looking deep into a person's life was like reading a book too long to finish. It was already past seven. Lin Yuan and I sat out on the patio and looked up at the stars. The burned land was as feral and fertile as it had always been, and the jungle hovered just out of our range of vision. The light from the stars in the north shone down power-fully. Waves rolled forward in the ink green river that separated Malaysia from Brunei—it was Friday night, and I could almost hear the stentorian whistle from the ferry as it set out, carrying all specimens of humankind in our direction, and the sound of the engines of imported cars as their overfed and lusty passengers landed on our bank of the river, drowning out the cries of the jungle creatures and pressing on like a martial bugle into the region of my birth. The extravagant, imposing palaces of Brunei heralded their own blessed existence with songs and revelry that would last into the wee hours, while the great belly of the South China Sea held its silence and the far-off Chinese mainland transformed and fissured, amoebalike, under the microscope of the Ursa Major constellation. I loved the tropical landscape just as night descended; its very savagery inspired in me two extreme and opposite desires: either to crawl along the ground and moan with abandon or to take up a pen and write a few obscure and complex and strongly pictographic Chinese characters. Lin Yuan held a cigarette in his mouth for a long time before he finally lit it and took a puff as strong as the first breath of fresh air of a party guest who had just escaped from the fire. Then he started to tell me the secrets about our two families that had been kept hidden for years.

There were only two women my father ever loved. Ten years ago, the Communists had tried to extort money from him. They had sent the woman in white to collect his "donation" once a month. Soon my father had, on his own initiative, changed his monthly donation to biweekly and then to weekly, so that he could see the woman in white more often. And he kept increasing the amount, in the hopes of making her happy. Even all this, though, could not still my father's longing for her, and if the woman in white had not reluctantly refused, he certainly would have cast my mother out of the house and taken the woman in white as his wife instead. After the woman in white was killed by government guns, thanks to my unwitting revelation, my father was wracked with despair. He considered following the woman in white into the realm of the dead. But after two years of this, his longing for the woman had changed into hatred for the government and the military, and he conceived of a decadelong blueprint for revenge. He became a member of the Communist

Party, kept offering them secret donations, and maintained relations with them for over ten years. He began expending a great deal of effort and money on spectacular parties, because he wanted to attract to our house the high-ranking government officials who were working to exterminate the Communists. Then, when the time was right, in cooperation with other party comrades, he planned to capture all the henchmen who had slaughtered his beloved. He wanted to wipe out in one fell swoop all the Borneo politicians who had opposed the Communists. If everything had gone well, he might even have been able to engineer a full-fledged coup d'état. Even if things had gone badly, the worst that could have happened would have been for him to die along with his comrades. My father had calculated for every exigency and had put in place 90 percent of the arrangements; the only sticking point was that the chief minister, who controlled the state's military apparatus, had not yet made an appearance. The seeds of my father's hatred grew into something more lush and more corrupt by the day, much like the seeds planted in my mother's labyrinthine garden. As he waited out those ten years, he descended into a life of utter debauchery and unchecked lust that lasted right up until he and Lin Yuan, on one of their sex safaris, met the teenage girl idiot in a Dayak longhouse. The core of my father's soul was shaken in a way that can only be compared to the way he felt when he first met the woman in white. His intuition told him that this girl might be the woman's reincarnation, and because of this he resolved to spend his remaining years with her. He forgot all about the revenge that he had spent over a decade plotting.

"Do you remember the bastard that your mother had with the Dayak man?" Lin Yuan asked me.

I nodded.

"Your father was unfaithful to your mother, but he would not allow your mother to be unfaithful to him. Do you know what he did with her bastard?"

I said I didn't.

Lin Yuan smoked in silence. It was as if he wanted to take the words I had just uttered and mold them into a tangible object so that he could hold it in the palm of his hand and measure for himself its solidity and weight. I didn't understand why Lin Yuan would doubt my sincerity.

"He fed it to a wild animal," Lin Yuan said. "He fed it to a croco-dile, the same way we used the monkey the time he and I stole the crocodile egg."

"Does my mother know this?"

"Your mother finally realized it that night when your father and I were talking about the crocodile egg."

I remembered my mother's piercing scream that night. Lin Yuan swung his head around and looked at me.

"I'm ashamed to say that I had something to do with your father's treatment of your mother," he said.

Lin Yuan had only ever loved one woman in his life, and that was my mother. When he disappeared in the jungle for a month before moving to Borneo, he was actually being held hostage by the Com-munists. The Communists had hoped to extort money from his fam-ily back in Taiwan, with the help of my father, who at the time was already a fellow traveler. But once my father learned what was go-ing on, he had interceded with the Communists on Lin Yuan's be-half, and they had set Lin Yuan free.

"Your father understood all along that he would eventually go bankrupt plotting his revenge, and he hoped that I would assist him with my own money. Then, once his plan had been executed, he was supposed to let your mother and me go off together and never come back." Lin Yuan held each cigarette in his mouth for a long while before lighting it, and he plowed all his bodily might into each strong puff he took. "Your father had known for a long time that I loved your mother. He was very eloquent and passionate when he spoke to the Communists. He professed his fervent support for their prin-ciples. He promised them that his plot would bring pride and glory to all the Chinese in the region and that it would lead the state's var-ious ethnic groups into a utopia of peaceful coexistence. But in fact your father was just taking advantage of the Communists' fanati-cism to satisfy his private desires and hatreds. Most incredible of all is the fact that your father took the exact same preacherly tone with me when he tried to convince me to help him with his plot. He sounded so sincere and determined that I almost had trouble telling if he was serious or not."

My father had married my mother solely because of Lin Yuan. This story begins with the two men's earliest and most primitive sex safaris, back when they were in college. Behind all the enjoyment and pride that both of them obviously got out of their games of romantic pursuit, there lay a ferocious spirit of competition, a battle of overweening egos. Each of them was always trying to demonstrate his superior ability to the other, but they hadn't yet managed to determine a winner. Then, when he met my mother, Lin Yuan sunk to the level of an infatuated schoolboy, and my father did not fail to take advantage of this. My father realized that the most direct route to victory lay in wresting away the girl his competitor loved, and that was why he set out to move heaven and earth to win my mother, a girl in whom he himself had no real interest but who haunted Lin Yuan's soul and his dreams. My father pretended that he was besotted with her, too, and my mother was moved by him and surrendered to him. It wasn't until my sister and I were born that she realized what his actual motive had been.

After Lin Yuan promised to provide financial support for my father's plot, his first order of business was to immigrate to Borneo and move in next door to us. That was the easiest way for him to stay close to my mother. When he suggested that they build a walkway to connect the two houses, my father designed it for him, but in a humorous, almost derisive style, as if he wanted to warn Lin Yuan privately that, as long as his revenge was not yet complete, he had better not even think about touching so much as a hair on my mother's head. I thought about the almost Zen-like conversations my father and Lin Yuan used to have and wondered whether all their talk about "returning to primal and simple things" and "elevating and purifying the soul" might have been oblique references to my father's revenge plot and to Lin Yuan's far-fetched hopes.

"I couldn't wait any longer, Su Qi." Lin Yuan took a sip of the hot coffee my mother had made. "Your father's plot was so outrageous. Your mother and I might have been a pair of doddering old fools by the time the chief minister decided to grace us with his presence. While your father and his idiot girl were playing house in the jungle, I told the girl's fiancé where they were hiding out. And I was right there watching them as they fought to the death. Only after your father died did I realize just how intensely he had worshipped that idiot girl. They had been living together for six months, and yet he hadn't sullied her, even once. She was still a virgin."

Lin Yuan took another strong puff on his cigarette and paused before going on. "Three days passed before anyone else found them. During that time I slept with the idiot girl."

I watched a few fireflies zipping around just above our heads, and I thought about the fireflies that used to cluster in brilliant hordes every evening around the stream that separated the garden from the jungle.

"Your father's body was still intact when I left the girl. I don't know how on earth his head vanished."

I thought about how my father had recorded in pictures his forty-seven days in the jungle, his angel girl, her humble animal servants, the celebratory flowers and fruit—my father had never in his life been as happy as he had been then.

"Do you despise me, Su Qi?"

I didn't respond.

"You could say that all he did to me was steal the girl I loved—not that that wouldn't have been enough to make me hate him to my very marrow—but in fact it was more than that. He's had me under his thumb my entire life. I blame him entirely for how Chunxi's mother died and for the fact that Chunxi is now in a coma."

I remained silent.

"If you understood your mother, maybe you wouldn't despise me. I just wanted to help your mother get what she wanted earlier than she would otherwise."

My mother had never loved Lin Yuan, and she never would, even after my father died. Lin Yuan understood this, but all he wanted was to spend the rest of his life near her, "like the last rays of the sun as it sets." He also wanted to honor the gentlemen's agreement that he and my father had had and see to it that my father's great revenge plot was executed. But the fire in the garden had not only saved the chief minister forever, it had also destroyed the revolutionary dreams of the Communists who remained in the jungle. Still, in a way, a portion of my father's plan had been carried out—several high-ranking government officials had been among the fire's victims.

Not long after my sister and half-brother died, my mother had started devoting all her attention to cultivating her labyrinthine garden. She absorbed the spirit of destruction and rebuilding from the local culture of burning blossoms. At my father's extravagant parties, she had observed the absurdity of human nature and had found her own opportunity therein. She had borne in silence the pollution of her labyrinthine garden by my father and his guests, and, like my father, she had silently developed a plan for revenge over the course of a decade. Day and night she labored to design an intricate labyrinthine fortress where anyone could easily lose his way, an effective rival to the jungle. Once she had completed this terrible trap, in which a person could spend an entire lifetime searching in vain for a way out, my mother planned to set the garden on fire while one of my father's parties was going on, immolating both the putrefying vegetation and the corrupt and fallen human beings within, my father included. At times my mother had wavered over whether or not to actually carry out this plan, but the licentious and unbridled acts that kept taking place in her garden, coupled with my father's persistent animal cruelty, shored up her resolve. She had no idea that my father had his own revenge plot. My father's sudden death had initially left her feeling discouraged; the greatest regret of her life was that she would not be able to watch him die as a result of her own decadelong effort. But in the end she had pulled herself together and done what she had long wanted to do. Burning that defiled garden may well have meant more to her than burning the people who had defiled it.

So the fire was, it turned out, an act of revenge that my mother had been designing for years. She had thought over and over again about how to trap people in the garden, so that they would have no way out. She had designed the winding paths and chosen the place where the fire would start with an eye toward the direction of the seasonal monsoon winds, to ensure that the garden would burn to the ground within seconds. If those young virgins hadn't interfered, no one would have escaped.

"Myself included," Lin Yuan said. "The strange thing was, when your mother confessed to me, I wasn't the least bit surprised. I even did everything I could to cover up for her, in spite of the fact that she's never cared whether I lived or died."

Lin Yuan kept on smoking, with the same peculiar motions. He seemed to be contemplating something for a long while before he spoke again.

"While the fire was still burning, two of my virgins told me that they had seen your mother set the fire. I took them into the jungle, and I killed one of them. The other managed to get away. Your mother doesn't know about this. For a while the authorities suspected that the Communists had set the fire, because one of the guests had seen a stranger in the garden. That stranger was a Communist comrade I had invited to the garden in preparation for our attack. But the cops couldn't find any proof that he was involved. Were it not for this, your mother's plan would have gone off almost perfectly."

"Who was the girl who got away?"

"Her name was Amma. The one I killed was her sister. I've already got some people on my payroll out looking for her. She's the only person I'm worried about."

Chapter 30

Two days later, an inconspicuous-looking imported car pulled up in front of our house. The driver got out and walked around to open the back door. A man with a thin beard, wearing a batik shirt and white pants, emerged from the back seat. The man rang our doorbell with a finger that bore an emerald ring.

I had been awaiting this gentleman's arrival for some time. On that night two days before, Lin Yuan had told me that someone would be coming to see me, but he had refused to tell me who. As it turned out, the visitor was the man who had had his wineglass knocked out of his hand by the wing of an owl while he was talking to Chunxi at one of my father's parties.

It was past four in the afternoon when the man arrived at our house. Two of Lin Yuan's green parrots flew around his head and then came to rest on the railing of the gate and did convincing imitations of the doorbell the man had just rung. After the fire, Lin Yuan had set loose all the wild animals in his menagerie, but the birds and the herbivores had not wanted to leave, and I frequently spotted them wandering around our house or the Lins'. Right after he passed through the gate, the man pulled out a handkerchief to wipe away the sweat on his face. His cheeks were as white and dry as the handkerchief, and both emitted a pleasant fragrance. In fact, only ten seconds or so had elapsed from the time the man left his air-conditioned car to the time he entered our air-conditioned house, not nearly enough time to make him sweat. But there he was, pulling out a handkerchief and patting his forehead with it, then carefully rubbing the handkerchief across first his left cheek and then his right, as if this was a required formality. I had only seen him before at the parties. Now, sizing him up in broad daylight, I realized that his skin was even whiter and softer than I had thought, just like the skin of an albino beauty snake; that the lines of his thick brows and red lips were tight and clean; and that the space between his eyes and forehead had a vexed, disturbed look that reminded me of the woman in white who always brought torrential rain with her. The superfluous elegance with which he daubed at his face and the daintiness of his fingers made all of him shimmer with the luster of moonlight and femininity, like some variety of nocturnal animal.

I sensed somehow that something in this man's blood connected him to the gloomy and hermetic world of the Sus.

"I am Mohammed Sallah." The man held out his right hand. "That name may be strange to you. In the past, I used a false name when I came to your house. Even Mohammed Sallah is not my full name. My full name is so long that sometimes even I cannot remember all of it. You may call me Sallah. Do you remember me?"

"Of course I remember you." I shook his hand. "An owl attacked you once. Another time you twisted your ankle dancing. You got sick to your stomach a few times. And we also played a game of chess together once, right?"

"Not just one game," the man said. "Three games. Each of us won one game, and the third was a tie."

"I think we may also have played the guitar and sung Beatles songs with some other guys. Do you still remember my name?"

"Of course I remember. You are Su Huan's son, Su Qi. I always addressed you by that name."

I invited the man to sit down and brought out a pot of coffee that I had brewed myself. Unlike most local people, he did not add a large spoonful of condensed milk to his coffee. Instead, he used his spoon to break a sugar cube carefully into two halves and mixed one half into the coffee. After a small sip of coffee, the man offered his condolences about my father. Then he expressed shock and sorrow over the tragedy in the garden.

"It's a good thing you weren't here when it happened," I said.

"How do you know I was not here?"

"That wouldn't make any sense. I've only ever seen you at night, so I had the impression that you were someone who only goes out after dark and so weren't likely to be at an afternoon party. In fact, right now I'm having a hard time getting used to seeing you in daylight."

"It is easier for me to go out in the evenings. In a moment I will explain to you why," the man said. "In fact, I was not here. After Chunxi's accident, I came here very rarely."

I was slightly surprised to hear him say this. Lin Yuan had only let a few close acquaintances know about Chunxi's situation. And this man in front of me now had only ever come to a few of my father's parties.

"I am the son of the reigning sultan of Brunei," the man said. "My relatives frequently disguised themselves as commoners and attended parties at your esteemed home, and I, once in a while, would come with them. Your mother, your father, and their good friend Mr. Lin all know about this, but they have never revealed my identity to anyone else."

I nodded.

"I began coming to your house perhaps four years ago," the man said. "In February 1975. It was the first night of the year by your traditional Chinese calendar. That was when I met Chunxi for the first time, and she and I talked for over an hour. If that owl had not ruined everything, we might have kept talking until daybreak."

I recalled the uninspired conversation I had had with Chunxi that night. "It was me who ruined everything," I said.

"I loved Chunxi the very first time I saw her. I cannot describe to you how strongly I felt about her. I am no poet, and I am no expert on affairs of the heart. Please forgive how crude and direct I am being." He was awkwardly rubbing his ring. "From that day on, coming to your house was the most important thing in my life. I still remember how many times I saw Chunxi, and what we said each time, and what we did. Su Qi, those were truly the happiest days of my life."

With this said, the man suddenly pulled out his handkerchief and wiped his forehead. He unfolded it, and then, turning it inside out, he folded it back into the same rectangular shape. Once he had put the handkerchief back, he took a small, casual sip of coffee. Maybe these actions were just intended to lighten the mood a little.

"Between that lunar New Year and the July when Chunxi and her family came to stay at your house again, I saw her seven times," the man said. "Each time we met, I grew even more certain that I wanted Chunxi to be my wife."

"Wasn't it more than seven times?" I said. "The year after that, that would be in February 1976, Chunxi spent another lunar New Year here. Then that July she and her mother moved here, and she was here right up until the accident in December. You're saying you didn't see her any of those times?"

"That is exactly why I've come here to talk to you today. Do you still remember Chunxi's twin sister?"

"Of course," I said. "She has a sister named Chuntian. But I've never met her."

"You are wrong about that. After 1976 Chunxi only came here once, and she was here only seven days before that terrible accident happened. What I mean is, the person you saw in February '76, the girl who wanted you to take her to see the dogfight in the garden, and the one who moved here that July, that was Chuntian. It was not Chunxi."

"How can that be?"

"I didn't know this until after the fact myself. Here is how it all happened. After Chunxi and I met in 1975, we were deeply in love. But we were both too bashful, and we both kept trying to sound out the other and never expressed our feelings directly. I blame myself entirely for that. In February '76, Chunxi's health took a turn for the worse, and she was hospitalized. But she still cared for me, and she asked her sister to maintain the relationship in her place. After that, her health did not improve until December '76, after they had buried her mother's ashes in Tai'an. The girl you saw in February '76, and again starting in July, was Chuntian, not Chunxi. Think about it for a moment. Given the kind of girl Chunxi was, would she really have asked you to take her to see a dogfight? I've also heard that you took her on a hike in the jungle. With her health as it was, would she have been able to withstand such a thing?"

"Why didn't Chuntian ever tell us the truth?"

"I was completely duped, too," the man said. "Even now I cannot be sure whether the one I loved was Chuntian or Chunxi. Perhaps you are facing the same quandary? But one thing I am certain of is that I was the one Chunxi loved and you were the one Chuntian loved. The problem is that neither Chunxi nor Chuntian could ever know how each of us felt about each of them. Chuntian may have known that you cared for her, but she must have suffered from not knowing whether your feelings were actually for Chunxi, the girl you had met first, because all the time you thought she was Chunxi. Think about it. On the one hand, Chuntian was pretending to be Chunxi so that she could carry on a love affair with me—if 'love affair' is the appropriate phrase. On the other hand, she was in love with you but could not reveal to you her true identity. If you had been in that situation, how would you have felt?"

"How do you know Chuntian was in love with me?"

"In December '76, after the Lins buried Chunxi's mother in Tai'an, Chunxi was finally able to come back here. Chuntian had told her that she could see me crossing the river on the ferry from your tree house. So that day, when your father was planning to hold one of his parties, she climbed up there before nightfall with a pair of binoculars, hoping to find out in advance whether I would be at the party. And, sadly, that was the night she fell. Everything I have just said is what Chuntian surmised after the fact. Of course, only Chunxi herself knows why she climbed up to the tree house alone. But perhaps she will never have a chance to tell us. Once I learned that I would not be able to see Chunxi anymore, I spoke to Mr. Lin and revealed my identity to him. One time, I went to Mr. Lin's house to see Chunxi—at the time you were already off studying in Taiwan—and I ran into Chuntian there. Chuntian confessed everything to me then and told me how much Chunxi had cared for me. It made me weep, Su Qi."

The man—or maybe I should say the prince—brought out his handkerchief to wipe his brow yet again. A black-and-white striped hornbill came sweeping past the window and landed on a dry, charred tree, emitting a sound like an infant crying. It immediately began pecking at the bark, and it carved out several tortuous, uneven holes. It was destroying the tree with remarkable speed.

"Chunxi went through two years of treatment, but there was still no sign that she was going to wake up. So I asked Mr. Lin if I could take care of her from then on. Chunxi was never sent to America. In 1978—that was two years after you left for Taiwan—I secretly brought her into the palace. She receives the best medical care available, and she will be able to live out the remainder of her life with me. Su Qi, I assure you, just as I assured Mr. Lin, that I will watch over her for the rest of my days, until she wakes up. And if she never wakes up, I will still look upon her as my wife."

I realized that tears were glistening in the prince's eyes, and I averted my gaze.

"The story about her going to America for treatment is what I told Mr. Lin to tell the rest of the world. I need to keep this a secret, because of my position and because of palace rules. Besides my closest relations in the royal family, only Chuntian, Mr. Lin, your mother, and I know about this. I apologize for hiding it from you at first." The prince shifted his gaze away from me, too. "There are many unpleasant, even lurid, rumors about what goes on in our palace. But no matter what happens, that sort of thing will never affect Chunxi. In general, the palace is a peaceful place and a lonesome, introverted place. Chunxi can recuperate there as well as she could anywhere. As for her changing places with her sister, both Mr. and Mrs. Lin knew about that all along. They were the girls' own parents. They would have known even if the girls had looked more alike than they did."

"So there's been no sign that Chunxi might wake up?"

"There hasn't been," the prince said. "She is still sleeping like a baby. The second time she and I met, she told me that she often dreamt of herself in a deep sleep in her mother's womb, when her body was not yet fully developed but still she was driven by a mad desire to come out into this world a little early. Sometimes, when I speak or read aloud to her, I sense that her eyelids and her lips are moving. Maybe she will wake up someday."

The prince handed me his calling card. Outside, an Oriental magpie-robin opened its beautiful, imposing wings on the railing of the patio and exposed them to the sun. A kingfisher was perched not far away from it.

"You are welcome to come to the palace to visit Chunxi any time. You may reach me at this number."

I took the card. "Where is Chuntian now?"

"That is precisely why I came to see you." The prince brought his gaze back to me. "Su Qi, after Chunxi's accident, you went to Taiwan and stayed there for three years. Chuntian may think that you have forgotten her, and that could be why she does not plan to see you again. She's come to the palace twice. Both times she seemed to have something on her mind that she could not say. She made herself a copy of the cassette tapes you recorded for Chunxi. Are you in love with Chuntian, Su Qi?"

When Lin Yuan, my mother, and I saw the prince off, it was already nearly six. The raucous cries of birds around my house evoked the labyrinthine garden's former glory. My mother questioned the prince in detail about how things had gone with the traditional Chinese doctor she had recommended to him for the old injury to his ankle, and the prince let her know that his ankle was almost entirely healed, though he still felt the pain now and then when he engaged in vigorous exercise.

"I have been told, ma'am, that on the afternoon of the fire you were asking whether I was there or not," the prince said just before he got into the car. "I wanted to let you know, ma'am, that I do not generally go out during the day. But I appreciate your concern nonetheless."

"I knew that you didn't go out during the day. But I was worried just in case," my mother said softly. "Wildfires start easily in weather like this. If you had by some odd chance come to that party, I would have warned you about that in advance. I would have told you how you could get out of the garden. But I never really thought that anything like that would actually happen."

"Thank you for all your concern, ma'am," the prince said. "I knew that you knew who I was four years ago, that time when you bandaged my hand."

"The world outside the palace isn't as simple as you may have imagined." I was almost jealous of the gentleness in my mother's voice. "Particularly our family. I just didn't want you to get hurt in any way."

When the prince's car was about a hundred meters away from our house, four more black cars pulled up behind it, and the caravan headed north and disappeared.

Chapter 31

Two weeks later, I was on a plane to Taiwan flipping through the new issue of the gardening magazine that had published a story about my mother's labyrinthine garden. The bird's-eye photographs had been taken from the hot-air balloon and showed with perfect clarity the anthill-like complexity of the garden's structure. They had been taken at the garden's most lush and overgrown period, the period when my mother had let the weeds run roughshod over it. These photographs only thwarted my desire to get a complete, integrated image of my mother's garden. In fact, portions of the garden as shown in those pictures did not look too different from the Borneo jungle outside the airplane window. Maybe I would never again see the perfect garden of my imagination. After I had finished reading the article, up there in the plane, the garden of my imagination had sunk only deeper into a morass of smoke, as if it were a virgin paradise that had never actually been explored. I inspected the pictures again and again, from all angles. I felt like I had when I was little, when I had felt like a boat drifting out of control over the relentless whirlpools and undertows of the azure sea. I remembered that day when I had sat in the tree house looking down at the garden and seen my mother like a roulette ball, leaping about and never coming to rest amid the pattering fragments that made up the kaleidoscope of the garden. The paths through the garden looked, at first glance, like cracks in a sheet of safety glass, spreading wherever they pleased, but in fact my mother had held firm control over all of them. They reminded me of the blue veins that would stand out on my mother's forehead, evidence of her fearsome will and her vengeful intentions. They made me think about sucking as a child at my mother's mysterious mammary channels, swollen and extending in their fullness toward the ultimate edges of the vast universe. I remembered my mother sitting at the window just off the patio, listening to my father and Lin Yuan discuss old times and gradually rotting away into a putrid empress dowager.

I examined each tree carefully. The ripe fruit that hung thickly on the trees made me remember my mother's bosom, ringed round with pythons, not a place for little monkeys and mice to venture on a whim. Those pythons and their profusion of vivid colors made me think of the tree of terror that had been planted in my mother's heart by a tiger.

I started to think that some of the paths resembled the brush-strokes of Chinese characters. It was as if my mother had been using her shovel and hoe as a brush for over ten years. Flowers and leaves were her ink, the pristine ground was her canvas. Stroke by stroke, she had sketched the things that were in her heart: a perfect palace of enchantment and a death trap.

The photographs taken from the tree house made my thoughts follow my mother's broad-brimmed straw hat through the flowers like a flying carpet. My carpet flew and paused and flew again. It disappeared for a time, and then it ascended to the bird's-eye angle of a hot-air balloon.

I saw my mother's naked body exposed on the tree house in the shape of a crucifix. My tiny convulsive cock swelled up to the size of a doorknob and lingered beneath the tree house. My father's white golf balls went flying past the fig trees. Lin Yuan was wandering around with his electric prods, pursuing whatever prey he could find. Arrogant lions, avaricious jackals, spiteful snakes, indolent hogs, gluttonous crocodiles, lascivious monkeys, and acrimonious nepenthes drifted around the garden. I saw what seemed to me a barbarous world overrun by carnivores.

I grew quite certain that I saw a few Chinese characters covered by the lush flowers and flourishing weeds. Maybe my mother had indeed designed the paths of her labyrinthine garden to form characters.

Then I finally read the sentence with which the journalist concluded the article: "The garden is divided into seven zones, and the plants in each zone are arranged in the shape of a giant Chinese character, but the mistress of the house would not reveal what the characters were."

After that, I inspected the seven zones even more intently, and while doing so I drifted off to sleep in spite of myself. Listening to an out-of-tune version of the old English-language song "Release Me" that was being broadcast on the plane, I saw myself changing from a rectangular, wavelike carpet into a green snake, thin and flat, that leaped and soared along the tops of the trees of the garden. My mother, with her red hair, was reading the Bible below me, while a golden tiger held her in its gaze.

Classes had already been in session for ten days. Catching up would not have been too difficult for me, but I wasn't much in the mood for schoolwork. Keyi had only been named a runner-up in the folk music competition, but the entertainment sections of all the newspapers had devoted the bulk of their attention to her, and all the girls in my classes were talking about her. I didn't get in touch with her until three days after I arrived back in Taipei. Keyi told me that the recording company was planning to put together an album of performances by her and the other competition winners and that lately she had been busy recording and doing concerts; the day after tomorrow, she would be heading south for a series of concerts at colleges down there. She also said that the only reason she had been named just a runner-up was that the judges didn't want anyone to think they were assigning prizes solely on the basis of contestants' looks—her beauty had been her downfall! That night, Keyi and some other prizewinners would be coming to my college to perform. She asked me if I would have the time to come see them and said that we should get something to eat together afterward. When I arrived, the place was packed, and I was forced to stand outside the auditorium, where I could hear the songs but couldn't see the performers. With some difficulty, I managed to catch a glimpse of a tiny corner of the stage just as Keyi's set was nearly finished. Then, with some aggressive determination, I managed to squeeze my way backstage, where I saw a guy who looked like a college student obsequiously holding Keyi's guitar and her bag. When Keyi saw me, she took the guitar from him and handed it to me, then took her bag herself and left the auditorium with me. Someone came up with a notebook and asked Keyi for an autograph. There was a touch of autumn in the air blowing through the darkened streets. We couldn't think of anything to say; Keyi tried to hold my hand, but I said, "You're a big star now. You'd better keep your distance." Keyi called me a nerd and insisted on taking my hand. We walked along, with no aim or consistent direction, and ended up at the coffeehouse that was frequented by all the artists. I ordered a cup of Osamu Dazai coffee. Keyi said that I was a dissipated youth—last time I had had a Yu Dafu, now I was having an Osamu Dazai; at this rate I was likely to end up committing suicide. She ordered a George Sand black tea and commented that it tasted no different from the Henry James tea. Then she asked me how things were at home. I told her everything, from the very beginning, except that just as before I said nothing about Chunxi, and I did not mention Chuntian or the prince either. Keyi said she could tell that I was hiding something, that something else was on my mind.

"Why don't I spend tonight with you, how about that? After this we won't have a chance to see each other again for a while. I'll be in class all day tomorrow, and then at night I'll be performing at another university. Day after that we head down south, and we'll be gone ten days, so when I get back I'll have a whole stack of schoolwork waiting for me."

"If you're that busy, you're probably best off going home early and getting some rest."

"You're mad at me for not contacting you earlier, aren't you? Come on, how was I supposed to know you were back?"

"No, no, that's not it. It's just that you can see how grumpy I look. I'm afraid I'll just depress you."

"The *reason* I want to stay with you is that you seem unhappy. Look at you! The girls who fall in love with you after me are going to have their work cut out for them."

When we left the coffeehouse, Keyi complained that she was hungry, and we went back to the same night market for a snack. The market was as crowded with throngs of people as ever. Keyi said she wanted to have beef noodles from that same stall, just like before. The stall's owner was still brusque and very busy, and the small bowl of noodles was still as big as a washbasin. Keyi was worried about hurting her voice and didn't want to have stinky tofu. A few people pointed at Keyi while we ate our noodles, but she didn't seem to care. I said, "After this I may not get many chances to eat noodles with you."

"Anytime you feel like eating beef noodles, just say the word, and I'll come eat with you, unless I happen to be busy," she replied.

It was after ten by the time we got back to my place. As soon as we got in the door, Keyi threw her arms around me and said, "Su Qi, you've lost so much weight. From now on I'll go with you to eat noodles every chance I get." The image of Chuntian's face in the dark, as broad and vague and pliant as the face of a half-formed human fetus, suddenly leapt into my mind. In my mind, the garden was a womb whose umbilicus was darkness, and within it Chuntian was being conceived a second time, growing up all over again.

Two weeks after that, my mother phoned to tell me that two young Dayak men had broken into the Lins' house at dusk the night before and had attacked and seriously injured Lin Yuan. Before they left, they had told my mother that they were Amma's relatives and had come to seek revenge for her and her sister. They also said that Amma had seen my mother set the fire and that if my mother revealed their identity to anyone they would take that information public.

"Did they hurt you in any way, Mom?"

"No. They said they would let me off easy this time for your sake, Su Qi. Was there anything going on between you and that Amma?"

I told my mother the basic story. I also let her know that she herself had at one point saved Amma's virginity from the lame foreman.

"Are they really not going to tell anyone, Mom?"

"I don't much care."

"Is Uncle Lin okay?"

"He's still in intensive care. He may lose his legs, but his life isn't in danger," my mother said. "I've already contacted Chuntian, and she'll be coming back in a few days."

I was silent for a moment. "Do you want me to come home, too, Mom?"

"Whatever you like."

The next day, my mother called again and said that, the previous evening, two middle-aged men had been hanging around the garden. They had knocked repeatedly on our door and seemed determined to get into our house, but my mother had refused to let them in.

"I recognized them. One of them had tattoos." My mother's voice quavered.

"What kind of tattoos?"

"I recognized him by his tattoos." My mother sounded as if she were in tears. "He hasn't changed one bit."

"The Dayak you went into the jungle with a long time ago?"

My mother didn't answer. The sounds of her weeping traveled clearly over the phone line.

"Are you sure you weren't mistaken?"

"Su Qi, the next time he comes to knock on the door, your mother just might open it for him."

"There was another man with him?"

"The other one was lame," my mother said. "It was that foreman, the one who thought of himself as such a Casanova."

"What was the foreman doing there?"

"After I led him into the jungle the second time, he never came out again. People say he drowned in the river. But I saw him here yesterday, with my own eyes, knocking on our door."

"Mom, why don't I come home."

I didn't believe my mother's story, but I thought that it might be her way of telling me that she wanted me to come home. My heart had not been in my schoolwork the past few weeks, and it seemed to me that the best thing would be to arrange for a formal leave of absence. I bought a plane ticket home for two days later. Keyi was supposed to have been back in Taipei by then, but she hadn't contacted me. I had read in the paper that she and several other singers were going to be giving a concert in a park that night. When I went over to the park that evening, I found that this venue, too, was unusually crowded. Keyi sang two solos and then sang a love duet with a male singer; at that moment I found myself thinking of Chuntian again. After the prince had left our house, Lin Yuan had given me Chuntian's phone number in America. I had wavered for several days before finally picking up the phone. Then I had to spend several more days sporadically trying the number before I finally got hold of a classmate of hers, who said that Chuntian was in Europe on a school-sponsored international exchange program and was staying with a host family there; she probably wouldn't be back for another couple of months. The girl had asked me if I wanted Chuntian's number in Europe. I had said no, that I would talk to her when she returned. After Keyi's performance was over, I went backstage and found her talking and laughing with the same guy who had been holding her guitar and bag the last time. The two of them were looking pretty intimate. Meanwhile, the singer with whom she had sung the duet was also hovering around her. I watched for a while, then turned around and left. After I had gone a couple of steps I thought I heard Keyi calling my name.

The doorbell rang not long after I got home. I opened the door and saw Keyi.

"Su Qi, were you at the concert just now?" Keyi blurted out.

"I was. I also went backstage to look for you."

"How come you didn't answer when I called you?"

"Too noisy. I must not have heard you," I said. "Plus, you were busy."

"Su Qi, you're jealous."

"I am not," I said.

"Honest?"

"Honest. I'm not."

"I didn't get back to Taipei until the middle of the night last night. I slept until noon. I just staggered through an afternoon of class. Then I found out the company had set up this concert! But there's nothing I can do about it. I'm new in this business, I need to make a name for myself. I was planning on getting in touch with you tonight. If you really weren't being jealous, how come you didn't say hi when you saw me? You came to the concert because you missed me and wanted to see me, right?"

"Whatever you say," I said. "I guess I was feeling lonely and bored. It's a good thing you came by. Stay here. We can talk."

"I came to see you precisely because I knew you weren't in a good mood!" Keyi said. "Not bad, Su Qi. You've made progress."

"Progress in what?"

"Before, even when it was obvious that you wanted me to stay with you, you still refused to take the initiative and say so."

I asked Keyi if she would rather go out for a walk or stay in, and she said she didn't care. She also said that she didn't have class the next morning and that she could stay with me all night. I said we might as well stay put for the time being and if we felt like going out later we could go out. I made a pot of black tea, and the two of us sat on the balcony in the rear of the apartment and gazed down at the bright lights of the military housing project. A few old men were sitting in a circle by the side of the road, chatting. There was a white dog among them, sitting on its haunches and looking like it was the one in charge. The girl in the wheelchair had just come back from her "walk" through the neighborhood. She took a key out of her pocket, opened her gate, entered her own yard, and then looked at the bright living rooms of the other houses. After that, she pushed her wheelchair over to a banyan tree and disappeared. Keyi said, "She's gone to hide so she can cry in private."

"How do you know?"

"She looked like she was about to burst into tears." Then Keyi said, "You keep frowning at me. Are you sure you're not jealous?"

I went ahead and told Keyi about the prince, about Chunxi, and about Chuntian. As I was doing so, I suddenly remembered the story Chuntian had told me, about the princess who had slept for fifty years, and I felt as if I were in a dream.

"So you weren't jealous at all," Keyi said. "I haven't known you for very long, but, still, it's been a while, and I thought I understood you. But it turns out it's not me you love, Su Qi. It's Chuntian. Were you afraid to tell me the truth because you didn't want to hurt me? So you wouldn't be hurt if I got another boyfriend? Su Qi, you should find Chuntian. No wonder you always seem so far away. I always felt like something was distracting you. If you want to know the truth, I figured out a long time ago that you weren't really in love with me. Don't worry, though. If Chuntian doesn't want you, I'll still keep you company until you're not lonely and not bored anymore."

"It sounds like you're in a hurry to get rid of me."

"Who matters more to you: Chuntian or me? Think about it."

"But I still can't figure out whether I'm in love with Chuntian or with Chunxi."

"But you know that Chunxi doesn't love you. You're very lucky—you lost a Chunxi, but you gained a Chuntian. And then you've always got me as a backup. But I should warn you—all I'm good for is helping you feel better when you're depressed. I won't be your girl for all eternity."

"I knew a long time ago that this would happen someday. I don't know why, but from the very first day I met you I had a hunch that you and I would break up eventually. Thank you, Keyi."

"What are you thanking me for? I should be the one thanking you."

Chapter 32

By the time Lin Yuan was transferred out of intensive care and into a regular hospital ward, his left leg had been amputated, and he had lost all sensation in his right leg. So it was already clear that he would spend the rest of his life in a wheelchair. His throat had been cut and his larynx seriously damaged, so when he spoke he sounded like an anguished animal. Every time I saw him, he would say terrible things about Amma and then tell me that I didn't need to worry about my mother. He had already made contacts, arranged some things with some people, so that even if the little savage decided to spill the secret no one would believe her. Nevertheless, after only a few brief days at home, I had already heard more than one rumor about my mother setting fire to the garden. Finally, under pressure from the friends and families of the casualties, the police came to our house again to investigate. I don't know exactly what the cops said to my mother, but I do know that she went into every interrogation carrying her Bible and looking sallow and half-mad beneath her head of scorched hair. The police came by several times but turned up nothing, and eventually they stopped coming. They had also questioned me about my mother's mental state, and I had said that she was just fine—the fire in the labyrinthine garden and all the terrible deaths had of course upset her greatly and left her feeling guilty; she had never imagined that a fire would start or that the guests would be scattered so widely through the garden when it did. I brought out the issue of the gardening magazine and told the police a little more about the garden, which had once been praised as one of the most beautiful in all of Southeast Asia. I let them know about all the sweat and tears my mother had poured into it: how she had hired an expert to design a complex drainage system to prevent damage during the long rainy season; how distracted with worry she grew every year just before the dry season began, worry both over how to keep the garden irrigated and over the possibility that it would be affected by the forest fires that raged every year; how she would exhort every visitor, child or adult, to be careful with anything flammable in the garden; how concertedly she sought to prevent the theft of any of the rare plants she had taken such pains to plant there. She had suffered the sight of my father's face so that she could obtain the seeds of those rare and valuable flowers; she had begged him, patiently and obsequiously, for permission to expand the garden. The look on her face as she showed guests around the garden had been enough to convince anyone of the satisfaction and pride it brought her. The wildfire that had destroyed the garden had not only spread to the nearby jungle—it had spread to my mother as well. Her discolored hair was the best evidence of how those flames had ravaged, and continued to ravage, her. As I was saying all this, my mother was pacing back and forth along the outdoor corridor. In the resplendent rays cast by the setting sun, her reddish hair resembled the creeping vines that spread along the corridor's walls. When the policemen walked by her on their way out, their hair and skin both seemed to tighten abruptly, as if they had just been singed by something. As soon as they were out the door, they went straight in the direction of the merchant who sold coconut juice by the side of the road, looking for something to slake their thirst. I consoled my mother, telling her that the cops wouldn't be back again, but she didn't seem to care. It occurred to me that she might not even understand who our visitors were. She reacted to the cops exactly as she did to the occasional friend or relative who dropped by. She treated them all like strangers; she seemed to have forgotten all their names and faces. As our house dropped further into tedium and overwhelming stillness, my mother's reactions to anything that upset that tedium and stillness grew increasingly violent. This was most apparent every time the doorbell rang, when she would stare out at our gate looking utterly absorbed.

"Who was it?" my mother would ask each time, after I had come back from answering the door.

"The man delivering the newspaper," I would say.

One day, she finally said to me, as she looked out the window at the setting sun, "Su Qi, if that Dayak man ever knocks on our door again, your mother will run away with him."

I reacted to that with extraordinary equanimity. Maybe by that point I had stopped paying any attention to anything my mother said.

I still had not seen the tiger my mother spoke of, even though she insisted that he lingered around our house every evening. I also had not seen the tattooed Dayak man, even though she claimed that one evening he had tried knocking on our door but had lost his nerve after he saw me. Nor had I seen the lame foreman, even though she said that he had tried several times to break into our house but had gone slinking away after she fixed him with her most withering look. And I most certainly had not seen Amma's relatives keeping watch on our house. My mother said that Amma's relatives suspected she wasn't keeping the promise she had made them and were planning on paying us a visit.

The wild grasses in the labyrinthine garden were gradually regaining their former vigor, and this inspired memories of my "fiery cock." The malignancy that my mother had driven away ten years before seemed to be spreading out in all directions from our house like a poisonous tide. My mother, who no longer had any interest in controlling it, was leaving it free to grow, just as she was giving her red hair leave to gradually obscure her beautiful face. At some point I suddenly realized that the garden I was looking at now was exactly the same virtual wasteland it had been when I was a child. Back then, the air in our house was filled with the stink of my sister's corpse, while the air outside was flush with the sweet fragrance of flowers and my mother's breasts. On the days when my father met with the woman in white, even his body gave off a scent of honey and sweet grass. Sometimes, I would fantasize naively about what would have happened if my father and that woman in white had run away together, if my mother and the Dayak man had been able to grow old together, and if my sister, my half-brother, and I had grown up together, playing hand in hand in the garden. Maybe that labyrinthine garden really could have been an Eden to all of us, including Lin Yuan, whose only option, short of forgetting my mother, was to spend the rest of his life lost and drifting there, an Odysseus on a sea of love. I also imagined, even more naively, what it would have been like if Chunxi—I suppose I should say Chuntian—and I could have spent our adult lives roaming the garden together, if we could have lived as recluses in some secluded spot and lost our way back, whether by our own choice or not, and never come out again for as long as we lived. Maybe it would have been like the time Chuntian and I had been walking in the garden and wandered by accident into the jungle: it felt as though we had traveled a great distance in the jungle, but in fact we had just been roaming in circles around the perimeter of the garden. Now, remembering that event in detail, I suddenly understood Chuntian's reaction as I hadn't before. As I sat in the parlor, looking out at the garden, all kinds of memories came rushing back to me. We had lost our way in the sunless jungle. I held Chuntian's wrist tightly and groped my way forward just as I had in the dark garden on the night the power went off. A giant tree trunk, with things resembling mushrooms wound all the way up and down it, gave off a phosphorescent green light that pulsated violently, like some kind of egg on the verge of hatching. I remembered Lin Yuan telling me that if I ever saw an area in the dark jungle lit up by phosphorescent light it might mean that there were innumerable human bones buried just ahead of me, that I was approaching a danger zone that had brought death to many people.

"What is that?" Chuntian had said, pointing at the green light.

"Maybe it's phosphorescent mushrooms. Or maybe it's the light given off by dead bodies," I said. "Explorers and researchers have been dying around here for centuries. No one ever found their bodies, so they got counted as missing persons. Most of the bodies were probably lost in the swamps, or in the rivers, or in quicksand, or else ended up in the bellies of animals. Half the pythons the natives kill have wristwatches in their bellies. Some of the people who died were poisoned or succumbed to strange illnesses, and their bodies melted into black puddles. Some people got lost and had their blood sucked dry by leeches, drop by drop. Then the ants nibbled at them until all that was left was a pile of bones."

Chuntian perked up her ears and cast her eyes in all directions, like rodent watching out for the Philippine eagle.

"We need to look out for things above us, too." I raised my head and stared up into the belly of the jungle. "Pythons like to hide above the paths that wild pigs and people usually take. When their prey appears, they come splashing down on you like a truckful of mud."

Chuntian raised her head and gazed up into the belly of the jungle for a long time.

"Don't just worry about what's above us, though," I said. "The jungle is full of quicksand, and swampland, and hidden precipices, and deep holes, and pools of water, and animal traps filled with sharp stakes."

"Su Qi, what would you do if I got lost in the jungle? Or what if I'm already lost, and the hand you're holding isn't Chunxi's but someone else's? Didn't you tell me that there's a monster in the jungle who likes to come to you in the dark and pretend to be someone you know? That he will lead the poor lost person all over the place until she dies of exhaustion? Can you be sure that the person whose hand you're holding now is me—that it's Chunxi?"

I leaned in closer to Chuntian, whom at the time I had not known was Chuntian, and once again studied her face, as vague and pliant as the face of a half-formed fetus.

"Su Qi, if I disappear from the human world one day, like a child who gets led away by a bad man and never comes back, will you go looking for me?"

"Of course I will."

"No, you won't," Chuntian had said. "You don't know it, but I've already disappeared."

"I don't understand."

"Sometimes in life you'll find yourself manipulated by some kind of power, and you won't realize it, just like the monster that leads people around the jungle. By the time you discover what's going on, you no longer have the strength to turn back. You've gone too far down the wrong road. Or, in other words, you're the one who's lost."

I mulled over the possible meaning of Chuntian's words.

"How about this?" I said. "Starting right now, I'll hold your hand very tightly. I'll go in front, you go behind, and we'll go forward like that, one in front, one behind. No matter what we run into, we won't let go of each other's hands. If one of us stumbles and falls, in quicksand or some other terrible place, the other person can pull them out."

"And what if they can't pull them out?"

"Then we'll have to let go," I said. "But, if you're the one who falls, I won't let go."

"I won't let go either, if you're the one who falls."

"No, it's better if you do let go. I'm too heavy. You won't be able to pull me out."

"Then I'll go down with you," she said. "How would I find my way out of the jungle without you? I'd just end up falling into a different trap."

"You wouldn't," I said. "If I fall into a trap, at the very least it will mean that you've cleared one obstacle and you have that much more hope of finding your way out."

"How would I find my way out of the jungle without you . . ."

"Just remember to head northwest. Once it gets dark, remember to keep going toward the North Star. Always keep it in front of you and to your right. Keep going straight, just keep on going, and eventually you'll come to the South China Sea. Don't worry. As long as I'm not the one who falls, I will never, ever let go of your hand."

I kept moving forward, holding her hand. Before long, we emerged from the dark jungle and came to the edge of a small stream. We took off our shoes and sat together on the rocks, shoulder to shoulder, and soaked our feet in the ice-cold water.

Two mudskippers, oblivious to our presence, chased each other around our feet, circling a dozen times before they disappeared behind a rock. A few smaller fish, their winding skeletons visible beneath their transparent scales, hung persistently around my toes. The jungle was silent enough that I could almost hear the sound of ripe wild durians falling to the ground somewhere off in the distance.

I lowered my head to get a better look at the small fish darting through the water near me, and when I lifted my head again Chuntian had vanished. So I followed the damp footprints she had left behind on the rocks. I followed them for a full fifty meters before I saw her, sitting on a tree branch that stretched out over the water and playing "The Swan" from Saint-Saens's *Carnival of the Animals* on a flute she had made out of leaves. An Oriental magpie-robin with an enormous torso sat just above her head with its wings unfurled, grooming its feathers.

I walked up to her and sat down beside her. Chuntian kept playing her flute even as told me a story she had read in a book: the story of the Postman Bear.

Chapter 33

The Postman Bear lives in the jungle, in a tiny log cabin surrounded by trees with trunks so thick it would take ten people to encircle them. If you are ever brave enough to walk onto his property, you might very well get lost, and before you even realize what is happening you will have become one more name on the Postman Bear's missing persons' list.

As you approach the Bear's home, you might decide to stop for a minute in front of a row of those towering trees. Maybe you will see a coil of stove smoke curling and lilting as it rises from the shrubbery; this will mean that the Bear is making his famous fruit tea, from durian, fig, hawthorn, and the skin of mountain bamboo. Maybe you will see a net twisted among the weeds; this will mean that the Bear has been collecting insect specimens. Maybe you will even see a fat, hirsute creature sitting on a rock with a fishing pole in his hand, drinking fruit tea; this will be the Bear, fishing for ghost fish, his favorite food.

But as you pass through the prickly grass, as you leap over boulders, as you make your way around more big trees than you can count, you will realize that the Bear is not there at all. The stove fire that you saw may still be burning bright; the sweet smell of fruit tea may still fill the kitchen; a copy of Kipling's The Jungle Book that the Bear is halfway through may still be on the windowsill. Maybe, in the prickly grass, you will see a page of drawings that the Bear has torn out of his sketchbook and thrown away; the white clouds in today's sky and the lines of the wind are sketched on the page in crayon. Maybe you can even see the reflection of the Bear in the river as he disappears behind a towering tree, his fishing pole on his back.

If you want to see the Bear, the last thing you should do is run rashly after him and annoy him. Instead, you have to wait until he comes to find you.

You should sit down in front of that row of towering trees, pull out a wind instrument that you brought with you, and start playing the songs you are best at playing. If you did not remember to bring an instrument, you may weave one from leaves or stalks of grass. If you do not know how to play any instrument, well, then, you can whistle.

You will not go awry if you play "The March of the Toy Soldiers" by Tchaikovsky, "The Swan," or "Yesterday" by the Beatles. People say that these are the songs the Bear likes best.

You may play for a very long time, until the sun goes down in the west, and the Bear still will not have appeared. But you must not lose hope. You must go home and come back again the next day.

Maybe then, the next day, after only one song you will smell the sweet smell of fruit tea, and a big, hirsute creature will suddenly plunk himself down next to you, sending the honey that you had brought with you as a hospitality gift for the Bear spilling onto the ground with a glug-glug-glugging sound.

In the scorching heat of the jungle, buffeted by the southwest monsoon wind, the Bear, sitting next to you, will wipe the sweat off his brow again and again. At that point, you will think that maybe you ought to look for another place to sit, someplace shady near the cool riverbank, a place where the Bear can soak his feet in the water or dunk his whole head under and refresh himself in the sweet water. Because the Bear, to be quite frank, is lazy and fat, and he hates the heat.

You will give the Bear the letter you prepared ahead of time, and when you do this it is best that you also add a brief explanatory narrative. You should tell the Bear that your friend has been camping out in the jungle for two weeks now, that you want to get a letter to him, and that you want him to reply.

Or maybe the story is that your friend went into the jungle to do field research six months before and no one has heard from him since. The search parties have already given up on finding him. Everyone else has abandoned hope.

You will take the questionnaire that the Bear will hand you, and you will fill it out with detailed vital information about your friend.

The Bear then takes the letter and the questionnaire from you, and he will stamp both with a postmark in the shape of a bear's paw. Sometimes the Bear will then offer you a cup of fruit tea, or take you to look at the butterfly specimens he has caught that day, or bring you down to the river to catch a ghost fish.

Finally, at a moment when your guard is down, all of a sudden, the Bear will disappear.

One afternoon—generally this will be at the time of day when the sun is strongest and the air is hottest—you will hear "The March of the Toy Soldiers" being played on a wooden flute. By the time you come outside, the music will have stopped. But you will see, stuck in a hole in the fence, a letter from your friend who is camping in the jungle, stamped with the bear-paw postmark.

Or maybe you will see the friend who has been missing in the jungle for half a year standing outside the fence, holding a thermos of fruit tea that the Bear has given him.

You will raise your head and look all around you, and only then will you see the Bear as he disappears into a flower patch, his fishing pole on his back.

Chapter 34

Our doorbell rang. My mother put down her Bible and looked out the window.

When I opened the door, I saw a girl standing in front of the iron gate, with long hair and a backpack on her back and a suitcase in her hand.

The first northeast monsoon wind of the year came blowing slackly by us. Both the girl's long hair and the withered grass and leaves in the garden rose slowly in the breeze like a succession of tidal waves. The sky was covered with dark clouds blown in from some distant place, and dampness was filling the air. I could smell sweat-scented moisture rising off the body of the girl with long hair. All this reminded me of the woman in white who used to make the rainwater flow down from the sky with such license, who used to make the rivers overflow.

"Chuntian," I couldn't stop myself from calling out. "Is that you?"